Red
Skies

BOOK FOUR IN THE

Tales of the Scavenger's Daughters

Also by Kay Bratt

Silent Tears; A Journey of Hope in a Chinese Orphanage

Chasing China; A Daughter's Quest for Truth

Mei Li and the Wise Laoshi

The Bridge

A Thread Unbroken

Train to Nowhere

Eyes Like Mine

The Palest Ink

TALES OF THE SCAVENGER'S DAUGHTERS

The Scavenger's Daughters

Tangled Vines

Bitter Winds

Red Skies

Red
Skies

BOOK FOUR IN THE
Tales of the Scavenger's Daughters

KAY BRATT

LAKE UNION
PUBLISHING

Text copyright © 2014 Kay Bratt

Published by Lake Union Publishing, Seattle
www.apub.com

Amazon, the Amazon logo, and Lake Union Publishing are trademarks of Amazon.com, Inc., or its affiliates.

ISBN-13: 9781503945166
ISBN-10: 1503945162

Cover design by Joe Simmons
Cover layout by Chelsea Wirtz

Printed in the United States of America

To my little sister, Misty.
If I were An Ni, you would definitely be my Mei.

"*When darkness is at its darkest,
that is the beginning of all light.*"

—*Lao Tzu*

Chapter One

M arigold—or Mari, as her family in Wuxi called her—kept her head down to keep the rain out of her eyes and the world from seeing her misery. She was exhausted. She'd finally finished dragging her stubborn camel to his shelter and was now running late in getting home again, but still something held her back, and she knew just what it was—or *who* it was. Without even meaning to or realizing it, she'd gone a block or so out of her way and now, heaving a sigh of sadness, she pulled the hood of her raincoat farther down on her face, then leaned back against the building to watch. Like a moth to a flame, she was drawn to the girl across the street, captivated by her plight. It was a red skies evening, the pollution of Beijing mixing with the lightly falling rain to create a dramatic scarlet backdrop as the young girl called out, her high-pitched but sweet voice imploring the passing pedestrians for a coin or two. *"Gei wo qian; gei wo qian."*

The sound of one lone coin clinking against the tin cup she shook echoed through the wind and drizzle, carrying itself to Mari along with scraps of memories from long ago. She'd never forget when she herself stood begging with her voice and pleading with her eyes for someone to notice her—to have mercy and give her just something so she'd be treated fairly at the end of the long night. Even though rescued from that life, reminders like the girl on the corner brought it all flooding back.

The girl looked about ten or eleven. She walked a few paces to the corner, then turned back and returned to her post, shaking her can louder. At first glance, she wasn't much to look at. Standing no more than four feet tall, she appeared delicate but determined. Her long hair looked dirty and unkempt, her clothes unmatched and ragged—the faded flowered pants short enough to show bony ankles above tattered shoes. The thin material afforded no protection from the cold dampness, and already she looked soaked through. If Mari's eyes could be believed, the girl shivered slightly.

Mari looked closer, and through the long, stringy hair and smudges of dirt on her tiny heart-shaped face, she could see evidence of a hidden beauty—unseen to most because they chose only to see a nuisance, if they chose to see her at all. Mari knew that the majority of people pretended street children were invisible. They refused to see or hear their needs, instead walking on by to their warm houses full of plentiful food while the children scrounged for a scrap here or there, working to be allowed any sort of shelter from the elements.

Mari wanted to go to her, but what would she do? Give her the small bit of yuan she'd made that day and then tell her husband she'd made nothing? Business was slow because of the weather, but would he believe she hadn't had a single customer? Not likely.

The girl stopped calling out, and her tiny shoulders heaved in a silent sigh. She suddenly looked so tired and desperate, prompting a passing woman to pause and dig in her purse, then shake her head. Mari couldn't hear her words, but she knew what they probably were— *sorry, I don't have any change.* She'd heard that herself at least half a million times.

The woman moved on, and the girl began her chant again, her voice weaker, her expression from afar even more desperate.

It wasn't the first time Mari had seen the girl. Perhaps it was the familiar look of hopelessness that had drawn her back for the second day in a row, or possibly even that she felt as if she were looking at herself as she had been so many years ago, before her Baba rescued her. Mari knew what it felt like to be passed from gang to gang. It was terrifying, and at that age, you either learned to swiftly swipe a wallet or purse, or you were pushed down to the lowest level of begging and posted on a street for eighteen or more hours a day. And that wasn't the only thing the girl would have to do if she remained on the streets. Eventually she'd be seen as just eye-catching enough to make a buck from lecherous old men. But those were thoughts Mari didn't like to dwell on.

Mari's blood boiled when a trio of teen boys walked by the girl and laughed at her, then one knocked the cup from her hands. It hit the sidewalk. The girl scrambled for it and the coin, but they were too quick for her. She grabbed the cup, but the biggest boy snatched the rolling coin and held it high over her head, then pushed it into his pocket before leaving her with only the sound of his sarcastic laugh lingering behind him.

That was the teaser coin, and Mari knew if the girl didn't make it up, her boss would be furious. Psychology wasn't just for the upper class—even thugs knew that if a person who had an ounce of compassion heard the clink of one coin, they'd be more likely to add their own contribution. People didn't realize how important that teaser coin was.

Stay away, Mari. Don't get involved, she tried to tell herself. Her life was already complicated enough. She couldn't add any more stress, or she'd fold. Simple as that. Her brain argued with her heart, but the stronger muscle won, and her feet obeyed. Before she knew it, she was crossing the street and stood before the girl.

"*Ni hao*," she said softly.

The deepest—and probably the saddest—brown eyes she'd ever seen looked up and connected with hers, and Mari felt the earth move. This child was her years ago, down to the young eyes full of premature wisdom a girl should not yet have. The skinny snip of a girl also could've been any one of Mari's sisters—other girls taken in by her Baba and Mama. Girls who, like her, found themselves alone in the world and were taken advantage of by depraved thugs.

The little girl backed up, immediately suspicious, as she held her cup to her chest. Mari slid out of her raincoat, then draped it around the bony shoulders and pulled it closed in front.

"You're giving me your coat?" the girl asked, hope evident in her face.

"*Dui,*" Mari answered. "And I'll replace the coin that bully took from you, too." She dug in her pocket, and instead of a coin, she pulled out a five-yuan note. She tucked it into the cup, wishing it could be more. But she couldn't go home empty-handed—even sedated, her husband would be angry if he thought she'd mishandled their take for the day.

"*Xie xie,*" the girl whispered, her eyes big as she eyed the bill.

Mari crouched down in front of her and touched her hand. "So tell me, which gang do you belong to?"

The girl froze, her eyes widening with fear at the mention of her boss. She'd never give them up—they'd scared her silent. Probably with threats of physical harm or even death.

"I know how it is," Mari said. "I used to be just like you. I worked for a street gang, too. Do you know your name? Can you at least tell me that much?"

"An Ni," the girl said, then looked up and down the street.

More than likely, she'd also been warned not to ever give her name, just in case she still had family looking for her, so Mari didn't believe for a moment An Ni was her given name.

Mari held her hand out. "Well, I'm Mari. It's nice to meet you, An Ni. Such a pretty name. Did you know you have the same name as a famous little girl in a book I once read? It was called *Anne of Green Gables*, a story about a little girl who was an orphan."

The girl hesitated, then appearing to struggle for the courage within herself, she reached out and clasped Mari's hand. "She was an orphan?"

Mari nodded. The book had been a favorite in her household, one of the many stories told to them by the light of the gas lamp in the evenings when they gathered as a family. A sweet memory—that was what her adopted parents had given her and what she wished for the girl standing before her. "She sure was, and my Mama used to say she should've been called Annie because it suited her better than Anne."

The girl mumbled so low Mari had to strain to hear her. "I like your clothes."

"*Xie xie*. I dress like this because I take photos of foreigners on the Great Wall. They expect me to look exotic, even if it's raining outside." Mari smiled back at her, holding her hand. It was ice cold and trembling, and the girl was probably shocked that someone was speaking to her like she was a human being and not a piece of rubbish. That thought brought Mari's father's face to mind—he was just a simple scavenger but was the kindest human being she'd ever known, and Mari felt a rush of homesickness. *What would he do if he came across the girl?* Mari knew instantly exactly what he'd do, and she felt a flush of shame. For a second, Mari let her imagination wander and consider how she could bring An Ni into her life. At over thirty, since she hadn't gotten pregnant before, it was unlikely she was ever going to give Bolin a child. Could the girl fit into their family somehow? Before the thought could grow legs, a man stepped out of the alley and stomped over to them.

"Who are you?" he barked out, then took a long drag on his brown cigarette.

Mari stood. She knew immediately from the looks of him that he wasn't the big boss. More likely he was just the right-hand man—but he was still dangerous. His steely eyes glared at her from beneath his shaggy hair, unflinching against her accusing stare. Dressed in black pants and a shiny black jacket, he definitely looked the part of a street thug.

Mari wished she could reach up and slap the smirk from his pocked face. But she kept her cool. "Doesn't matter who I am. I was just saying hello and giving the girl some money."

He started at Mari's feet and examined her all the way up to the tip of her head before releasing the cigarette smoke directly into her face, letting it waft around her face in a cloud of stench. He pulled at his jacket, shaking off the drops of rain in a gesture to make himself appear collected. "You wouldn't be thinking of trying to take my property, would you? Because I got a lot invested in this girl here—my sister. And I was just about to take her home."

An Ni looked terrified. She slipped out of Mari's coat and handed it back, then stepped closer to the man, silently showing her loyalty. An Ni knew the ropes—that much was obvious. The fear on her face told Mari that she didn't believe anyone could help her, and one wrong step would result in punishment so severe that most couldn't fathom it. But what the girl didn't know was that Mari knew about it all too well, and she wouldn't be the one to cause her more pain.

Mari accepted her coat and quickly put it on. It was still warm from the small body that had worn it briefly. She looked at An Ni again, but the girl refused to meet her eyes.

"No, actually I was just lending her my coat, but since she's done with it, I'll move along. I'm sure you just forgot she was standing in the cold rain with no protection. I'm leaving." She almost choked on the words, but she knew that if she challenged the bully, the girl would pay. Even the local police would do nothing. The gangs in Beijing ran everything, and if An Ni was to ever have a chance, she would have to be sneaked away—they'd never give her up easily.

In the world of street children, especially in Beijing where foreigners were prevalent, the little beggars were a commodity passed around by the gangs until they'd grown too old or hardened to turn heads and reap sympathy any longer. An Ni still had many good begging years left in her, but looking into her eyes was like staring into the soul of an older, much wiser person. It took all her willpower, but Mari took a step back.

The man took another long drag then flicked his cigarette at Mari's feet. "I think you just made a very wise choice."

Mari straightened as tall as she could and walked away, refusing to look back. But something told her that she and An Ni weren't through crossing paths yet. Somewhere, someday, they'd meet again. And if her father had taught her anything, it was that her responsibility was to be kind to everyone, but especially those in despair. As she made her way home to her small apartment, Mari hoped she'd have another chance to prove that she had half the heart that one old scavenger possessed.

Chapter Two

An Ni huddled in the doorway of the produce shop, just out of the falling rain, her knees to her chin to keep her body warmer as she thought of the curly-haired woman. For a moment—just one shining second—she'd thought it was her chance to escape. But then *he'd* come back and caught them talking. Even though An Ni had brought in her share of money for the evening, her punishment for interacting with the woman had been watching the other kids fight over her share of steamed rice. Li Xi—the oldest boy in the group, nicknamed Little Dragon—had laughed at her, taken a deep drag on his cigarette, then blown smoke in her face. She didn't cry. She wouldn't give him the satisfaction. He was always the appointed boss if Tianbing was away, and his mean streak never stopped, especially if he saw any weakness.

"Xiao Mei, can I have some blanket?" she whispered to the girl who lay curled behind her. An Ni's feet ached after standing for so many hours, but more than that, her body begged to be warm again.

Xiao Mei moved closer, bringing the blanket over An Ni's legs. Xiao Mei wasn't her real name, but she hadn't been with them long enough for Tianbing to decide what she'd be called, so like the other new girls before her, she was Xiao Mei until further instructions. An Ni didn't even remember her real name any longer, but it didn't matter. The lady had said An Ni was a pretty name—and now she'd decided she liked it.

She'd asked Tianbing where she really came from after the last new arrival had wailed for days about her Mama and Baba. Tianbing only snickered, showing his brown teeth, and then told her she'd been born under a rock, and if he hadn't come along, she'd have grown into a slithering snake. An Ni knew he was lying. She also knew that she wouldn't be a street child forever. She'd had a dream, and just before it had faded away with the morning light, she'd been told someone was coming for her—someone to free her. For a moment, she'd thought it was the pretty woman, but now she knew it had to be someone else. She shivered once, biting her lip to take her mind off the pain in her legs.

Li Xi was still bragging. "I climbed in that window and stuffed my jacket full of food before the night guard even turned around. Then I was out of there and off the train in seconds," he said. "You should've seen me."

Guo Ji, the younger boy that followed Li Xi like a puppy, high-fived him.

An Ni's stomach growled and she wished for just one of the apples or dried noodle boxes that Li Xi had snatched and turned in. She hadn't eaten anything but a partial corn on the cob since early that morning. She felt grateful for that, though it was just leftovers thrown down by a toddler holding on to his Mama's neck. An Ni had stared him down, almost willing him to drop the cob, and when he did, she'd jumped in fright, scared she might have some sort of secret powers. But when she tried it again on a girl who walked with street candy in her hands, it hadn't worked. So blind luck it was, apparently.

Li Xi came around from another doorway and stood over An Ni and Xiao Mei, blocking out the light from the streetlamp. "Guess what I heard, Snake?"

An Ni didn't answer him.

"Xiao Mei is being traded soon. Tianbing is negotiating a buyer for her, and she'll soon be headed to colder climates."

An Ni shivered again. This time it wasn't from the dropping temperature. It was fear, plain and simple. An Ni didn't want Xiao Mei to go. She knew from experience the girl would have to be broken in—taught the pecking order and the new gang's brand of expected respect. She herself almost hadn't survived her training period with Tianbing, and her ribs ached from the memory of what they'd experienced at the tips of his shiny black shoes.

Xiao Mei didn't react to the news. An Ni turned her head so that they wouldn't see the rogue tear that slid down her face. Not for herself, but for Xiao Mei. She felt the girl's tiny arm slip around her and squeeze gently for support. Xiao Mei was still innocent and wouldn't be able to save herself—that much was for sure.

Chapter Three

By the next afternoon, the rain that had relented the evening before decided to make a return visit. With one hand on the tattered rope, her ladder over her shoulder, and one hand clutching her camera bag, Mari led the camel down the rocky path to the parking lot. In her cheap plastic slippers, her feet were already soaked, and since she'd run out of the apartment late and forgotten her raincoat, the colorful outfit she wore would soon be wet, too. With her long, dark hair already damp, it would be a long walk to get the camel to his shed, and then back up the hill for her equipment, then a long walk to the bus stop where she'd get her ride close to home. Even thinking of it exhausted her. She just hoped the weather was a passing shower and wouldn't turn into a thunder and lightning storm. Her small patio garden could use the rain, but only if it continued slow and steady, instead of becoming the torrential downpour that threatened.

The camel grunted behind her and stopped. Mari turned around and faced it.

"*Guo lai,* Chu Chu." She urged it to come along. It stood its ground, glaring at her in defiance. It was no secret that he preferred to be handled by her husband. The beast hated women and always had.

Mari tugged again. *He will not win this battle.* Yes, the camel was cranky and tired, but so was she. At least she had been for the last few months, since her husband had fallen off the blasted animal and hurt his back. Now the business—their only livelihood—was totally in her hands. No longer did she simply bring customers in with gentle smiles and persuasion, hand them off to Bolin, then sell them a photo. Now she had to bring them in, get them dressed in traditional Chinese garb, help hoist them onto the camel, then take their photo. What had always been too much for even two people now fell on her shoulders alone.

Finally Chu Chu moved forward a foot, and Mari sighed in relief, despite the pinch the ladder was making in her shoulder muscle. Then the camel stopped again. *What does the stubborn animal want?* Mari had already fed him, and she'd even covered his back with an old plastic tarp because she knew he hated the rain. Why did they have to own such a snippy old creature? Was he too drunk from the beers she'd given him? She knew alcohol wasn't good for Chu Chu, but the tourists loved it, and Bolin made her promise she'd do it to give them a better chance at more tips. Now besides him being stubborn and drunk, the rain was making him smell horrid.

She looked behind the camel to see people hurrying down the lane, too inconvenienced by the rain to continue their sightseeing on the Great Wall. They walked—some ran—with their bodies bent and newspapers, bags, or umbrellas over their heads to keep from getting wet.

On each side of the road, the street merchants with small shops worked fast to pull their items in so they could close the wooden shutters and save their merchandise. It'd be a tough afternoon for most; because of the rain, they'd lose a lot of sales before nightfall. Mari cursed under her breath. She'd really started to hate her life and the competition that was such a big part of the Great Wall experience. But they were lucky. Permits to work at the Great Wall of China were hard to come by, and even with it, the government still got the largest piece of profit. It'd taken them three years to finally secure a permit for their meager business. Still, it had been better than working the farm. At least with their new life, they had some time left in the day that wasn't dictated by watering, seeding, picking, or caring for animals.

Mari looped the strap of her bag around her neck and pushed the ladder higher on her arm so that she could use both hands to pull the camel. She dug her heels in and whistled, then pulled.

Chu Chu didn't move an inch.

"Hello! Uh . . . *Ni hao* . . ."

Mari turned to see who was witnessing her embarrassing moment of tug-of-war with the camel and found herself face to face with a tall, light-haired foreigner with the bluest eyes she'd ever seen. He looked like what the elders called a foreign ghost.

"*Ni hao,*" she answered, then went back to tugging on the rope. Her humiliation reached a new level.

"You speak English?" he asked from over her shoulder.

Mari wanted him to go away. It was times like these she wished she was still a girl growing up in the warm comfort of the small neighborhood *hutong* in Wuxi. She missed the days when everyone knew her as the local scavenger's daughter.

"Yes, I speak English." Of course she'd had to learn basic English in order to do her job well. Most of her customers didn't speak Mandarin, other than the occasional *ni hao* or *zai jian*. And learning English was one of the few things she'd done that her sisters hadn't—something her parents proudly bragged about. But obviously this stranger assumed she was too poor or illiterate to speak another language. She stopped moving and took a long slow breath to calm herself. It wasn't the man's fault that her camel was a devil.

"You have your hands full. It looks like you're leaving—or trying to—but I wanted to see if you have time to do one more photo. You're the girl that does photos of tourists on the camels, right?"

She pushed a wet strand of hair out of her eyes. "I'm one of them, yes. But it's raining." She pointed at the sky, as if the man needed to look closer.

He laughed, and Mari was taken aback by the way his voice rang out, deep and pleasant, but strong, too. Strangely, he was not the least bit perturbed by the weather.

"I can see that. But it's like this. If you'd take just one more customer, you'd help me out tremendously. I'm staying here in Beijing for a while, but my boss—see that man coming up the lane?—he's come from the States to check up on me and sightsee while he's here."

Mari shrugged. *How is that supposed to affect me?*

The man leaned in close and lowered his voice. "This will sound so silly, but here's the deal. He leaves tomorrow, but he promised his bratty kids he'd get a photo of him on a camel at the Great Wall. I can take a photo, but I don't have access to a camel. And if I don't make this happen, he'll *lose face*—as you people say here—and there'll be hell to pay."

Mari stepped back to get some space between them. He talked so fast, she only caught fragments of what he was saying. The intensity of his stare felt like he saw clear down to her soul. She didn't like it, either.

She looked over his shoulder. There, huffing and puffing with a face as red as the inside of a ripe watermelon, was the biggest man she'd ever seen. Even in the cool rain, the *laoban* looked overheated but determined as he trudged up the steep walkway. He carried an umbrella, so Mari assumed the wet sheen on his face was sweat, not rain. He also wore a scowl that made him look like he was dragging the thunder right along with him.

"*Dui bu qi*, I was just leaving," she apologized, but she needed to go on home. She really didn't want to unpack her camera, set everything back up, then get even wetter just for a few renminbi. She tugged at Chu Chu. He resisted. Again.

"Look—please. I'll pay you triple what you usually get. And your camel doesn't look ready to go, anyway. Please." His voice went up an octave as he looked quickly over his shoulder and saw his boss man getting closer.

Mari felt a rush of sympathy for the man at having such an angry-looking *laoban*. At least she didn't have anyone but her husband to answer to, and he was in too much pain to care much about anything other than getting the medicine he needed to keep him out of his head.

She wavered. Her first impression was wrong—looking into his eyes, she saw intelligence, but also something more. Something deeper and intense. Something interesting.

He smiled, showing that he took her hesitation as agreement. "Great! You'll do it. Here, let me lead your camel. Where're we going?" The man reached over to take the rope from Mari.

"Wait. I didn't say yes." She jerked her hand back, keeping Chu Chu attached to her. The poor foreigner didn't realize her camel would never move for him. He didn't just hate women—he was also racist and hated anyone not Chinese. Just getting photos with them perched on his back was hard enough, but for a foreigner to lead him was out of the question. Chu Chu would spit right in the man's face, if he got close enough.

The fat man arrived and bent over, putting his hands on his knees while he breathed deeply. Mari studied him. He was at least a head shorter than the light-haired man. She'd seen big foreigners many times, but this guy had no business trekking around in his condition. She wondered about his lungs and hoped they would hold out. She was wet and tired and didn't need to be part of a dramatic medical situation.

The fat man looked back and forth between them. "Are we ready? I have a meeting at the hotel in two hours," he said, then slowly stood and examined Mari from head to toe.

Mari felt naked under his gaze, and it sent a shiver of revulsion through her. She knew her clothes were beginning to stick to her body, and the flimsy gauze of her costume left little to the imagination. She mentally berated herself again for forgetting her raincoat.

The nicer—and slimmer—one immediately came out of his jacket and took the ladder from her, then draped the coat around Mari's shoulders. It was huge, swallowing her up and giving her instant relief from the chilly rain. He nodded approvingly. "Here, you can use my jacket until we leave."

She met his eyes, and a look of understanding passed between them. His expression told her he knew his boss was a creep, but he needed her help anyway.

"Can we do this?" he asked. "It won't take long."

He waited for her to answer, and Mari could sense his silent plea. She sighed. She never could say no.

"Fine. But I'll lead my own camel." She turned and took a few steps. But to her continued embarrassment, Chu Chu still refused to move. She cursed him under her breath, then begged him to behave. He still stared blankly ahead, not responding.

"Let me try," the tall one said, taking the rope. He swung his backpack around his shoulder and then used both hands to grip the lead.

Mari's hands were chapped and sore, so she just let him have it. He was stubborn, obviously, so she supposed he'd have to see for himself that Chu Chu didn't like foreigners. But to her amazement, the man began trudging up the hill and her stupid camel calmly followed as if he'd known him forever. The fat boss trailed behind them both as Mari stood watching, her hands on her hips.

The man leading Chu Chu turned around for a moment, smiling at her. "You coming? I don't know where you want us. Can you lead the way?"

Mari threw her hands in the air, wondering what she was getting into. Then she let them flop to her sides and jogged to catch up to them.

Could this day get any worse? At least with one more customer she'd be able to bring home a profit. Bolin would be pleased—if she could get him awake.

Mari quickly scrubbed the potatoes and sliced the peppers, then added them to the sizzling oil in the wok. After a quick glance across the room at her husband sprawled on the couch, she balanced the empty strainer on the pile of dishes in the sink, wishing again that she had more counter space. She knew she shouldn't be ungrateful when so many had nothing, but the truth was she hated their stuffy apartment in the high-rise building. Bolin had acted as though they'd won the lottery when they'd finally been approved for the loan to buy it, but this place—it didn't come close to feeling like the home she'd left behind when she'd agreed to marry Bolin. But surprisingly, he wasn't even bothered by the unkempt look of laundry hanging out of every window of the grayish building and sagging balconies supporting plants and trees that wilted from the incessant pollution. Each time Mari walked up the street and their building came into view, she couldn't repress a sigh of disappointment.

But perhaps things would change and her life would one day be what she'd hoped for when she'd accepted his proposal. And who would've thought that her taking the chore of visiting the vegetable market each week would net her a husband? She remembered the first day she'd laid eyes on him. He had been working hard to unload the baskets of vegetables from his father's truck, the sheen of his sweat glistening on his muscles as he worked. He turned and caught sight of Mari, a glimpse that had startled him enough that he'd dropped the basket of turnips he carried, which had rolled quickly right to her very own feet.

She'd laughed and bent down to help him gather the vegetables and he'd stopped moving, put his hand out to stop her, and told her to do it again.

"Do what again?" she'd asked.

"Laugh like that. I've never heard another laugh like yours, and it sounds like music," Bolin had spoken softly, mesmerizing Mari with the intensity of his request. Of course, she couldn't laugh on command, but she'd returned to his stand the next week.

And the week after that.

He'd told her that, with her petite frame and wild hair, she reminded him of a princess from long ago. She smiled when she remembered all the things he used to tell her—courting her in fifteen-minute increments as she picked through his vegetables. Their meetings were short but packed with anticipation and hope.

His Baba, the grumpy old farmer, had at first tried to dissuade their attraction, but when it continued, he began allowing Bolin to take an hour off when Mari came by. When Bolin told her he knew he wasn't much, but he wanted to marry her anyway, Mari had told him he had to come to her home and ask her Baba. He'd come that very afternoon, and the rest was history. From then on, he'd tell her to let him *hear her music* when he wanted her to laugh. The sound always made him smile and he'd tell her he'd found the best wife in China.

She looked over to the couch. Despite the racket she made preparing their dinner, Bolin still hadn't moved. She hadn't laughed like that in years. No longer did he ask to hear her music—now he didn't want to hear anything from her or anyone else.

She sighed and turned back to their dinner. At least one thing had gone her way for the day. Bolin was still sleeping, and she was able to get out of her wet clothes and even soak her freezing feet in hot water for a few minutes before starting dinner. She was exhausted, and her body ached from her nose to her toes, but she still had her household duties to finish before she could even think about going to bed.

She suppressed a smile as she thought back to her last customers. The man—named Maximilian but who went by Max, he'd told her—had almost had a nervous breakdown when his boss couldn't fit on the camel. She should've known his backside would be too large to squeeze between Chu Chu's humps, but he'd wanted to try anyway. Finally he'd settled for photos of himself standing on the stepladder beside the camel. Max had still paid her very well for her time, and if she wanted, Mari could probably even take a few days off this week with the extra funds. But she wouldn't. They needed to save all they could for the upcoming winter when the tourist season wasn't so busy. It would be her first cold season working without Bolin, and Mari didn't know how she was going to manage it. Already her body ached day and night from all the manhandling of Chu Chu.

"Mari . . . where's my pills?" Bolin called weakly.

"I've got them, but you need to eat something first. Remember, the doctor said not to take them on an empty stomach."

"*Aiya*, bring me my pills. My back is killing me."

Mari looked over the wok and saw Bolin struggling to sit up. His hair was too long, and it stuck up all over his head. She needed to wash it, if he'd let her. Sighing, she went to her purse and removed the small bag. She opened it and took out the bottle, then shook two capsules into her hand. She poured a glass of water and took it and the pills to Bolin.

"Fine. But if you get queasy, don't blame me. I'm making your favorite—sliced *tudou* and peppers." He was a vegetarian, and though Mari had tried to tell him a bit of meat would help him gain strength, he still refused it.

He took the water and pills from her and swallowed them greedily. Mari felt a rush of sympathy. He wasn't the same man she'd fallen for and married, but it wasn't his fault. Pain and a constant feeling of helplessness were bound to change a person. And Bolin didn't have anyone else to take his frustrations out on. She looked at his body, too thin from months of lying around. The doctor had told him to begin exercising in small doses, but Bolin refused, saying it hurt too much. She knew why it hurt, too. He'd let his muscles shrivel up to nothing.

19

Mari couldn't help a vision of the foreigner, Max, coming to her. After they'd gotten the photos, he'd not only led Chu Chu to the shed a mile from the wall, but he'd also carried her bag of equipment, along with his own. He'd even toted her small ladder over one arm so she wouldn't have to go back. He hadn't let Mari carry anything, and that gesture stuck with her—it'd been a while since anyone had treated her that way. It made her think of her Baba and how, from the day he'd found her, he'd acted as if she were a precious treasure.

"Bolin, do you think you might want to get up and take a walk down the hall after dinner?"

"No, Mari. I can't—and stop asking me!" He handed her back the emptied glass and turned over on the couch, facing the wall. He'd be asleep within minutes.

Mari went back to the wok and picked up the wooden spoon, stirring the potatoes. She wished she had someone to talk to about her day and all the strange people she'd seen. She thought of An Ni and, like she'd done a hundred times that day, mentally scolded herself for not going to check on her. She glanced at the hump of blankets that was her husband and considered telling him about the girl, but she knew what he'd say: *Leave it alone, Mari.* Bolin had never had a heart for others, and Mari thought that came from the hard life of a farmer's family. In their world, it was difficult enough just to feed those under the same roof, let alone look out for strangers. Bolin wasn't cruel—he'd simply grown up a different way than she had.

She looked at her desk. "I got a letter from Mama yesterday." She picked up the paper and unfolded it. She'd read it twice already, but since she couldn't think of any other conversation to start with Bolin, she figured he might be interested, or at the least she could keep him awake until she could get some food into him.

He didn't respond from his place on the couch.

Mari put the lid on the potatoes and leaned against the counter, gazing at the gracefully drawn characters that made up her Mama's handwriting. She felt she could almost hear her voice, as gentle as a tender breeze on spring leaves. "Mama says Peony is still struggling—she doesn't want to accept that she has any foreign blood racing through her veins."

She looked up. There was still no response from Bolin, but just thinking of her little sister brought a lump to Mari's throat. She hoped her husband felt a thread of guilt that she hadn't gotten to go home to be there when Peony had first been contacted by the woman who'd abandoned her on a park bench years before. Her little sister had slipped into a short depression, and the sisters gathered around her—giving her support after that one square of paper had rocked her world. Mari was the only one who couldn't afford to come home, and Bolin should've felt bad about that. But she doubted he did. He could only think of one thing, one obsession. And traveling a few hours to comfort someone else wasn't it. Losing himself in the haze of his painkillers was his only focus these days.

Mari blinked back the tears that threatened to come—tears of homesickness and thoughts of everyone gathering without her. Her Baba had offered to wire her enough for a train ticket, but even if she did make herself accept money from him despite knowing his own struggles, how could she have gone and left Bolin all alone? She'd had to decline and, even worse, make up a story to tell her family about why she couldn't be there.

She straightened her shoulders and took a deep breath. What was done was done. At least her sisters and parents were there for Peony. As her sister had grown older and noticed the stares she received from others, Peony had finally come to the conclusion she wasn't strictly Chinese. Still, Mari appreciated the total honesty their parents had always maintained with all their daughters. They'd always told all they knew about the birth and abandonment circumstances of each girl and how she'd come to be a part of the family—*flowers in the Zheng family garden*, as her Baba liked to say.

"She also said the *hutong* is planning to have their biggest new year's celebration ever."

Bolin grunted. Mari knew he really didn't care about any of it, but she was going to keep talking even if he didn't. She smiled when she read about Jasmine and how she was learning to read. At least that was an outlet that might give her another means to communicate. Jasmine wasn't deaf, but for some reason, she had never spoken since she'd joined the family. Mari hoped that her parents could find someone to teach her little sister sign language. That would be her best opportunity for communicating when she got older and was ready to go out into the world.

She read on. "And listen to this—Ivy and Lily are starting to look more and more different."

Her sisters were twins, and despite the fact that one of them was blind, for years they'd looked nothing less than identical.

"Is dinner ready?" Bolin asked, his voice barely more than a mumble.

She scanned the letter to the end, looking for anything else that might interest Bolin. She skipped over the paragraph about the youngest in the family. The last time she'd visited, the toddler was just learning to walk. Just the visual of her sisters standing over what only months before had been a snuggly little infant, holding her hands as she wobbled along in her first steps, made Mari's heart ache for that one milestone she'd never achieved—motherhood.

"And Maggi Mei is getting better at sewing—it's something she can do when everyone else is too busy to entertain her. Isn't that great, Bolin?"

He grunted again. There was more she'd like to share with him, but she knew he wasn't listening. No longer did she feel she was a part of a marriage; now they were more like caretaker and patient—and Mari was lonely. Back at home, they were all involved with each other—each day most likely filled with laughter and an air of festivity, despite their hardships. But here, Mari struggled every day to just make ends meet, and she had no one to share it with, because she didn't want anyone to know. She'd continue to return letters to her mother, full of fairytale details of her adventurous Beijing life, until she could figure out a way to get back on track. And first things first—she had to find a way to turn Bolin back into the strong man she'd married. Even more than his assistance in providing for their tiny family, she missed the intimacy between them—that feeling that she wasn't alone in the world. She missed his arms around her at night, his voice whispering in her ear. This person—this new cold thing that lay quiet and lifeless before her now—he was only a shell of the man she'd married, and she wasn't going to stand for it anymore.

She took a deep breath and pulled back her shoulders before she slid the wok off the heat and pulled two bowls from the cabinet. She looked at Bolin again, willing him to wake up—wishing for one of the smiles or kind words he used to be so generous with.

He remained still. She sighed and prepared herself. It would be a battle, but she would have victory tonight, even though getting him to actually eat would probably be harder than getting Chu Chu to move.

Chapter Four

"N*i hao,*" Mari heard someone behind her calling out. She turned and was surprised to see the foreigner, Max, strutting toward her. She didn't have the energy to force a smile, but she waved half-heartedly. Yet another difficult night with Bolin had led into an even more difficult day. She'd had only a few customers, barely any tips, and the stubborn camel was giving her a headache.

Max jogged the last few feet until he stood before her. "How are you?"

Mari looked at him and then back at the camel. Couldn't he see? She was exhausted and aggravated—the story of her life, lately. It was ironic that people used to tell her she had the most musical laughter and lightest spirit they'd ever known. If they could all see her now, they'd not even recognize her.

"I'm fine. Just taking this stubborn creature back to his shed for the day." Chu Chu glared at her under the fringe of coarse hair that mostly hid his eyes. She looked up at the stranger. What did he want? *Were the photos not good enough?* Mari looked around him and didn't see the fat boss man anywhere in sight. "What do you need? More photos? You'll have to come back tomorrow, and this time I mean it. I'm done for today."

Max reached out and put a hand on Chu Chu. Mari expected the difficult camel to rear his head back and show his yellow teeth, but surprisingly he allowed the gesture.

"I'm shooting my own photos today. This is one of my favorite places to take in the scenery. Then I saw you and wanted to thank you again for what you did."

Mari raised her eyebrows. "You came all the way out here—probably by taxi, as I don't see many of you people on the buses—and made your way past the aggressive shop owners and souvenir hawkers, to climb this rigorous wall to *look at the scenery*? Please." When the words were out, she realized she probably sounded very rude. For once she wasn't proud of the way she'd picked up English so well from the many books, lessons, and practicing at the English corner with foreigners. The young university students passed along more than grammar, and Mari knew her sarcasm was a remnant of those long days of practice and striving to emulate their inflections.

Max nodded, and his face took on a serious expression. He looked over the wall at the steep mountainside and wild terrain. "Really. I do it all the time. If you avoid looking at the flashy cable cars, the hawkers pushing all the mass-manufactured junk, and the thousands of rude tourists—the history underneath it all is phenomenal. Can you imagine, when this wall was being constructed, it was called the longest cemetery in history because of all the workers who lost their lives and were buried along it?"

Mari shrugged. It sort of stung that a foreigner knew more about her own country's history than she did—but she wouldn't let him know that.

He pointed toward the west. "And out there, thousands of hostile Mongolians threatened to charge, and the Chinese stood their ground and pledged death before destruction."

Mari watched him talk, saw the excitement shining in his eyes and heard the rise and fall of his voice as he mused about history he had no connection to. It was interesting to her, this man's evident love for China.

"Anyway, I try to capture candid pictures of people. Have you ever watched their faces when they're looking at something amazing and letting their minds explore the possibilities of the scenes before them? If you can get them in that split second when they forget the chaos around them and let themselves be immersed in what might have been—it's magical."

He was right, but she wouldn't tell him that. Seeing the wall for the first time *was* magical. She still remembered the day she and Bolin had traveled to Beijing, full of ideas and excitement, ready to shed their humble beginnings and make a new life. Their first stop had been the Wall, a monument even their own fathers had not had the honor of seeing yet. Bolin had stared out over the ledge, obviously so proud that he was going to get a chance to be more than a farmer. His enthusiasm was contagious, and he'd inspired Mari that day, too. But now that moment felt like at least a century ago. Their magic had faded.

"Are you a photographer?" Mari asked, curious now. He spoke like a poet, and unlike any foreigner she'd come in contact with.

"Photojournalist," Max said. "I'm independent, but that man you saw—my *laoban*—he's sponsoring my time in China, hoping I'll get a scoop that no one else has. Something he can take credit for. He'd like to stay here himself, but he says China is a hardship he can't handle. But he wanted to come to this part of the wall because he'd heard about Nixon visiting it way back in the early seventies."

"In what way is China a hardship?" Now Mari really was curious, and not about President Nixon—she'd heard all that before. She was always enthralled with how other countries felt about China, and despite her own troubles, she couldn't imagine ever wanting to live anywhere else. Her country had more history than any other place in the world, after all.

Max looked embarrassed and cleared his throat. "Well, you know, the food. He thinks—well he's an idiot, and I don't think this—but *he* thinks it's unsanitary here. He's afraid if he stays longer than a few days, he'll end up with some crazy infection or illness. But I love China." His face reddened, and he switched subjects. "Hey, listen, want me to pull your camel back to the shed? I remember the way."

Mari hesitated. If Bolin found out that she was having more than a business conversation with a strange man, he'd be angry. But then, she was tired, and Chu Chu walked so much better for Max than for her.

"Hao le," she agreed. The faster she got the camel back in the shed, the faster she could get home. And she might even have time to stop by the block An Ni had been on and see if the girl was there.

Max held the rope tighter and gave it one pull. Chu Chu began walking behind him as if he were the gentlest creature on earth. Mari felt like kicking him in his gently swaying rear. But she kept up with them, grateful for the respite from tugging the animal for another mile.

"Were your *laoban's* children satisfied that their father was a true adventurer?" Mari found it hard to believe that one photo of the man on a camel could mean that much—but still, she'd paid their entire month's electric bill with the generous tip.

Max laughed. "I guess they did, because he hasn't called me with any butt chewing since he was here that week."

"Butt chewing?" Mari asked.

Chu Chu decided at that moment to move forward—or more accurately, lunge forward—and Max had to drag his heels in to stop the animal from pulling him down the walkway.

Mari caught up to them and grabbed the halter.

Chu Chu stopped fidgeting immediately, and Mari let go, glad to let Max handle him. "You were saying? What is a butt chewing?"

"Oh, sorry," Max laughed again. "Just American slang that means he hasn't given me any negative feedback on my job lately."

She nodded. Americans were strange. She much preferred to work with the Europeans—at least their English was comprehensible. She'd learned the language from books and unfortunately, books did a shoddy job of presenting actual casual conversation. Now she felt like an idiot.

"Oh, *dui.*" She hoped he'd step up his pace. She needed to get home; Bolin would be eagerly awaiting his next medication and would be angry if she was late.

Mari looked at her watch as Max waited for her answer. He said he wanted to ask her questions about Beijing—get her take on the city. She knew she should be getting right home, but honestly, the man had helped her get stubborn Chu Chu to his shelter again. Not only that, but he'd carried most of the equipment, giving her sore muscles a break. He'd saved her at least an hour and maybe more. Would one cup of tea really be too much to agree to? With one glance at the hopeful expression on his face, she made up her mind. It had been ages since anyone cared to spend time with her, so she wasn't going to feel guilty for making a friend.

"*Hao le,*" she agreed. "I'll go but I really can't stay long."

His smile grew so broad, it covered his face. He took her arm and led her across the path, made treacherous by the old stones, to the bottom of the hill and over to the parking lot, chattering as they walked. Mari expected to take a taxi, but instead they stopped in front of a small, blue van, and Max tapped on the window.

"*Aiya!*" The driver jumped, startled out of his nap. He sat contorted in the driver's seat, his legs somehow propped on the dashboard. The noise sent him clumsily working to get back into a proper position, then he leaned over and unlocked the door.

Max opened it and held his arm out, inviting her to step in. "My chariot."

Mari hesitated before getting in. She'd heard of the crazy serial killers the West seemed to breed relentlessly, but would one as chivalrous and kind as Max really have found his way to China? And why would he have come here, when there were so many naïve women walking the streets in America, who were surely easier to get to? She was being silly. There was no way he meant her any harm.

She followed her instinct and climbed in. Max went to the back and stored all their stuff in the rear hatch, slammed it, then returned to the passenger side and climbed in. He gave the driver instructions, and they were off.

She leaned back in the seat to take the pressure off her aching feet. She had to admit, it was nice not to stand around and wait for a taxi to take her to her bus stop.

"Rough day?" Max asked after setting his camera gear on the floor at his feet.

Mari nodded. "Lately it's always a rough day."

"Don't you have someone to help you with all that? It seems like a lot for one person—especially one as small as you. I hate to say it, but I can tell that camel is a handful."

She looked at him, but his intense gaze told her he didn't mean anything flirtatious by it. He was truly curious. "I used to, but my husband got hurt and now he can't work. I'm just handling things until he gets better. Then he'll be back and take charge again." She hoped she sounded more confident than she felt. These days, she wondered if Bolin would ever be well enough to leave their apartment. She couldn't even get him off the couch.

"I'm sorry to hear that. How did he get hurt?"

Mari took a deep breath. The truth would make her husband look like an idiot. But a lie would make her feel like one—so the truth it was.

"You see how stubborn Chu Chu is, right? Well, he never likes to be ridden. We work hard enough just to get him to stand still so we can get the photo shots."

"Aw, that camel isn't so bad. Looks to me like he's just old and tired. I can imagine when I'm a senior citizen, I won't want a bunch of people on my back, either," Max said and winked at her.

"He is old. But he's not *that* old. Anyway, he was being obstinate one day about going to his shelter, and Bolin—my husband—got angry and leapt on his back, then kicked at him as though he was riding a bull. Chu Chu started charging, then stopped abruptly and threw Bolin over his head. Since then, my husband's been in agony because his back really hasn't healed."

That made her think of Bolin's medication, and she felt a flush of guilt that he was waiting for her.

"Man, that sounds awful. Can't the doctors do anything for him?" Max asked.

Mari reached in her bag, rummaging for the pills. "They say his back is not broken—it was just strained. They gave him these pills—hold on, I can't remember the name."

She pulled the bag closer to the window for more light and opened it wide. The pills were not there. "Oh no. I hope I didn't drop his medicine. It was in my bag last night—I'm sure of it."

"Look again," Max urged her. "We can go back if we need to look at the wall."

She rummaged some more. She vividly remembered putting the bottle back in her bag the night before. She was always careful. The pills were strong, and she didn't want Bolin getting them and taking more than he should.

"They aren't here. I hope they fell out last night and are at my house." She knew Bolin would have no reason to think she'd left them behind, so he wouldn't look for them. She just hoped she got to them before he stumbled over the bottle.

The driver pulled to the curb, and they got out of the car. Instead of heading to her regular bus stop, she followed Max to the noodle shop.

Inside they sat at a corner table, and Mari tried to hide her smile at Max's somewhat intelligible attempt at ordering *cha* and the special of the day, *Běijīng Jiǎozi*. The server—a small-framed and shy girl—watched him talk then turned to Mari for translation. She complied and reiterated that they wanted green tea and dumplings. Max threw his hands in the air as the waitress walked away, scribbling their order on her pad.

"What? Isn't that what I just said?"

He looked so incredulous that Mari let out a laugh, then covered her mouth. She nodded. "It's your face. You are too white. She doesn't expect Chinese to come from you, so her ears aren't attuned to it. But yes, you said it correctly."

He rolled his eyes. "I was in here yesterday, and they understood me just fine."

But then he smiled, and Mari knew he wasn't really upset. She liked that in him. Most of the foreigners she dealt with got frustrated and short-tempered when they couldn't be understood or things didn't go their way. She'd seen more than one stomp away, cursing to themselves that they'd ever come to China, this reaction usually brought about after they'd become winded while walking along the wall, or when too many souvenir hawkers had pushed them past their limits. What some didn't understand was the difference between selling five postcard packets or none might mean the difference between feeding their family that night or going hungry. Jobs weren't easy to come by in China, and tapping into the foreign tourist market was usually one of the last resorts for those who couldn't find other less frustrating work.

"Where did you learn to speak Chinese?" Mari asked.

Max dropped his eyes to the plastic menu on the table and played with the curled-up corner. "My daughter."

"Oh, is she a teacher?"

He looked up at her, and Mari thought she saw a flash of pain before he camouflaged it with a smile. "No, not officially. But since she became old enough to speak, she's been infatuated with China. We—well, really *she*—decided we'd try to learn to speak the language, and eventually, we'd come here."

"Did you also have a formal teacher?"

Max let out a small chuckle. "No, but believe me, my girl is relentless when she sets her mind to something. She probably taught me more than any teacher could. She made up these crazy little flash cards and pasted them all over the house—labeling every item in sight with the Chinese word. At dinner several times a week we weren't allowed to use English. We could only speak Chinese. She's a tough little cookie, and I found out fast that if I wanted my dinner, I had to focus. There were nights I went hungry for hours until I learned the proper words for *pass me the chicken*."

Mari laughed at the story he painted, and Max stopped.

"Your laugh. It's so—how do I say this?—infectious. It sounds like music."

Mari felt her cheeks burning, and she realized that she hadn't laughed in such a long time. "*Xie xie*. That's what my husband used to tell me."

Max was quiet for a minute, then started back in about his daughter. "Honestly, my daughter took to Chinese much better than me. But then, she was the most determined to learn. By six years old, she could say her colors, numbers, and even speak some simple sentences. By seven she could name every object in the house with its Chinese name. By eight, she'd stop Asian people at the store or wherever and ask them if they could speak Mandarin, then delight them with her gift."

The waiter came and set two mugs and a steaming carafe of tea on the table. Mari picked it up and poured Max a cup. "I'm sure they were very intrigued. Were they American, like your daughter?"

"Oh, they were intrigued, all right. I don't know if they were American, but most of them were enchanted at the way she interacted with strangers. And it made me so proud, I felt like busting each time she did it. China was her thing—at nine, she'd recount hours of history and legends. Her Mama used to tell her if she spent just half the time working on her math that she did reading about China, she'd be a genius by high school. But she wasn't interested in math—her mind was on seeing the Great Wall and visiting Xi'an and the soldiers."

Mari watched as he enamored her with stories of his daughter, then suddenly he stopped talking and brought his tea to his lips. For a moment he'd looked happy and excited, but now he shielded his eyes from her and was stone quiet.

"Why didn't you bring her here with you, if coming to China was her dream?" she asked.

Max stared out the front windows a moment, then set his cup down and stood, looking from one corner of the shop to the other. "Is there a bathroom in here?"

Mari pointed at the far wall. "Yes, just over there."

"I'll be back," Max said, his voice grave, as he walked away.

Mari watched his suddenly stiff back and wondered what had changed his mood so abruptly.

She stared out the window at the corner that the girl, An Ni, had stood at several nights ago. She hadn't seen her since, but she had thought of her often and even dreamed of her the night before. In the dream, An Ni had beckoned her closer, pulling at her to get to her ear as if to tell her a secret.

Mari was startled out of her thoughts by the clattering of dishes as the waitress returned and placed the two bowls of dumplings on the table. She left chopsticks, and Mari asked her to bring a couple spoons just as Max returned.

He sat down across from her and cleared his throat. "Are you available as a guide?"

Mari picked up a dumpling with her chopsticks and sucked the juice from it, then swallowed it. "A guide?"

"Yes, as you can see, my Chinese isn't that great—even with the relentless lessons from my daughter—and I'm planning on visiting a few more sites and could use someone to translate the history there." He lifted his bowl and slurped the broth, looking like a local to Mari as he waited for her answer.

"But I have to work at the Wall," she finally said, though to be honest, she dreaded each morning that she trekked to the shed, retrieved Chu Chu, then led him up the Wall to face another exhausting day.

"Let your camel rest. Maybe that'll put him in better spirits. Work a few days for me, and I'll pay what you'd make at the Wall."

Mari hesitated, thinking. If she accepted his offer, she could make some extra money, maybe even enough to catch up on the bills, and Bolin never needed to know.

Max plucked a business card from his wallet and, holding both corners, presented it to her. She appreciated that he took the extra effort to do it the Chinese way, holding it with both thumbs outward as though extending a gift of friendship, and she accepted it, then read it.

"Keep my card and call me tonight if you decide to take me up on my offer," Max said, then stood. He peeled a pink bill from the stack of money he pulled from his pocket, and he laid it on the table.

"You want to wait for your change?" Mari said, pointing to the bill. "It won't be even half that. She'll bring you back some money."

"I don't want anything back," Max said. "The rest is for that waitress. She looks like she could use it."

Mari picked her bag up from the floor, and with one last look at the money on the table—more than she'd made all day—she followed Max out the door. She couldn't help but shake her head. Foreigners and their hastiness to part with their money always amazed her.

Max watched as Mari walked away, her tousled hair swinging to the sway of her hips. He'd met a lot of women in China, and thus far, none of them had piqued his interest like this one. And it wasn't anything sexual. He wasn't looking for that complication in his life, and as far as he could predict, never would again. But this girl, there was just something about her—something deep and perhaps haunting. Something familiar. He'd been drawn to her from the very moment he'd seen her dragging her stubborn camel. And if he was being truthful with himself, he thought maybe he'd seen his own broken spirit in the mirror of her eyes. He'd love to know more, but he didn't want to intrude on her privacy. Maybe like him, her demons were too many to tell. Yet it was startling to him, this feeling of wanting to connect with another human being after the last few years of such self-imposed isolation.

And she'd almost gotten him to talk about things he hadn't been able to discuss before. He'd come close—even straddled the line of spilling it all—but thankfully, he'd stopped himself before she could see what a weak man he really was.

He grabbed his bag and threw it over his shoulder, then walked along the street, taking care to give way to the passing pedestrians. It was nearing the dinner hour, and people had more pep in their step, probably heading to their homes—a safe place away from strangers and a reason to feel optimistic about the future. He'd had that once, then lost it. But he still marveled that he was finally in Asia. Getting to travel to China on assignment was bittersweet, but he knew it was the right thing to do. He'd been pulled here by a force that felt almost not of this world, a force he'd finally caved to, and then he'd made the calls to make the trip happen.

But hovering beneath his determination to journal about the icons of history, combining words and his photographs, he couldn't shake the deep sense of loss that followed him with each step. This wasn't his dream—and he wasn't supposed to be the one doing the discovering. Yes, he was here—*she'd* led him to this place, and so far, he loved it more than he'd thought possible—but even that thought made the reason for him coming even sadder. Made the fact that he was alone more heartbreaking, if that was even possible.

He stopped suddenly. A crushing burden of guilt smothered the bit of relief he felt at avoiding the memory of her face—the crinkle of her nose, and the sound of her laughter. He'd left it hidden in that deep void of his heart, but only for a moment. When he could breathe again, he put one foot in front of the other, focusing on nothing but the path before him.

He made his way home to his small and dark, temporary apartment. He'd allowed himself a brief reprieve from his self-penance of solitude, but now it was time to go back in his shell. Tonight, he would get some work done. He'd sit there, and his fingers would connect with his brain—pecking out the details of the last few days. If he willed it so, maybe it would happen. But what if he couldn't? What if his night ended just like every other night had for months? Would he be strong enough to keep it away?

Doubt started creeping in, causing his hands to shake and his mouth to water, craving the taste of oblivion. As he'd sat across from Mari, he'd not felt the usual yearning. He'd only thought about the petite woman with the almond-shaped eyes that, like his, hid a hurt that couldn't be touched or healed easily. And that laugh. Her laugh came as a close second to one of the most melodious laughs he'd ever heard.

But it wasn't enough. The monster awaited him—waited to consume him. There'd be no more reprieve. He walked as fast as he could back to his apartment and the bottle that had owned him since the day his life had crumbled.

Chapter Five

Mari climbed the stairs quickly, anxious to get up to their apartment and check on Bolin. She was only an hour and a half late, but he'd be angry if he was awake and waiting on his medication. *The medication I've possibly lost.* She stepped a little faster as she prayed the bottle was lying on the floor or possibly even on the kitchen counter. For a little while, she'd allowed herself to relax and forget about her troubles at home, but now she felt guilty. Bolin needed her, and if he found out about Max—even though he was just a customer she'd had a conversation with and nothing more—he'd be livid.

Out of breath, she finally reached their floor and jogged down the hall toward their door, the last apartment. Many of the other residents left their doors standing open until after dinner, giving her a glimpse of family life the way others lived it. When she saw them, it never ceased to amaze her how different they were from the neighbors she'd grown up with. Here, in the city, no one bothered to get to know anyone else or even to lend a helping hand. In her hometown, neighbors were like family—and when someone was down, they rallied.

She passed the Zhao home and saw their daughter sitting at the small table, hunched over what was probably homework while her mother stood in the kitchen, tossing something in a steaming wok. The girl reminded her of An Ni, and Mari felt another streak of guilt. She should've been back over there sooner to check on the girl. But this girl didn't live like An Ni—that was for sure. On the couch behind her, the girl's father relaxed with the remote control in his hand, his feet crossed and resting on their small coffee table. Music played from somewhere in their home, and the scene brought a lump to Mari's throat. They were what she and Bolin had planned to be but had never reached. She looked away and continued on to her own, much less comforting, life.

At the door, she dug in her bag and found her key, then quickly entered, looking straight at the couch to see if Bolin was there.

He wasn't.

She pushed back the first stirrings of alarm. Bolin was always on the couch. She dropped her bag and went to their small bedroom. He wasn't there, either. She backed out and went to the bathroom, peeking around the open door.

"Where the hell have you been?" Bolin looked up from the floor where he squatted over the toilet hole.

Mari backed away, giving him some privacy. She leaned against the wall in the hallway and took a deep breath. Her first lie to her husband was about to leave her lips, and she didn't feel good about it. She paused, then diverted the line of questioning.

"Bolin, your pills weren't in my purse today, and I'm sure I put them there. Do you have them?"

He answered with a grunt.

She heard him moving around, then listened as the sound of water running drowned out his mumbling. Finally he emerged, shoving past her as he headed back to the couch. Mari was taken aback when she caught a whiff of his body odor. She wondered how many days it had been since he'd showered.

"I didn't hear you," she said. "Do you have the pills?"

He reached the couch and stretched out, turning his face to the wall. "*Shi de*, I have them. They're mine, Mari, and I'm not a child. I can keep up with my own medication."

She felt a flash of relief that she hadn't lost the pills. They wouldn't have been able to replace them this week. It was hard enough finding a doctor that would let them leave with medication, as most of them demanded that the patient shuttle back and forth to the hospital to get their drugs given intravenously. But she'd pleaded with the doctor, telling him how hard it was for Bolin to move around and walk, until he'd finally relented. He'd never believe they'd lost a bottle of the expensive drugs and would probably think they'd sold them.

"The doctor told me to keep them, and you know that. When you're sedated, you don't remember how many you've taken. I want them back, Bolin." Mari went to the kitchen and opened their small refrigerator, leaning in to take inventory of the few supplies they had left for the week. She took out a head of cabbage and a carrot, then pulled an onion and ginger root from the wire basket hanging over their sink. She wished for a nice, thick slab of pork. Just once she'd like to cook something she wanted and not have to cater to Bolin—especially when he barely touched what she worked so hard to make.

She sighed. She was being petty, and she knew it. He was sick—and they couldn't afford pork anyway. So what did it matter? After plugging in the rice cooker, she grabbed the soy sauce and pulled the cutting board from the nail on the wall, rinsed and threw down the first vegetable, and started chopping.

"How's Chu Chu doing?" Bolin mumbled from the couch.

Mari looked up. Bolin was showing interest in something other than sleeping. That was progress. She went to a cupboard and pulled out a small bag of rice, measured some out and poured it into the rice cooker. After adding the appropriate amount of water, she placed the lid on and locked it down, then returned to her cutting board.

"He's okay. Still stubborn as can be. The man who brings the hay didn't show up for two days but I gave Chu Chu some cheap fish I got from the market, and he was happy."

She wanted to talk about Bolin, and his health, and their future. But even talking about the camel was preferable to his usual silence. She plugged in the wok and poured in some peanut oil, then went back to chopping.

"He likes dates, if you can find some," Bolin said, and Mari thought she heard a touch of sadness in his voice. *He misses Chu Chu.*

And that was good news, that he still felt connected to something, even if it wasn't her. She wouldn't ruin the moment by telling him they couldn't afford dates. And truth be told, she'd been giving Chu Chu all kinds of things to eat when she couldn't even pay the hay farmer. He'd had plants, grass, and even a few bushes she'd found along the highway and pulled up for him. The stubborn animal had one redeeming quality—he wasn't finicky when he was hungry.

"Okay, I'll try to pick some up from the market. Say, Bolin, do you think you'd want to sit up and watch some television after dinner? There might be something good on the Hong Kong channel," Mari said as she threw everything into the sizzling oil. She hoped they'd get to spend some time as a couple. She really needed his touch—any touch—to make her feel anchored. Lately she almost felt like a ghost moving through life, pushed aside and ignored by everyone.

He didn't answer.

Mari put her spatula down and walked over to the couch. Bolin was sound asleep, his hand curled around his pill bottle. Gently, she pried his fingers off and took the bottle, tucking it into her pocket. She bent and kissed the top of his head, then pulled the coverlet from the top of the couch and spread it over him.

She stood staring down at him, her arms crossed as she examined his profile. He'd aged, she could see that, and the deep grooves that had appeared between his eyebrows showed his constant irritation with his new reality. Even in his sleep, they no longer disappeared—they were a permanent part of this person who had taken control of her husband and buried him underneath a new being who reeked of addiction and depression.

On the table she spotted their engagement book and picked it up. The first page showed them dressed up and posed at the garden park. While they hadn't been able to afford a fancy wedding, her Baba had splurged and paid for the day of photo taking. She and Bolin had laughed, and they'd had so much fun that day. Her smile disappeared as she looked closer.

The faces on the pages of the book were like strangers to her now. Where was that joy? Sapped out of them by real life, she supposed. Now they couldn't even afford to waste a day at the park, much less have a photography session there. She'd be lucky to pull enough money together that month just to cover their living expenses and have anything to eat. She closed the cover on the book and set it down. Seeing how they used to be—and confronting the truth of how much they'd changed—made her so sad.

She just had to get them back to where they were before. But until then, it was up to her to keep them afloat. She remembered that she still had Max's card in her bag. She could call him. But should she leave Chu Chu and do something different? Maybe earn some better money? It was tempting, but she knew Bolin wouldn't approve of her working with a foreigner.

A plume of smoke from the kitchen reminded her of their dinner cooking, and that once again, Mari would be eating alone. She sighed and slowly made her way back there to finish up, so that she, too, could shut out the world by letting sleep overtake her.

Chapter Six

The flames licked at his face as Max breathed shallowly to filter his air. It was hot. Hotter than anything he'd ever felt. So hot that he just knew it was comparable to the pit of fire only spoken about in pulpits and bedtime prayers. The heat burned his nose, and the hairs on his arm stood tall, guarding against the scorching they knew was to come.

But he kept going, inching closer. Why couldn't he move faster? His legs felt as if they were encased in concrete, and the harder he pulled, the heavier they got. He stopped, dropped to his knees and coughed.

Then coughed again, this time so hard he felt his lungs straining to burst.

He was losing his breath—and taking in nothing but black smoke. Finally, he reached the side of a fire truck and crawled past it. He didn't have much farther to go now. He looked up, and through the haze of smoke and flames, there she was.

She screamed for him, and he lunged.

He awoke. Drenched in sweat, his body burned from the heat he'd created with his thrashing. Max looked around the small, dismal room, trying to figure out where he was. The clock on the bedside table flashed four fifteen—morning time.

He sat up and swung his legs over the side of the bed, propping his arms on his knees as he held his throbbing head. He didn't even remember lying down the night before, nor did he remember how much of the tall bottle of Chinese liquor he'd downed before he'd succumbed to the welcome black void. *Bai jiu*, they'd called it and laughed at him when he'd handed over his money. The words translated to *white wine*, but Max thought it should be called firewater, like the Indians used to say. The stuff was harsh, but it had at least put him out of his misery and into a deep, silent sleep—but only for a while, because it never stayed silent or empty. His demons always chased him until they found him, then haunted him until his mind could take no more and he woke in a frenzied state from one nightmare or another. Fires, drowning, car crashes—always a tragedy he was trying to avoid but never quite succeeded in escaping.

He eyed his laptop sitting on the table across the room. He remembered being infuriated with it when once again he'd been unable to string together enough sentences to make him worthy of being called a journalist. *Writer's block.* It was relentless. If it didn't yield soon, no one would give him any more opportunities, and he'd be officially washed up. Emotionally and professionally.

On that thought, he stood. He needed a shower. He knew it was only his imagination, but the stench of smoke and fear surrounded his body like a cloud, overpowering what should have been a reminder of the booze he'd consumed.

He went to the bathroom, turned on the water, and used it to try to rub away the fatigue. The man in the mirror stared back at him, a look of contempt stretched across his face.

A new day.

Another twenty-four hours to carry the pain and regret of his past. Another chance to redeem himself before he knew he would flounder again and try to find peace in the bottom of a bottle.

He cursed at himself, then looked up at the ceiling and glared, pointing a finger at what he couldn't see. He didn't know what he believed anymore, other than the fact that a merciful God would've put him out of his misery long ago.

Five hours later, Max entered the small noodle shop to sip his green tea and wait for Mari. The bald-headed owner was getting to know him quite well now—after more than a half-dozen visits—and had greeted him like an old friend, causing the locals to stare and mumble at his tall frame and pale hair. Max was getting used to the staring. But with the convincingly genuine greeting, for just a moment, he'd almost felt like he belonged in the small community. But the feeling disappeared too soon, and the reality hit him square in the gut—he no longer belonged anywhere.

"Zao, peng you!" The old man called out as Max headed to his usual table. It was interesting what a bit of respect and a generous tip would do for a person. The man had smiled at him through gaps in his teeth, then waved at the waitress to bring tea and a bowl of congee, and to hurry with it. Max nodded his approval. He didn't like or dislike the locally favored breakfast of bland rice porridge, but since he was trying to make an effort to feed his system more than a bottle of spirits each day, he'd swallow it down.

He looked at his watch. Ten minutes, and she should be there. *If she doesn't back out.* For weeks he'd stumbled around Beijing on his own, looking for a story, struggling with the language and finding his way. So he was glad she'd called him and agreed to take him around.

She'd sounded sad on the phone and almost a bit desperate. So perhaps this deal would be good for both of them. Moving around the city would be easier with a guide, and though he could've hired any number of young men or women trained to do the job, he'd not felt the need until he'd met Mari and realized she'd be good company. And he'd need that company. Today would be hard, but it would knock one more place off his list. He brought the cigarette to his lips and took a deep drag, then held his breath to keep from choking. He didn't want anyone around him to know the Chinese brand was harsher than his own American ones. He could probably go to the upper side of town and shop in the expat markets, pay twice or three times the usual price and get the comforts from home, but he didn't want to do that. He was here to really *feel* China—to become a part of it and, in turn, let it consume him until he'd finished what he came to do. That was the promise he'd made, after all. And if nothing else, he was a man of his word. Today might squeeze his already broken heart a little tighter, but he'd found out by experience that the heavy sadness wouldn't kill him.

He looked up from his cup just as Mari came through the door. Today she'd dressed less flamboyantly, but even with the darker—more common—outfit of slacks and a sweater, her wavy hair and the sparkle in her eyes lit up the small shop.

She quickly crossed the room and settled herself across from him, dropping her bag on the floor at her feet. "Good morning."

Max smiled. *"Zǎo shàng hǎo."*

Mari nodded, and her first smile of the day found its place. "Very good. Your tones are getting much better."

He found a bit of courage. *"Chī le ma?"*

Mari let out a laugh, and Max felt a burst of happiness at the sound, then felt ridiculous for it.

"No, I haven't eaten. Have you?" Mari answered.

Max shook his head. "That's all I got for now—it's exhausting to think in Chinese. But I think the old man has sent for some congee. You want a bowl?"

As if on cue, the old man approached their table, and he and Mari began a conversation too fast for Max to keep up with. The man bowed, nodded, then backed away and headed for the kitchen.

"That's an awful lot of talking to ask for a bowl of congee," Max said.

"I told him to forget your order and bring us something different."

"And that is . . . ?" Max was usually open to trying anything, but with his stomach so sensitive lately, he thought he'd better ask.

"Just wait. You'll love it. We call it *yóutiáo*. The owner said it's his treat today because you've become a regular here."

Max couldn't help it, he felt something wasn't exactly right about that. He hadn't known too many Chinese to just give anything for free.

His expression must have shown his reluctance because Mari chuckled. "You're right to be suspicious. The truth is that he assumes you only know how to ask for congee, so he wants to introduce you to a more expensive breakfast. If you like *yóutiáo*, he'll make more money later when you return for it each morning. He's not making a whole lot on your simple breakfast of congee and tea."

Max nodded. Now that made more sense. And if he did like it, he'd ask for it again because, to be honest, the thought of more congee didn't do much to tempt his waning appetite.

"Did you sleep well?" she asked.

He looked away, then back at her. "Well enough." And that was true. He didn't deserve to sleep any better.

"So are you ready to tell me where you want to go today?" Mari took out a small book and started flipping through it. "I bought a Beijing tourist guide. We can choose something popular from here if you like."

"I want to see a *hutong*," Max answered.

Mari continued to look through the book. "*Hao le*, a *hutong*. They have listed several historically preserved ones in here. Let me see—"

Max reached across the table and put his hand on hers to stop her from flipping more pages. "No, I don't want to go to one set up for tourists. I know which one I want to see."

She stopped moving and closed the book. "Oh, okay. Which one?"

Max wanted to maintain eye contact, but he couldn't. He looked over her head and watched the people scurrying by on their way to their next life moment as if they were losing precious seconds. And if they only knew what he knew, they'd know they were.

Finally, he found his voice. "The one where my daughter was found when she was a few days old."

Max helped Mari up into the rickshaw, then took his place beside her. Mari leaned forward and gave the driver his instructions, then she settled back against the seat, not completely relaxing. Max thought she looked as if she wanted to leap from the moving pedicab.

"It's a good thing we're nearby. That'll save us a lot of transportation money today, since we don't have to hire car taxis." Mari said, then scooted over as far as she could.

Max appreciated that she'd understood that the subject he'd raised in the noodle shop was too sensitive and personal to continue until he was ready. "Yes, that's why I took the small apartment in this area. I wanted to be close. Anyway, I'm glad you're fine with taking a pedicab, as I'm down a few hundred renminbi. I lost my wallet in the train last week." It looked to him like the touch of his leg made her nervous, so he moved as far over to the right as he could. With a small distance now between them, she seemed more at ease.

The driver yelled out to offer them a small lap blanket, and Mari replied they didn't need it. It was a little chilly, but it felt good. Along with the satisfaction in his belly from the tasty *yóutiáo* deep-fried dough sticks that she'd shown him were to be dipped in huge bowls of steaming milk—it was nice to have some company for the day, and if he was being truthful, it was an added bonus that the company was Mari. He didn't want to admit it, but lately, even being in the middle of thousands of people, he felt so alone. And who was he kidding? It wasn't even just because he was in a foreign country. He'd felt alone for a long time now, anywhere he'd gone.

"Was your wallet snatched by a pickpocket?" Mari asked.

He shrugged. "Maybe. But I didn't see anyone."

He didn't know how or by whom; he only knew that when he'd gotten off the train from his short trip to Shanghai, his wallet had been gone. Luckily he didn't carry his credit cards in it—he'd learned a long time ago to keep his cards and some backup cash in a money clip, safely in his front pocket. And he never carried his passport; instead he kept a folded-up copy in his wallet. But the biggest loss had been worse than losing money—all his photos were gone. He didn't even have any saved on his phone. Now, far from home, he had to rely on his memory to picture her face.

Thinking of faces, he scrutinized Mari's profile. While he could tell she was a usually happy person, it appeared to him that she hid a certain sadness. Maybe even something like his. He didn't mind the silence, but she looked uncomfortable, and Max didn't want her to feel that way.

"So can you tell me a little about the *hutong*?" he asked.

"I can't say I know much about this particular *hutong*, as I've never been there. They are all different, but in a way, the same. They are a much better place to live than the towering apartment complexes most Chinese live in now. I was lucky—I grew up in a *hutong* in Wuxi." A small, contented smile eased across her face, and Max could see a good memory had been unearthed because of their conversation.

"Well, that's a surprise. I thought you were a big-time Beijing city girl. Wuxi's quite small, isn't it?" If Max remembered right, Wuxi was famous mostly because of its sprawling Lake Taihu.

Mari nodded. "Compared to Beijing or Shanghai, it's definitely small. But Wuxi is growing now, with all the foreign companies bringing their businesses there. When I was little, though, I truly only knew the boundaries of our *hutong* and just the few streets around it. So it felt like living in a village."

Since the day Max had read that his daughter was found in one of the small, winding alleys of a *hutong*, he'd been enthralled with them.

"Tell me more."

Mari sighed, then visibly relaxed against the back of the hard seat. "The *hutong* was a charmed place to be a kid. We lived in a one-room house, but I never felt we were lacking for anything. I remember our little stove fighting the cold in the winters, and our open windows when we were hot in the summers, but within those walls, I felt safer than I ever have in my life, before or since."

"Was there any crime in the *hutong*?"

Mari laughed softly. "Not really. Just little stuff. But my Baba was Chairman of the Neighborhood Conciliation Committee, so we probably knew more about what was going on behind closed doors than anyone else."

"Neighborhood Conciliation Committee?" Max was truly curious, and he loved to hear her talk in her perfect English, even if she did stumble over some words.

"It was a half-official and yet half-volunteer group. They were— I'm not sure I know the right word for it—*mediators*? They settled frustrations or small arguments within the *hutong* and neighboring streets."

He nodded. *Mediators* definitely sounded like the right word. "But what about the police?"

"The committee was first set up to help out the local administration, but really, just like in the old villages, there has always been a community leader. In your American roots, it would have been like the chief of an Indian tribe. The police are a last resort—only called in if weapons or serious injuries are involved. Most everything else can be settled without officials."

Again, her intelligence astounded him. Obviously, even though she was raised in a small community, she was well-read. But her reference did amuse him, considering his blond hair and blue eyes were as far from an Indian heritage as could be.

"It sounds complicated for your father."

"*Dui*, it could be, but he had a committee to help him. And he was very respected in our *hutong*, so his word—and his final decision—was rarely challenged. His two-year term was renewed for decades because my Baba is a wise man and just to have him in the room usually settled people down. He continually reminded everyone that our goal was to live in peace with one another, to be a support to those around us. And there *was* a lot of peace and support. If a family was doing poorly and couldn't afford a meal, they'd usually find vegetables or eggs on their front stoop. Or if their children needed something their caregivers couldn't provide, the neighbors came together to make it happen. In some ways, even though there were hundreds if not thousands living in the small community, it felt like a huge extended family,"—she smiled, and a small dimple showed on one side of her mouth—"but a family always has issues, you know?"

Max nodded. He knew probably better than anyone the complications, twists, and turns a family can be faced with. Some that could bring a family together, with others having the ability to tear them apart until everything they stood for was nothing more than a useless pile of rubble.

The driver turned a corner sharply, and the pedicab hovered on two wheels for a second, then settled down when the pedaling quickened.

Max spied a group of high school kids walking briskly on the walkway, laughing and jostling each other as they pointed at him. With his light hair and eyes, he knew he stood out, but he hoped Mari wasn't embarrassed to be seen with him. As for him, he found her stories about her family absolutely fascinating. "Do you remember any of the cases your father decided?"

Mari nodded. "There were some that were so petty it bordered on ridiculous, but since many of the houses shared a kitchen between them, and some of them shared water access, a lot of arguments were over one or another using all the hot water, or leaving a mess in their shared kitchen shed, or using one another's food supplies without asking."

Max couldn't imagine, and the more Mari talked about the hutong, the more captivated he became.

"Sometimes it got more serious when a neighbor was accused of stealing a bicycle, or even other more valuable things. We all lived quite close. Maybe too close, some would think. I remember once when one of the elderly neighbors came to Baba because she knew that a woman was stepping out on her husband with another man. She wanted Baba to tell the husband about his cheating wife."

"What did your Baba do?"

Mari looked embarrassed. "He brought the woman to our home, and my Mama counseled her. First, she got to the root of the problem. It seemed the man was being abusive to his wife. When that came out, my Mama took her under our roof for a few months while my Baba counseled her husband."

Max's mouth dropped open. "And you are telling me that the couple got back together?"

Mari nodded. "They really did love each other, and the man the elderly woman had spied with the wife? That was her brother, coming in the evenings to talk to her about returning home. After a few months of counseling, my Baba was able to make the young husband understand that life would always be full of ups and downs, but his wife would be there to help him get through it, that to take his frustrations out on the one who loved him the most was robbing him of his own good fortune."

"Do you think they really stayed together?"

Mari laughed, and the pleasant sound even startled the driver, who cocked his head back. Max could understand how he felt and almost chuckled. Her laugh no longer caught him off guard, but it was still really something amazing.

"I know they did. The last time I was home for a visit, I saw them passing their grandchild back and forth in their front courtyard, arguing over who he looked the most like."

Max didn't answer. Her life sounded like a storybook tale. Even something he would've loved to have been a part of. That reminded him—his daughter *was* a part of such a community. *Or she possibly was at one time.* Or at least she'd been found in one.

The driver stopped pedaling and spat out a few unintelligible words.

"We're here," Mari translated, then hopped out of the cab.

Max hesitated for a moment. He reached down and patted the paper he knew was in his pocket, then he climbed out after her. For a second, he wished he'd brought his camera. But he knew whatever he found would stay burned into his heart forever, with or without the memory of a photo.

Chapter Seven

An Ni was wide awake and aware that the big kids were up to something. Xiao Mei was still sleeping, huddled against her back. An Ni was grateful for the girl's warmth, though the icy cold of the concrete they lay on still penetrated her clothes and the coat that Tianbing had grudgingly given her, making her legs stiff, as if they contained clay instead of blood. She'd been awake for hours, wishing for the sun to come up and warm them, if even only a little.

She felt something crawling in her hair and reached up and scratched. She knew what it was—lice. They all had it, and even the cold temperatures couldn't kill the relentless creatures. More than any other part of her life on the streets, An Ni hated the lice and the anguish and embarrassment the tiny bugs caused her.

From the doorway near theirs, she heard Li Xi mumbling to one of the other boys and the sounds of cards slapping the pavement. They'd been playing poker for hours. An Ni didn't see how they went day after day with barely any sleep, but she knew they did it to stay warm.

Sleeping was hard enough on concrete, but when you threw in plunging temperatures, it was agony.

She heard someone stand, then footsteps came closer until Li Xi was standing over them. She knew it was him—she could feel it—but An Ni kept her eyes closed, hoping he'd go away if he thought they were asleep.

A kick found its way straight into her ribs, and she gasped, her eyes flying open.

"Stop pretending, Snake," he snarled.

An Ni sat up, holding her side. She looked up at him, trying to see his face through the shadows. "What?"

"Get up. We're going."

She shook her head. If they weren't there when Tianbing returned, they'd be in a lot of trouble. Li Xi was bad enough, but a few kicks to the gut were nothing compared to the punishments their boss would heap on them for stepping out of line. "I'm not going anywhere, and neither is Xiao Mei. We aren't getting in trouble."

Li Xi used his foot again, this time to rouse Xiao Mei. For her, he was gentler, An Ni noticed. "Tianbing didn't come back and I know he won't be rolling in until the afternoon tomorrow. He's somewhere warm and safe—and left us cold and hungry. We're going to fix that, but this time, you have to help."

An Ni could tell he wasn't going to leave her alone. She and Xiao Mei sat up at the same time. The little girl used her fists to rub at her tired eyes. It reminded An Ni that she was no longer the youngest, since Xiao Mei was at least four years younger than her own eleven years. She felt sorry for the girl and had since the day Tianbing had led her into their group, wide-eyed and terrified, still crying for her mother.

"I want to go home," she whined, and An Ni put an arm around her.

Xiao Mei was so new to street life, snatched from right under her family's nose only weeks before, then brought to the streets of Beijing where she'd be like a needle in a haystack to find. But still, An Ni knew Xiao Mei still hoped someone would lead her home. An Ni didn't want to tell her that soon her memories would fade and she'd remember nothing but her new, harsh life on the streets. Eventually, fear and hunger would replace everything else and consume her thoughts, crowding out any memories of her life before.

"This *is* home," Li Xi snarled. "Get used to it. You two have three minutes to get up and be ready to go." He stomped around to the other doorway, and An Ni heard him giving orders to the two boys there.

"But where?" An Ni asked.

Li Xi poked his head around their doorway again. "Night train. And this time you're getting on, too. You're going to start earning your keep—more than just a few coins. Tianbing's been too soft on you. If we have to do it, then you should, too."

An Ni stood paralyzed with fear. It wouldn't do any good to tell him that she didn't want to mess with any trains, that they scared her with their loud noises, smoke, and speed. He'd just laugh and make it worse. When Tianbing was gone, it was easier just to do what Li Xi told them to do. And he'd make sure they were back in their places before Tianbing returned. He always did. He was just as scared of the man as they were—maybe even more so, considering the long red scar that ran down his face was from their leader's own hand.

They walked until they were about a mile from the station. The night was quiet, everyone else in her part of the world was asleep, and the moon shone, surrounded by at least a million stars. As they hiked, An Ni stared up until she got dizzy, but even then she didn't want to look away. The stars had always made her happy, for they were a reminder that the world was huge and that, though her place in it for now was

small, there was much more to see and explore one day. It was simple—
the brilliance of a million twinkling stars gave her hope.

When she stumbled over a bump in the sidewalk, she tore her eyes
away from the sky above her. Walking warmed An Ni, but she hoped
that by some miracle, there'd be no trains tonight. She and Xiao Mei
followed the boys, listening to their chatter as they bragged about past
train adventures. An Ni was sure that Li Xi had snuck into many, but
she thought the other boys were probably exaggerating.

"My legs are tired, An Ni," Xiao Mei whined as An Ni pulled her
along.

"Come on, run! I hear it coming!" Li Xi took off running, and the
boys followed.

An Ni looked around and saw a grove of trees a few yards from the
road. She gave Xiao Mei a push toward them. "Xiao Mei, I don't want
you near the train. Go to those trees and wait there until I come back
for you."

Xiao Mei began to cry and held on to An Ni with all her might.
"No, don't leave me, An Ni, please."

Li Xi called out for her again, and An Ni knew if she disobeyed,
she and Xiao Mei would suffer later. She'd have to be mean, but it was
for Xiao Mei's own good. "I have to go, but I promise I'll be back for
you. Now go on." She was firmer this time, and she peeled Xiao Mei's
fingers from around her and gently pushed her. The girl stumbled and
fell, falling onto the ground and looking up at An Ni as if she were
suddenly the enemy.

An Ni felt a rush of guilt for being too rough as she ran to help
her up.

Xiao Mei slapped her hands away. "Why are you being so mean,
An Ni? I don't want to go over there by myself, it's too dark." She held
her palms out, and An Ni could see that they were speckled with gravel,
and probably stinging.

Li Xi yelled again, and both she and Xiao Mei jumped. He had stopped to wait for them, and he was angry.

"Xiao Mei, listen to me. If you don't go hide over there, Li Xi is going to make you jump onto a moving train. What if you fall? We have to hurry, but please—go there and wait for me. I'll be back, and when I do, I'll have some food for you. I promise." An Ni hoped the mention of food would convince her, and it did.

Xiao Mei ran to the grove of trees, and An Ni took off to catch up with Li Xi. Jumping on a moving train was the last thing she wanted to do, but the alternative was to take a beating first from the boy, then probably again later from Tianbing when Li Xi told on her for being disobedient. Maybe a train was the lesser evil after all.

The closer she got, the louder the train became. Even though they were running, she could feel her legs getting weaker and trembling. She'd never even been close to a train, much less climbed on one that was moving!

It finally came around the bend, chugging as it moved toward them. Li Xi was the first to it, and he pointed out what he thought was the dining car. When he got close, he leapt between two train cars and disappeared for a moment, then poked his head out and waved the boys closer. He looked proud as he balanced on the metal piece that connected the two cars.

An Ni's side ached where Li Xi had kicked her earlier, but she kept running. She still had a ways to go to catch up to them, but as the train was moving toward her, it wouldn't take long. As she ran, she saw the two boys jump, one by one, onto the narrow platform Li Xi stood on.

Finally she was near enough to see the expressions on their faces, and though one of the boys looked scared, the others were smiling— happy they'd made it and high from the rush of the danger. The car they clung to came closer, and Li Xi held his hand out.

"Grab my arm and I'll pull you up!" he called to her.

Once again An Ni wondered why she had to do this with them—the boys could've done it and been back before morning. Why take along two girls? She gasped for breath as his brown hand came closer. She resisted her urge to jump back from the train, and instead, grabbed hold of Li Xi's fingers and was yanked into the air. She jerked her legs up—afraid they'd be eaten by the zooming track below—as she scrambled to find her footing. The other boys laughed.

Li Xi held his hand up for them to be still. "I don't know why you sent the little one away, but I don't have time to deal with it. We have only another few miles before the train picks up speed. We gotta hurry. Follow me."

Now An Ni was trembling so hard she could barely function. She looked at the scenery flying by, knowing it was taking her farther from Xiao Mei, and she'd have to walk back a long way.

Li Xi moved from the metal connector to the rusty ladder attached to the side of the car. For a second, An Ni thought he was going to climb to the top of the train car. She prayed he wouldn't, because then he'd expect her to follow. Instead, he focused on the two windows. One was open only slightly, but the farthest one over was open enough that a body could slip through. Li Xi went from the ladder to the first window, using it as a foothold, then grabbed the frame of the second window and stepped over. He slid his legs through, and then his body disappeared. The boys quickly followed, then Li Xi poked his head out the window and waved to An Ni.

She was finding it hard to let go of the handle she'd found. With it under her hand, she felt that she wouldn't be blown off the train and fall to her death below. She clung to it and tried to still the dizzy feeling that was taking over her head.

"*Guo lai,*" Li Xi called out to her to come to him.

Slowly, An Ni moved until she could put one foot and one hand on the ladder. She inched over until both feet balanced on the bottom step. Taking a deep breath, she began to climb. With each rung, her fingers hung on like claws, almost refusing to let go to climb another few inches. But she did it, and when she reached the rung that brought her level with the window, she closed her eyes and just did it. She reached out and grabbed it, then swung herself over. When she found footing in the open space of the windowsill, she made the mistake of looking down at the ground—a brown blur as they picked up speed. Her vision swam before her eyes, and she felt a hand on her arm.

Li Xi grabbed her in a tight grip, and together with him pulling and her climbing, he jerked her into the window, and she landed on the floor, her butt hitting it soundly. She scrambled to her feet, and then Li Xi used his hand to push her back down again.

"Stay down and be quiet," he said as he looked around.

The other boys were squatting, as if they were on a steady street corner casually throwing dice and not just seconds away from a bloody death on Beijing train tracks. They looked at her and laughed. She knew she looked pale, because she'd felt the blood drain from her face the second her feet had hovered between the windows.

"You're a chicken, An Ni," Li Xi spat out. "I knew it."

An Ni didn't argue with him. She *was* terrified of heights—and, of course, clinging to moving objects. She looked around at the rows of seats with tables between them, lines of cabinets overhead for storage. Luckily, the car was empty.

Li Xi held his finger to his lips. "Everyone spread out and look for food or anything valuable. Stay in this car." He went to the corner of the car and walked behind the counter, opening and closing cupboards. He began to toss out small containers of instant noodles, and the boys picked them up, stuffing them into their jackets.

An Ni stood and wandered over to a table. She opened up the seat, guessing it was storage. It was empty. She went to the next one and opened it. Empty again. Behind her, she could hear the boys finding things and knew she'd better come up with something.

She went to the next table and seats. She blinked hard and then put her hand on the seat to flip it open. Before she did, something caught her eyes. Something dark was wedged in the crack behind the faded yellow seat. She pulled on it and was rewarded when a man's wallet emerged. She glanced around and saw the boys weren't paying her any attention, so she dropped to her knees under the table and put the wallet to her nose. It smelled like real leather. Could she be so lucky?

She opened it and felt a rush of defeat. Other than a few scraps of paper and some dog-eared photos, it was empty.

"An Ni, where are you?" Li Xi called out.

She stuffed the wallet into the pocket of her pants and crawled out.

"What the hell are you doing? Hiding?" His hands were on his hips, and the look in his eyes was thunderous.

An Ni stood, went to the counter, and stood beside the boys.

"We need you to carry some of these," Li Xi had found a refrigerator, and in it, they'd struck gold. He set at least a dozen frozen entrees out on the counter. The sight of the food moved An Ni's stomach, and it rumbled loudly. Even as scared as she was, her hunger loomed.

"How can I carry them and get off the train safely?" she asked, looking over his shoulder at the window. The train was picking up speed. She felt a shiver of panic.

"I don't know, but you're going to. Figure it out, just like we do." Li Xi told her, then slid six of the trays across the counter toward her.

An Ni looked around and saw the trash bin at the end of the counter. She opened it, and thankfully, it was empty. She pulled the liner out of it, then tucked her six trays inside, tied a knot in the plastic, then threw it over her shoulder.

Li Xi grinned at her. "Good idea. See—you can be smart if you just stop and think."

He opened a few more cupboards until he found a roll of bin liners. He pulled off a few and tossed them at the boys, taking one for himself.

The boys scrambled to stuff their goods inside, then mimicking An Ni, tied knots and got ready to go.

Li Xi led them to the window, then turned around. "This is easy—I've done it a million times. Just do what I do and don't let go or jump until I tell you. But when it's your turn to go, you gotta move fast. Don't hesitate, or you'll be sorry."

He climbed out the window, and An Ni watched as, like a monkey, he maneuvered himself over to the other window, then back to the ladder, then all the way over until he stood on the connector again. One of the boys climbed out after him, then did the same.

"Let An Ni go next, and when you hit the ground, tuck your legs and curl into a ball," Li Xi called out, then pushed the first boy hard, sending him flying off the train and onto the ground. The boy rolled, and the bag of loot flew from his grip. But An Ni waited, and when he stopped rolling, he stood and held his arms up triumphantly.

He was okay. But still—what if she wouldn't be? She slunk back into the train car, unwilling to go next. The last boy looked at her, raising his eyebrows, then shook his head as he climbed out the window and disappeared.

An Ni knew she'd be in trouble for disobeying, but she couldn't stop the trembling that had come back to her. She was going to get hurt; she just knew it. Then who would take care of Xiao Mei? Or for that matter, who would take care of her? But . . . if Li Xi had to climb back in the train to come after her—that would be worse.

She went to the window. She first stopped and stuffed the lumpy, cold bag of plastic food trays under her shirt, then tucked the material into her pants as tight as she could. She needed both hands and didn't know how the boys had done it while holding their stuff.

She hesitated when she heard a door behind her. She turned and saw a man—the conductor by the looks of his uniform—coming down the aisle toward her.

"What are you doing in here?" he demanded, stomping faster and coming closer. An Ni could see by the rage in his face that he wasn't going to be lenient. Visions of the police and handcuffs swam before her eyes.

She bolted to the window and put one leg out just as the man reached for her. She felt his fingers skim her hair, and she panicked. She saw Li Xi's hand stretched out, but the man was so close she could smell the garlic on his breath, and she lunged away from him, hoping Li Xi would reach her and pull her to safety.

The last thing she saw was the browns and greens of the swirling ground coming up to meet her much too quickly, then everything faded to black.

Chapter Eight

The tree-lined street was narrow, but Mari was accustomed to dodging parked bicycles, pedicabs, and small vehicles. Other than the highways, most streets in China were just as crowded as this one. But she smiled as, behind her, Max tripped more than a few times and let out several well-known expletives during their trek. Finally they moved into the oldest part of the *hutong*, where more hazards awaited them in the thick tree roots that spotted the walkways.

They eventually navigated to the main entrance of the *hutong*, obvious by the four huge characters engraved over an archway. Though they'd passed plenty of crumbling bricks and walkways, Mari was impressed to see the old doors that flanked the even older wall. A red sign bolted to the concrete was separated with characters on one side and English on the other. Max stopped in front of it and read as she waited. A caricature of a chubby policeman at the corner of the sign pointed to the words below.

**WELCOME OUR COMMUNITY. ACCORDING TO CHINESE LAW,
ALL FOREIGNERS SHOULD REPORT LOCAL POLICE STATION
WITHIN 24 HOURS OF VISITING THIS AREA.
WE APPRECIATE YOUR COOPERATION.**

Max looked at her and raised his eyebrows. She shook her head. Checking in wasn't necessary, and no one really complied anyway. Why give the local police a reason to follow and be suspicious? She'd learned long ago to stay as far away from the authorities as much as possible to save a lot of undeserved discomfort. And with what had happened to a local citizen only months ago when the local *chengguan* picked him up and accused him of begging, then proceeded to manhandle him to the point of breaking his nose—there was even more reason not to initiate any communication. The foreigners just didn't have a clue when it came to local police antics. She waved Max away from the sign.

Next to the wall, two old men served as watchmen to their neighborhood entrance as they perched on wooden stools. One called out, *"Jīdàn,"* as he pointed to a basket at his feet, filled to the top with brown eggs speckled by dirt and hen feces.

The second man stared and sipped at a steel-lined cup of what could be green tea, though she bet it was something closer to warm beer—or at least it would be later that evening when the local beer seller made his rounds door-to-door, calling out his brew for sale.

"Bu yao, xie xie," she declined the man's loud offer of cheap eggs as she slipped by the men and into the *hutong*. She wasn't exactly sure where Max would want to go, but she hoped just a cursory tour would satisfy the intense longing she saw in his eyes. He was lucky—many of the *hutongs* had been cleared away when the city was preparing for the Olympics, but by chance, this one remained untouched.

As they walked, she could see Max taking in everything greedily. She didn't think he missed anything, not even the scrawny mother cat and her kittens as they crept through the bushes that lined the walkway, two tumbling against one another as they wrestled. He even paused when, in the courtyard shared by two small houses, an elderly woman picked through a bucket of walnuts held by an old man still wearing his nightclothes.

To Mari, the sights and smells were all familiar, and a memory of her old neighbor, Widow Zu, came to mind. The woman used to give them fresh eggs, and Mari's Baba and Mama returned the favor with vegetables and other treats. The old woman always looked out for Mari and her sisters, even spying to keep them in line—another set of eyes when their Baba and Mama weren't aware of what was going on right under their noses. The *hutongs* were that way. Neighbors were like family.

"This is just amazing," Max said, stopping at a dry fountain in the middle of the main courtyard.

"It is, isn't it?" Mari replied. She thought about how, so often when she was younger, she took her home for granted, even took the entire *hutong* for granted. This kind of place—it was rare to find any longer. Even the feel of it was nothing less than magical. Why the younger generation all strove to live in high-rise apartments and penthouses, she just couldn't understand. For a moment, a wave of homesickness washed over her, and she felt that she could almost smell the sweet scent of her Mama, feel the warmth of her arms enveloping her in a tight hug.

She sighed and thought of Bolin. Maybe she should try to find a way to get him to Wuxi. Her family didn't have a lot of room, but they'd find a way to make it work if she said the word. Perhaps there, with family around, he'd improve and regain his will to live again.

She wished it were that easy. She could hear him now, still trying to hold on to everything. *What about our business? Our camel? Our apartment we worked so hard to secure?* He wouldn't consider that he'd left her to figure out how to keep it all while he succumbed to his addiction. So many complications, and she didn't know the solution to any of them.

Max's voice brought her back to the present. "It's like this place is lost in time. But right here,"—he thumped on his own chest—"I feel it. It's the heartbeat of the city."

"You're right, Max. This is where real Chinese are born and raised, where the best people with the kindest intentions are molded. From *hutongs* just like this one."

Max nodded. "And to think, just a mile or so away, the people have iPhones stuck to their heads as they walk around in their expensive designer clothes or ride in their luxury cars, all competing to make the most money and own the finest toys. I can't imagine giving up the peace that this place brings." He'd stopped walking and now stood looking, taking time to examine the small houses and courtyards.

"Do you know where you want to go in here?" Mari asked. She'd seen a few curious people looking their way, pointing at Max. She knew he was hard to miss with his fair looks and tall stature. She also knew it was only a matter of time before someone—probably someone in charge—approached them to ask why they were there.

She watched as he seemed to be thinking intensely, then he nodded. "I'm sorry. I was thinking that here, in this place, is where I should find a story to write. Something real—about the people and relationships—not some hyped-up political garbage like they want me to find."

Mari wasn't sure what he meant.

Max shrugged. "Excuse my rambling. Let's get back to why we're here. My daughter was found east of the fountain in this main courtyard, nestled on the ground between two jasmine trees that the locals call the Twin Trees."

Mari turned and led him east. His directions were precise, and she hoped he'd find what he was looking for—if it was something tangible. If it wasn't, she hoped just finding the place would bring him the satisfaction she could tell he longed for.

As they walked, she decided she'd made a good decision to be his guide. He was easy company, so much less demanding than other foreigners she'd worked with at the Great Wall. She almost hated to charge him for her time, as today was the first day she'd felt relaxed in a long time. Seeing Beijing through his eyes, she saw more than the usual day-to-day struggles and smog-filled skyline. Because of his fascination with parts of the city—especially the older, historical or undeveloped areas—Mari remembered again why she and Bolin had been drawn to build a life there. She remembered the history and the amazing tenacity of the people there who refused to be beaten, always rising up again to rebuild their city after each defeat. Truthfully, Max was a salve to her usually discontent spirit. She felt she should be paying him.

They passed more walled courtyard homes as they turned down a few more lanes, trying to continue east. Some boasted remnants of pairs of stone lions on either side of their thick, red doors. Other entrances were flanked by bags of trash or stacks of papers to be recycled. Max was getting to see some of the most basic living conditions, even previously big houses that had been converted to small one-room homes, with several families all sharing kitchen and bathroom privileges. She wondered what he thought of that.

"Such character," Max murmured as he followed. "This has to be the most amazing part of Beijing."

Mari laughed. "Yes, I guess you could say that, though the residents of the other remaining *hutongs* may argue that their neighborhood holds that title."

They wound down a few more alleyways as Mari looked for anything that could be the Twin Trees. Each time she found a few, as they approached they turned out to be something other than jasmine trees. Behind her, Max mumbled again.

"I'm sorry? I didn't catch that," she said.

"Oh, nothing. I was just remembering something my daughter told me about Genghis Khan."

"Was it that he and his army reduced all of Beijing to rubble, then the *hutongs* were designed and built to crisscross the city and offer more protection?"

Max laughed, and Mari felt a flush creep up her neck and over her face. Why was he laughing at her? Did she use the wrong English? Maybe she shouldn't have come.

"I'm sorry. It's just funny because that's almost word for word what she said. Except she didn't sound like a tour guide."

"Your daughter must be a historian," Mari answered, still feeling a bit indignant at his amusement. She moved toward a man using a bucket of steaming, soapy water to clean a gate that lead to a well-kept courtyard. "We're going to have to ask someone about your Twin Trees, because I don't see them."

The man stopped washing his gate and stood, waiting for them to approach. He held the dripping sponge, appearing impatient to get back to work.

"*Qing wen,*" Mari said, asking him to excuse her interruption. "Can you tell me if you have a landmark called the Twin Trees here? A set of jasmine trees, I believe."

The man shook his head, then went back to working.

Mari turned back to Max and shrugged. "I guess not."

They started walking again, but the man called out.

"They aren't jasmine trees. They're pomegranate trees, and you're going the wrong way." He pointed behind them, the way they'd come. "Go back to the last crisscrossing of alleys and turn left. That'll lead you to the real center of the *hutong*, and your Twin Trees."

Mari felt a rush of emotion. She couldn't believe how much it meant to her, that she helped Max find the site he longed to see. She wanted to please him. "Come on, Max. I should've known anyway. In China, the pomegranate tree is favored because the fruit has so many seeds."

Max looked at her, confused.

"*Seed* and *son* sound alike in Chinese. The older generation believes the more sons, the more blessings, so they plant the trees when they have a chance. It would be a perfect place to leave an unwanted daughter for a symbolic explanation of why they couldn't keep her."

Max's curious look was replaced with one that she could've sworn bordered on anger. He walked beside her, but he didn't speak.

"Have I offended you?" she asked.

He shook his head. Then he hesitated for a moment, staring into space before he looked back at her and nodded. "Actually, you did. She wasn't unwanted. I just want to make that clear. I don't know why her birth family gave her up, but I know she wasn't unwanted. Use any other word you want, but not that one."

Mari swallowed hard. She'd hit on a sensitive subject. "*Dui bu qi*, I'm so sorry. I didn't mean it to sound that way. My English word—it was chosen too quickly."

Max stared straight ahead as they walked, and Mari felt her heart drop. He was mad at her, and it didn't feel good. She stopped and put her arm out, making him pause, too. He turned to her.

"Let's go," he said, his voice devoid of its usual warmth. "I need to see the place."

"We'll go, but first, please believe me, I'm truly sorry." Mari didn't know why, but it was important for her that he know her sincerity. There was only one way for her to make him see that she didn't take the subject lightly. "And Max, I didn't know my birth parents, either— though I don't call them birth family. The word *family* would imply that there was a bond between us. I remember nothing of the sort. I don't know if I was abandoned, lost, or taken from them. But my Baba and Mama found me on the streets and took me in. I'm adopted."

Max's eyes bore into hers, as if he searched for truth. Then he nodded, and the warmth flooded back into his voice. He reached out and touched her shoulder. "I overreacted, and I'm sorry. Thank you for sharing a part of your life with me, Mari. You make a good point about family versus parents. And I accept your apology."

Mari began walking again, this time feeling more in step with him than before. She'd never really shared her past with anyone other than close family, but saying the words didn't feel as awkward as she had thought they would. With Max, they almost felt natural, as if telling him was meant to be. And he'd respected her privacy by not asking anything further. Now she longed to see the Twin Trees, too. They moved faster to the crossing the man had spoken of, then turned as instructed.

A few yards later, just as the man had promised, they came upon the center of the *hutong*. It was an area much more well kept than the rest of the neighborhood, probably as a memorial to the ancestors who'd lived and died in the neighborhood. The lawn was nicely manicured, and the shrubs and trees were precisely groomed. A large koi pond was the focal point, and water gurgled into it from a fountain made of rocks. Mari spotted the Twin Trees behind the fountain.

She could tell the exact moment that Max saw them, too, as his stride increased with purpose. He quickly left her behind, and she slowed even more, giving him the distance he needed. When she saw a bench, she moved to it and sat down.

Max continued until he was at the trees, then he stood between the two spindly trunks. As Mari watched, she saw the slump of his shoulders and the dip of his head, almost as if he were praying. She wondered again why his daughter hadn't come with him to make this pilgrimage, especially since he'd said she was so entranced with China and her own history. But as Mari knew, children grew into adults and then had their own agendas—schedules that were much too busy to fit in childhood dreams. That was probably the case with Max's daughter, but still, it was sad to see him experience such a special moment alone.

Finally he turned. She waited as he made his way back to her.

"How old was your daughter when she became yours?" Mari asked, her curiosity overcoming her good manners. Immediately she thought of the scolding her Mama would have given her and she wished she could take the words back.

"She was officially declared my daughter when she was nine months old, but I think she belonged to me—or I belonged to her—the second she was born. It just took a few months, and many miles, for us to find our way to each other."

He said the words so sincerely and solemnly that Mari believed it, too. It could only be true, for the man's love for his daughter shone through his very being. She wondered if perhaps that was the way her own Baba felt about her, even though she was not made from his own flesh and blood. They'd always been close, but she had to admit, she hadn't shared any of her recent troubles with her parents for fear that they'd think less of her for her failure to make her marriage thrive.

"Do you want to see more of the *hutong*?" she asked, ready to move on to a safer subject.

Max smiled. "No, I've seen all I need to see. We can go."

Mari was relieved. She really needed to get up to the shed to check on Chu Chu.

"Can I leave you at the street? I need to go see about my husband's camel." They walked closely together as the lane narrowed.

"How about I go with you?" Max asked. "I've nothing better to do."

Mari considered it for a moment. She looked at her watch. She still had a few hours before Bolin expected her home. If he was even awake enough to see the time.

"That'll be fine, if you're sure you don't mind. It's a long way up there."

He took the lead, guiding her out of the *hutong* and back onto the street. "I don't mind. And you need to tell me how much I owe you for today. And if you're free again tomorrow, I have somewhere else I need to go."

Mari waved at a taxi, and the driver hit his brakes, then backed up to them on the curb. Max opened the door for her and they climbed in. She didn't have an answer for him, as she didn't know what tomorrow would bring. She thought of An Ni again, then her landlord. She needed to get her priorities in place—if she didn't earn more money, she and Bolin might be joining the girl on the street soon.

One stop at the farmer's market for a bundle of hay that Max insisted on paying for, and a half-hour taxi ride to the small dirt road that held the shed that housed Chu Chu, and Mari was exhausted. Max knew the way, and she let him take the lead and carry the hay as they walked.

"I probably shouldn't ask, but where in the world did you find a camel to buy for your picture-taking business?" he asked.

Mari laughed. "We bartered for him with a neighboring farmer in my husband's village. The old man used Chu Chu to carry heavy loads, but when Bolin presented a fat cow, he gladly traded."

"Should I ask where you got a cow?"

"It's fine. I know, this isn't India—you don't see cows just walking the streets. Bolin grew up in the country and his father is a farmer. Our wedding presents were few, but from his parents, the cow was one—and to Bolin, she represented a new venture and the city life he'd always dreamed of."

"And you? Did you also dream of city life?" Max asked.

A vision of the *hutong* in Wuxi, her hometown, came to mind, and Mari shook her head. "I would've been happy staying close to my family, but a wife's place is to follow her husband and support his dreams. I want Bolin to find success. I want to build a family with him." She kicked at a few rocks in the road.

"Well, I for one can't wait to see that stubborn camel of yours. I think he's got quite a personality," Max said, and hurried his pace.

They walked another few minutes until the shed came into view. Usually, when Mari got near enough that Chu Chu could hear her, he started to snort and make some noise—usually to show his impatience. Today she heard nothing.

"That sure is a sturdy-looking shelter you have for your camel," Max said.

Mari agreed. "It's been here for ages. During Mao's early reign, he didn't care about the Great Wall, and the guards turned their heads when the peasants and farmers foraged it for raw materials. Many a farmhouse, barn, and reservoir were built with its stones."

"That's a shame," Max said, and Mari could tell he meant it.

"It is, but the upside is that those structures built long ago with the strong materials of the Wall remain standing, for the most part. We were able to rent this one for a fairly decent price." She walked up the trodden path to the double doors and pulled her keys from her bag. After a few seconds of rifling through the ring, she opened the padlock and removed it from the bracket, then opened the doors.

"Chu Chu?" she called, wondering why he was so quiet. She walked into the dim building, and immediately she could see that he wasn't standing in his stall, which meant he was lying down. "Oh no, he's down. He must be sick."

"Maybe I should go first," Max said from behind her.

"No, he doesn't really know you," Mari worked her way over the messy floor, stepping over soiled boxes and old towels, pushing away a wave of irritation at Bolin for using the shed as a dumping ground for everything. "Chu Chu, what are you doing lying—"

She stopped mid-sentence. The camel wasn't in the stall. She was dumbfounded. Where was he? Bolin couldn't have been there, and she had the only key.

"What is it?" Max asked.

She finally found her voice. "He's not here. He's gone."

"How can he be gone? Is there another way out of here?" Max put his hand on her shoulder.

Mari looked toward the back of the shed. "There is, but it's bolted, too."

Max strode past her and to the far wall, pushing against the double doors. Mari felt another jolt of shock when they opened right up, and the light from the blue sky flooded in.

"But—how—"

Max disappeared outside and then in seconds was back, holding up the padlock for her to see. "They cut it with bolt cutters."

That much was obvious, but Mari couldn't form a reply. All she could do was stand there as thoughts of their financial demise floated around her head. She and Bolin had no other way to make a living. He was temporarily—maybe even permanently?—disabled, and she didn't have any other skills. The camel was their one link to building a business to cater to foreigners—and everyone knew with enough time, any business that dealt with *waiguorens* would flourish.

What would she do now? Work in a noodle shop? Sweep the streets? She felt a wave of dizziness. They'd lose everything.

"Mari, are you okay?" Max was coming at her.

She was still struck with disbelief.

"Mari!" he called out to her, then he was there, his eyes filled with concern.

She looked up at him and shook her head. He'd never understand. He came from a country that was known for abundance—complete with easy ways to get help from the government when people fell on hard times. Being absolutely alone and helpless wasn't something he'd ever know. How *could* he understand?

"I've got to go home. My husband will be crushed." Mari turned, her mind on nothing but the look she knew she'd see on Bolin's face.

And she should feel guilty. It was her fault. She was the one to blame for leaving Chu Chu alone, and probably gave the thieves ample time to get far enough away for him never to be found.

Chapter Nine

The flights of stairs felt longer than they'd ever felt before as Mari trudged her way to the third floor. She thought of An Ni and wished again the day hadn't gone so wrong. She'd wanted to look for her, had even planned on doing it that evening on her way home. But she wouldn't have done it with Max beside her, and he'd refused to let her walk home alone. After he'd accompanied her to the local police precinct to file a report, Max had insisted on seeing her all the way to the door of their building, saying she was in no shape to navigate the city alone. He was right. She was shaken, and she really didn't want to face Bolin. He'd depended on her to step up and take care of things as he tried to get a grasp back on life. But she'd let him down—she'd let them both down. If she hadn't been gallivanting around town with Max, their camel would've been with her. Instead who knew where he was or if he was being cared for? For all she knew, he was being used to carry too-heavy loads, or even worse, being butchered.

She shuddered, then stopped to get her breath. Bolin never would admit it, but he loved that camel. Mari knew he saw it as a symbol of his independence from his family. And he'd also never admit that it hurt him when his parents refused to support his decision to go to the city. Bolin wasn't the only child, or he'd have never gone. A farming family was allowed more than one child, and Bolin was born after a sister. He was the heir his father had prayed for, but his sister was the one with farming in her blood, not Bolin. He'd told Mari that it was clear his sister was born to be a farmer. He'd hated the country life. But their father couldn't see past his son's need to do something different. They hadn't spoken in years.

Mari dropped to the stair, sitting down with her head in her hands. The image of his parents swam in her head. Bolin always thought he'd make it big, then show up in his tiny town and make them proud with gifts of red envelopes stuffed with money, to get them to change their minds about disowning him. His dreams just hadn't happened for him, and Mari knew that was part of his depression. He felt like a failure. She didn't understand, though, why he couldn't let her into his thoughts, share his disappointment with her, instead of shutting her out. He didn't grasp the fact that she'd also left everything and everyone she'd ever known behind to come with him to Beijing. It was sad, but the truth was that they were together but both alone.

She stood and took a deep breath. Time to face him, because she wasn't going to hide behind reality as he'd been doing. Her Baba and Mama had always taught her to take hardship by the horns and wrestle it to the ground.

Their floor arrived sooner than usual, and Mari felt as if she were taking the walk of shame, passing other apartments with open doors, happy voices, tantalizing smells of pork simmering and vegetables steaming. Signs of normal life, a life that she couldn't have, as she made her way to her own too-quiet home to give her husband news that would only make him feel worse.

At the door she hesitated only a second, then unlocked it and turned the knob. The house was quiet as usual. Only the television droned on, a soap opera blasting dramatic music as a scene between two lovers played out.

"Bolin?" she called out as she dropped her bag on the table.

She looked over the kitchen counter at the couch. There he was, his back to her, like always. Mari didn't know how he spent hour after hour sleeping, day and night, only waking up to medicate once again, then going back to it.

He moved, and Mari knew he was awake. She went to him and sat on the small piece of couch his body and blanket hadn't claimed. Putting her arm on his back, she leaned down. "Bolin, are you awake? We need to talk."

He turned over, surprising Mari because she didn't have to coax him. She caught his odor—unwashed and reeking of desperation.

"I'm out of pills, Mari. You have to go to the doctor." He handed her the empty bottle that he'd been clutching against his chest. His hair stood up in tufts, much too long and in need of a haircut. Another expense they couldn't afford. "Did you hear me? I need you to go get me more."

Mari sighed. She did have some money, thanks to Max and her impromptu tour guide job—but she'd planned to use that for their rent. It wasn't time for him to be out of medication. "You took all those today?"

He nodded, looking like a scared little boy. Mari didn't have the heart to even yell or scream. It was done. But she was disappointed beyond belief.

"You told me you were an adult and could hold on to your own medicine. Remember, Bolin? You acted like I was the bad guy, treating you like a child. And now look—you took it all."

He shook his head in denial. "It's not my fault, Mari. I just got confused last night. And I need a bigger dose anyway. Those aren't helping me. I'm still in pain, and I can't sleep."

Mari stood up. She didn't want to fight with him. But she knew the doctor was not going to give him anything stronger. She already got the feeling that the doctor thought her husband was milking his injury and should've been up and around by now. A part of her—the unsympathetic part that she tried to squash—tended to agree.

There was only one way to do it and that was to just put it bluntly. "Bolin, I need to tell you something. Chu Chu was stolen."

She jerked back when Bolin sat up as if a string were attached to his head and someone jerked it upright.

"Stolen? What do you mean? Stolen right out from under your nose?"

Now for the kicker. Mari felt small.

"No, stolen from the shed. I didn't have him with me today." She pulled her shoulders back, ready for his attack.

Bolin's eyes narrowed until she couldn't even see his pupils. "What were you doing, Mari?"

"I had a different job. It's been difficult lately getting customers for photos, and I was offered a good fee to be a guide." She kept the irritation out of her voice, hoping he'd drop it. But she also didn't want to tell him more about Max.

Bolin picked up a throw pillow and buried his face in it. He mumbled something and rocked back and forth.

"What? I can't understand you," Mari said, trying to pry the pillow from him.

Bolin dropped it, then screamed at her. *"I saw you!"*

"What do you mean, you saw me?" Mari felt the earth shift under her.

"I saw you with *him*—the *waiguoren*. He had his arm around you, Mari. You were out with some foreigner and let Chu Chu get taken!"

Was Max's arm around her when he walked her to the door? Mari couldn't remember. If it was, she sure hadn't known it. But of all things for Bolin to see, nothing could be worse. He had a serious dislike for the relationships that local girls forged with foreigners, feeling as if they were selling their souls—their heritages—for a sum.

"It's not like that, Bolin. He was with me when I went to the shed to check on Chu Chu, and I was—"

"See! Why did you take him to the shed? What were you going to do there?" He pointed his finger in her face, and Mari saw rage. She'd never been afraid of Bolin before, but now—this was a new side of him.

"Bolin, please calm down. You aren't being rational. He's just a customer—someone wanting a guide to help him get all the details so he can write a story about China. I swear." She pleaded with him now, begging him to hear the truth through his haze of anger.

Bolin took some deep breaths, then put his hand to his head. He lay back down and turned to face the back of the couch. He was shutting down again. "My head hurts. I need my pills. Please."

Mari got up, grabbed her backpack, and left the apartment. They hadn't put together a plan. She didn't know how they'd pay their rent, and it was due in two weeks. But her husband's pills were more important than the roof over their head. He obviously cared for nothing other than getting his fix.

For a second, she thought about calling her parents. They'd do what they could, but Mari knew their life was a struggle, too. She would not add to it. She'd just have to figure it all out herself, just like she'd been doing for months.

Three hours later, she'd had no luck scoring any street drugs for Bolin. In her defense—not that anyone was accusing her, but she did feel guilty—before she'd hit the streets, she'd called the doctor, and he'd refused to refill Bolin's prescription for more pain pills. He insisted that she get Bolin to see him so he could be re-evaluated.

Mari knew from the doctor's tone that if she pushed him, he'd declare Bolin an addict. Then where would they be? The doctor had the authority to have her husband committed, or even jailed if he felt it was warranted!

She turned the corner, tired but anxious to see if An Ni was there. From her days on the street as a child, she remembered that if she didn't make her quota of coins, many nights she was forced to keep begging late into the early morning hours, hitting up the patrons leaving bars and parties, encouraged to pull at their drunken heartstrings.

She strained to see, but as she got closer, it was obvious An Ni wasn't there. Mari wished she could get the girl out of her mind. She had enough going on and enough stress. She didn't need to be thinking about a little street urchin, but she just couldn't help it. She'd been drawn to her and couldn't stop wondering about her. She stopped at the exact place where she'd talked to An Ni, hoping that waiting would make her appear.

Two boys stepped out of a dark shop entrance and Mari jumped.

"What do you want?" The biggest one asked, a dark scowl on his face.

Mari stared at him, wondering if he was a part of An Ni's gang of beggars. When he shrugged sarcastically at her, she almost laughed at his forced bravado. But she wouldn't hurt his pride—she could sympathize too much.

"I've seen a little girl here before," Mari said. "Her name is An Ni. Do you know her?"

She could tell by the sudden, quickly masked surprise on his face and by the shuffling away of the younger boy that they did indeed know An Ni. Yet the bigger one shook his head.

"Listen, I know you don't want to tell me. But can you just say if she is okay or not?" Mari opened her bag and took out a five-renminbi note. Precious funds to her, but if it got her an answer, she'd gladly give it up.

The boy snatched the bill as soon as it saw the light of the streetlamp. "She took off, and I doubt she'll be back here again."

Mari narrowed her eyes at him. "Did she take off, or was she traded?"

More surprise showed on his face that she knew street talk.

"I used to be just like you and An Ni," Mari said softly, hoping their connection would spring more information from his lips.

The boy looked her up and down, then crossed his arms. "You're wearing a warm coat and nice clothes. You're clean, and you look well fed to me. I'll bet you have a home to go to—somewhere out of the rain and cold. You're nothing like us." He spit on the ground at her feet, then turned and stomped away.

Mari didn't blame him for the sudden anger. She'd spent many years with the same heavy burden, even after she was rescued. Only when she'd finally faced her anger and broken down wailing—finally letting out all her sorrow—in the embrace of her Mama's gentle arms was she able to let it go. She knew what the boy was feeling.

Rejection. Isolation. Fear.

It wasn't easy to watch people going by on their way to protective and loving homes as you scurried into a dark hole somewhere, searching for warmth never to be found. She knew he lay awake at night—cold, hungry, and wondering, *Why me?*

She didn't know what fate had in store for the boy, but she did hope he at least would spend the money on a hot bowl of noodles or rice for himself and his friend. And that was all she could do.

She turned and headed away, ready to hit one more street in her search to get Bolin what he needed for his relief.

Chapter Ten

An Ni opened her eyes and stared at the shadows that moved above her. She wasn't sure where she was, but it definitely wasn't any of their usual shelters. She didn't see a trace of any building, overhang, or culvert. Instead, what looked like trees—tall and almost bare of leaves—were her ceiling. Where was she? Where was Xiao Mei? Had they already taken her away?

Train. Window. Jumping.

Now she remembered. She struggled to sit up, but an agonizing pain streaked through her leg and all the way to her hip, sending her flailing backward again.

"An Ni, stay still," a small voice said. Xiao Mei appeared over An Ni's face, leaning down to talk to her. The girl pulled at the small blanket, tucking it around An Ni even more.

"Where am I? What happened?" The pain from her attempt to rise made her dizzy, and she closed her eyes to still the swirling trees.

"We're in the woods. You dove out the window. Li Xi couldn't reach you, and you hit the ground and rolled."

It was coming back to An Ni now, though she didn't remember the impact after her dive out of the window. "Where's the boys?"

"They ran when you didn't wake up. Li Xi's scared he's going to get a beating because of your leg."

"My leg? What about my leg?" An Ni tried again to sit up, propping herself up to look down at her leg. What she saw made her even dizzier. The blanket—and where it had come from, she didn't know—was short, only covering her torso. Her legs poked out, and her right leg lay at a strange, skewed angle. And it hurt. Badly.

"Oh no. Don't tell me I've broken it." She remembered that more than a year ago, one of the kids in their gang had stepped out in front of a car and broken his leg. He'd gone through a lot of pain, but Tianbing had never taken him to the hospital. Instead, he'd fixed him up himself, and the boy's leg had finally healed—or she guessed it did, even though he'd still walked with a bad limp until the day he wasn't with them anymore.

Xiao Mei looked at her, eyes big with fright. "I don't know, An Ni, but I thought you were dying. You wouldn't wake up."

It was still night, so An Ni didn't think she'd been out long. "How long was I out?"

Xiao Mei scrunched up her nose and looked at the sky. "You slept through the rest of last night and all day today. It's nighttime again and I was getting scared. I walked all the way to the station and snatched this baby blanket when the Mama wasn't looking. I didn't want you to be cold again."

A whole night and day? The alarm ran through An Ni. She'd been out that long? Then she was filled with warmth for Xiao Mei's sweet spirit. She'd thought that no one cared about her, but Xiao Mei did. Then confusion swirled once more.

"But how did I get in here?" From her place on the ground, she couldn't even see the train tracks.

Xiao Mei smiled. "I dragged you, but I didn't touch your bad leg,

I promise. I think it took me a couple hours—you're really heavy, An Ni. I rolled you, too, sometimes. I was afraid if someone saw you from another train car, they'd call the police, and they'd take you away."

An Ni struggled to get her legs under her but gave up after a few seconds of agony. Poor Xiao Mei, she must've been terrified. And no wonder she hadn't woken up. If her leg was broken, she'd probably passed out over and over from the pain of being moved. But Xiao Mei wouldn't have known any better.

Xiao Mei smiled and ran over to a tree, grabbed something, and came back. In her arms, she held the plastic bag of dinner trays from the train. The ones that An Ni had risked her life to steal.

"These fell all over the ground when you rolled, but the boys were so scared about you that they didn't pick them up. I waited until they ran and then I got them all and put 'em back in the bag." Her smile disappeared. "But I already ate one. Sorry, An Ni."

"Don't be sorry. You did good. And I'm not gonna call you Xiao Mei anymore, because now you're such a big girl. Now you're just *Mei*. And I'm proud of you. But," she said through her clenched teeth, "we've got to get to some shelter. It's going to be too cold out here tonight."

She wasn't worried about herself as much as she was the little girl. What if she passed out again and something got Xiao Mei? A person? An animal? Anything!

"We need to get you to a hospital," Xiao Mei said, her voice trembling.

To An Ni, Mei looked twice her age, her eyes full of fear and the knowledge that this was a serious problem—them being left out in the woods all alone. As bad as Tianbing was, at least on their part of the streets, most people knew he was their protector and didn't mess with them. Here, anyone or anything could get to them. She realized her teeth were chattering, though it wasn't cold enough for that yet. And An Ni didn't know much about injuries, but she did know there was something called shock. And she hoped she wasn't in it.

"No hospitals. You know they won't take me without an adult. Just let me think a minute."

Xiao Mei sat down beside her. They were quiet for a minute, then the little girl looked at her. "An Ni?"

"What?" An Ni said, her mind distant as ideas took form then were rejected quickly.

"We can't go back there." Xiao Mei spoke softly, almost too low for An Ni to make out her words.

"Go back where?"

"To Tianbing. Please don't make me go back there. And he won't come looking for us, because you know the boys aren't going to tell. He doesn't know where we are. We can get away."

Something in her voice made An Ni stop thinking about the pain and focus her attention on the girl.

"Why, is something bad happening to you?" She felt silly even phrasing it that way. Everything about their life was bad. *Bad weather, bad food, bad people.* But she knew from stories she'd heard that it could always be worse.

Xiao Mei hesitated, then nodded. It was in the way she slowly bobbed her head that the realization came over An Ni.

She was filled with fury—so much that it overrode the pain. Xiao Mei was hardly more than a baby. If one of the boys had—if they'd— she couldn't even form the words in her head.

She played over the last few weeks in her memory and remembered that after the few times Tianbing had taken Xiao Mei away for hours and then brought her back, she had been especially silent. "Tell me, Xiao Mei."

Xiao Mei started to cry, rocking back and forth as she squatted on the ground. "No, don't make me, An Ni. Please."

An Ni reached out to her, and, ignoring the streak of pain the movement caused, she pulled her into a hug, then just held her as the girl cried. "Sh. You don't have to talk about it. And we won't go back. I swear. I'll promise you this, too. I'm going to find a way to get you home. *Hao le?*"

Xiao Mei sniffled, then used her fist to rub at the tears on her face. "Okay. But you called me Xiao Mei again."

Through her pain, An Ni had to chuckle at the girl's spunk. *Mei.* She'd try to remember. She didn't know where they'd go or what they'd do, and she might not be able to find a way to get her home, but she did know one thing—she would not let Mei go back to Tianbing's gang. But first, they needed shelter until they could figure out some things.

"Okay, Mei, I can't see outside the line of trees. What's out there other than the train tracks?" If she remembered right, they'd walked about a mile or two from the station, along a deserted edge of Beijing.

"Nothing, except a tiny building sort of close to the tracks. It's no bigger than an outhouse."

That got An Ni's interest. An outhouse-sized building would be plenty big for her and Mei while she thought things out. "Really? How far?"

"Not far." Mei looked out, over An Ni's shoulder.

"But are you sure it's not being used? How do you know?" An Ni didn't want to try to make it there and find out someone was in it. Someone who might call the police. Tianbing had lots of friends who were police, and An Ni didn't trust any of them.

Mei shrugged. "I didn't see nobody."

An Ni attempted again to get up, but her leg just wouldn't cooperate. She thought for a minute, then turned to Mei. "Mei, I need you to find me two sticks. Real strong ones." She used her hands to motion to her groin area. "Get me one that is about as long from here to my foot. The other can be as long as from my armpit to my foot. Try to find some that have forked branches on the end. Just bring them to me and let me look at 'em."

Mei jumped up and began scouting around for long branches.

"Wait—I just remembered, the branches need to hang longer than my foot, so my leg doesn't touch the ground. You might have to get them from the trees." An Ni sat up, ignoring the shooting pain, and began tearing the little blanket into strips. She was going to make some homemade crutches like she'd seen Tianbing do before. She'd stored everything she'd seen in the last few years up into her head. She didn't need him. She might only be eleven, but she could do everything he could and more.

And she'd find a way to get her and Mei away from the street life. She *would*.

She bit her lip, concentrating on tearing the material to keep tears from falling. *I will do it,* she chanted to herself. *I will do it.*

Chapter Eleven

Mari paced in front of the noodle shop, impatient for Max to arrive so they could get the day started. Fall was coming fast, and just in the last few days, the air had turned crisper, causing the people around her to already start wearing scarves and thicker coats. She shivered and hoped the sun would come out from behind the haze of pollution, then looked at her watch again. *Hurry up, Max,* she thought. The faster they began, the quicker she could get home. She continued to pace, letting the cheap soles of her rubber boots slap the sidewalk with a satisfactory thump to keep her mind distracted.

A week had passed since they'd lost Chu Chu, and in that time, Bolin had barely said two words to her. She'd tried to talk to him, discuss a plan to get them out of their current financial mess, but he'd offered nothing. She should've known that spending their last funds on more medicine—this time from the black market because the doctor refused—would send him back to his hazy world of not caring. But he'd cried and begged, so she'd relented. And he hadn't mentioned Max again. Now it was up to her to pay the rent that was due in less than a week. And after hitting the Internet cafés to search online for jobs and trudging up and down the shopping streets looking for signs in the windows, Mari had decided to call the one person she knew would help and not ask questions.

Max.

A bus came to a screeching stop on the street directly in front of her, and Mari watched the harried people load, many pushing against the other in their worry to secure a place. When it finally pulled away, Max was crossing the street toward her, a smile on his face.

Mari wouldn't let herself appreciate the feeling of comfort it gave her, that another human being was happy to see her. This was a job—a minor emergency, really. But if Bolin found out this was how she'd pay the rent, he'd probably come out of his haze long enough to go stark raving mad. He and his distrust of foreigners bordered on ridiculous, but Mari didn't want to hurt him. So she'd keep it quiet. She didn't want to—she'd been taught not to—but she'd have to lie to him and tell him she'd caught a short-term job doing something else to get the rent.

"*Ni hao*, Mari," Max called out as he waved.

"Max." She nodded at him, keeping her distance.

He stepped onto the curb and gestured toward the noodle shop. "*Zaofan?*"

Mari couldn't help but laugh at his pronunciation of *breakfast*. She had to give it to him, though—he tried. Still, despite the rumbling in her belly, she didn't want him buying her food. "I'm okay. Have you eaten?"

He shook his head. "Mind if we get a quick bowl of noodles?"

She shrugged and followed him into the shop. The owner waved and called out a greeting, pointing to the table that Max had claimed as his usual spot. They crossed the room and sat down.

"You look different," Max said as he dropped his camera bag to the floor at his feet, then bent down to push one of the straps under the leg of his chair. Now no one would be stealing it, and Mari was impressed to see him take the precaution.

She reached up and smoothed back a few stray hairs, ran her hand down her ponytail. She probably did look a bit boring, with her dark jeans and bland, gray sweater. But she was feeling drab. No wonder she'd unconsciously chosen clothes to match. "I'm dressed to blend in. And my hair was being extra difficult this morning, so I tied it back."

"It looks good. And I like your rain boots," Max said, smiling again.

"Are you making fun of them?" Mari knew that some were ridiculed for their obsession with the cartoonish icon Hello Kitty, but the truth was, she'd found the boots at an outside market for a fraction of what they would've been in a store. Normally she might've chosen the same boots with a different pattern, but her tiny size was limited to just Hello Kitty styles. It was embarrassing, to say the least.

"No, I'm not. Really. My daughter's room was decorated in Hello Kitty when she was younger. We learned to ferret it out in every shopping mall in the area. Clothes, toys, books. She took it to another extreme though, with all the stuff she collected."

The waiter brought them a kettle of steaming tea and two small porcelain cups. Mari raised her eyebrows, noting how the owner no longer served Max with paper products but had moved on to the fancy stuff.

"You talk as though she collected it in the past. What about now? Is she too old for Hello Kitty?"

Max stared into his cup for a moment, then looked up. But he still didn't make eye contact with her. "At my house, yes—her room is stuck in a time warp. But at her mother's house, she finally moved on to a more grown-up theme. My wife—I mean my ex-wife—hired a decorator. My daughter said her new room was all candles, silk, and bamboo. Sounds to me like some kind of spa or something in there. And I told her that, but she said her mom thought it would make her at peace with her mind and body—or some nonsense like that."

Separate houses. Ex-wife. So they were divorced. That answered a lot for her. And Mari could only imagine how spoiled his daughter was, having two houses, two bedrooms, and being passed from father to mother as they both competed for her affections. She'd heard that American children were usually given every material object there was. Computers, iPhones, iPads. Here she was probably the only one in the city still using a flip phone, and even it was left at home for emergency use only. Who Bolin would call in an emergency, she didn't know. Over the last year, he'd shut them off from all their neighbors so completely that no one even looked at her when she passed by.

She was self-conscious that she didn't own a computer, but they were lucky to even have a television, and especially a refrigerator. The small fridge had been their first New Year's present to each other.

"Your daughter, what was it like when you first saw her?" Mari asked, thinking briefly of the first time her own Baba had walked up to her on the street corner and looked down at her. The first thing she'd remembered was his kind eyes. Then he'd handed her an orange, and she'd been taken aback by how big his hands were. Minutes after he'd asked her about her life on the streets, he'd looked at her and told her that if she wanted to, she could walk away with him and be a part of his family. It was her first time trusting a man, and her first experience with trusting her instincts. She knew now that she'd made the best decision of her life—she'd conquered her fear of the man who controlled her, and then she'd become the first of many daughters her new parents would bring under their roof. They'd been poor, but the love she'd had from them was worth more than any amount of money or gadgets.

"When I first saw her, she wouldn't come to me," Max said softly. "I think she was scared. But soon, I won her over with her curiosity to feel the beard I wore back then. One day, maybe a week after she came home, she held her arms out to me and came willingly. Then she grabbed my beard with both her chubby little hands and pulled my face to hers. She pressed her forehead against mine and giggled like crazy. That was our moment."

Mari let him talk, watching the intensity of his emotions when he spoke of her. It was hard to believe a father could be so enamored with a daughter of a different heritage, but obviously this one was.

"I always said that was the moment I melted like butter. When my daughter got old enough to talk, she'd ask me to tell her about the time she made me melt like butter." He smiled as he wrapped his hand around his cup of tea and stared down into it.

The silence settled around them. Mari didn't want to be too intrusive, and his sudden reticence warned her not to pry even more. "So," she said, "you want to see the underground tunnels?"

Max nodded, then dug in his pocket. He pulled out a piece of paper and unfolded it, then spread it on the table. It was well worn, and Mari could tell he'd studied it many times before. She couldn't read it from across the table, but it appeared to be some sort of list.

"Yeah, that's the plan. If I can find a story there, that'd be great. But either way, I need to see it." He took a pen from his pocket and marked something on the paper. Then he folded it carefully and put it away.

The owner brought two bowls of noodles—he hadn't listened to Mari decline hers—and set them on the table. She almost pushed hers away, but her good sense and her rumbling stomach kept her from being too proud.

"So let's eat up, then get out of here," she said, and she lifted the bowl to her mouth, grateful when the first taste of the warm broth hit her tongue.

"Isn't there an easier way in here?" Max asked as he stepped down and joined her in at least six inches of water. He stopped to snap a few photos, almost blinding Mari with the flash.

Mari peeled the end from her ball of string, then tied it to the flaking banister. She led the way down the stairs, slowly and carefully, as she let the string out and searched the narrow passageway for any swimming rats. They could've taken the easy route to the higher tunnels, where migrant workers paid a small fee to live in the tiny bedsized private alcoves that served as rooms. Max had been astonished when she'd told him the damp tunnels were home to laborers who came to Beijing from faraway villages and couldn't afford the aboveground housing expenses. But Max wanted to go deeper to the older and restricted tunnels, so they had to go through more of a hardship to get there. She hoped her boots held up and didn't leak.

"No, not if you want to see the real thing. I could always take you down to the ones set up for foreigners to tour and make you pay a bundle. But you wouldn't be seeing anything authentic. This one, I can promise you, leads to the real deal. But we have to go through some rough spots to get there."

She felt badly that she hadn't told him to wear something to keep his feet dry. But when she'd called him, she was already embarrassed to be asking for work, even though he'd offered to begin with. His attire hadn't crossed her mind when he said he wanted to see the old tunnels beneath Beijing. Most of the accesses had been closed up over the years, in addition to a huge chunk being demolished to make way for subway routes. She'd had to make a lot of calls, but finally she'd gained information on where to go to find an unbarred entrance. Ironically, this tunnel started in a small and tightly packed children's clothing shop, and they'd moved several racks of winter coats to get to the door. The entrance was one of those city secrets—and another source of income for the old couple who owned the shop.

"I want to see the oldest part of this you can show me," Max replied, and splashed behind her. "My daughter did a school report on these tunnels and how Mao ordered the tangle of corridors and rooms to be built for a place of protection from the Cold War. It just boggles the mind to think of the money and manpower this endeavor took."

That reminded Mari. A few of her precious bills had slid into another hand to get permission to go through the shop and the hidden closet to this specific tunnel, so Mari hoped the trek was worth it and Max would pay her well. She'd been too embarrassed on the phone to ask him what fee he would give her, but he'd been generous before, so she hoped he would be again, which meant she needed to give him his money's worth. It also meant she was glad she'd paid attention to her Mama's history lessons around the table each night.

"*Dui*, they started it in 1969 and dug for almost a decade, making it big enough to hold thousands of evacuees. Back then, rooms were sectioned off and outfitted to be hospitals, school rooms, and even a few theaters." She gave a small snort. "Old Mao loved to keep up culturally."

Mari led him down a side tunnel, then up a small concrete stairway to a large door left ajar. She pushed it open and stepped aside, giving Max a look. It was dim but a bit of light from the larger tunnel filtered in, illuminating the room enough to see. Max snapped more photos.

"Most of the lights went out when the tunnels flooded."

"It looks like this was meant to be some sort of laboratory," he said, pointing at a few discarded overturned stools and the remains of long slabs of countertops against the wall.

"See the mold?" she asked, knowing he couldn't miss it. It layered everything in the room, cottony, greenish fuzz on every surface.

Max whistled and stepped back. "Whoa. We shouldn't get too close. I've never seen mold that big or ugly."

"Actually, part of the plan for sustaining life down here was to cultivate fungus for the people to live off of, but you're right. I can't afford to get sick, either." She thought of Bolin. Who would be there to care for him, if not her? If they were both down and out, they'd be in more trouble than she could shake a stick at.

She backed up and wound the string back around the ball as they retreated to the main tunnel, then took another smaller one to the left. The light got dimmer the farther they traveled, but they could still see well enough. Mari pointed out a few dangling electrical wires, urging Max to avoid touching them. They passed a large room that appeared to be a bathroom, soiled, muck-filled stalls cased with stained porcelain tiles. A few crates of tattered and dirty towels told Mari the room might have been used more recently than she had first believed.

"Fascinating," Max said as the shutter on his camera flipped rapidly.

Mari nodded in agreement. "Years ago—before the Olympics came to China—you could get a tour down some of the older tunnels by guides dressed like soldiers. The tours took you by old busts of Mao and other relics from the Cultural Revolution days."

Max followed close behind her, putting his hand on her shoulders to steady her once when she stepped on a deeper part of the floor and almost lost her balance.

"I can't imagine living down here for months with no fresh food or water—no natural light," he said.

"There would've been water. According to reports, almost a hundred wells were dug. And surely you know the Chinese people are made of strong stuff. They've been through and survived things that Americans can't even imagine. Even my father was put through abuse and terror during the revolution. See there?" She pointed at some characters scrawled on the wall. "It says *dig deep and don't pass enemy secrets.*"

Max took a few photos of the sign but was silent. Mari led him deeper, and they passed other doors, closed off and bolted. A few open tunnels showed what appeared to be deeper water, urging them to continue on until finally she turned him around and headed back to where they'd began.

As they traveled closer to the surface, they passed a lot of discarded items. Mari saw old traffic signs, rusted bicycles, and even dead potted trees she was sure once dotted the streets during the Olympics.

Max finally broke the heavy silence. "You said your father experienced the Cultural Revolution?"

Mari nodded, forgetting for a moment that her Baba's past wasn't something he discussed. He still harbored many scars from the period of time that cost him his dignity and even his family.

"How old was he when it all started?"

Mari could hear the curiosity in his voice and was sad she couldn't fill in every detail. But some things were kept under their own family roof. "He was sixteen when the revolution started, but he was a few years older when Mao called people of every age and size to begin digging. He wasn't anywhere near Beijing, but the story spread far and wide. It's told that the people used anything they could find to dig—shovels, garden tools, and even pieces of wood torn from the city wall."

"Everyone started at the same tunnel?"

Mari laughed. "No! They dug all over the place! Even in many courtyards in the *hutongs*, too. But mostly the biggest courtyards. In some of the tunnels, you can hear the families overhead having dinner, aware but not caring that their homes sit over their country's history buried in deep, dark tunnels."

"Fascinating," Max whispered behind her. "I'll bet your father is full of stories."

She finally got to the beginning of their string and untied it from the banister, then tucked the ball into her pocket. She led him up the stairs to the wooden door, then knocked for the shop owners to come open it.

When the door opened, she was startled to find the couple cowering behind a policeman, and he wore a thunderous look on his face. He gestured for them to come out.

"What's this?" Max whispered behind her.

"Sh, let me handle it," she said. She led the way out into the light, following the official to the street outside. He turned and pointed at the curb, telling them to sit down. Mari pulled Max along with her, doing as he said.

Max's long legs looked ridiculously uncomfortable as he crouched on the curb. But Mari put her finger to her lip again, warning him to be quiet. The official paced in front of them, talking on a cell phone. Mari couldn't understand his dialect and only picked up a few words. She definitely caught on that he was discussing a foreigner being in the tunnels. Finally, he shoved the phone in his pocket and glared down at them.

Switching into the official language of Beijing, he asked to see their identification.

"Do you have your passport?" she asked Max.

He shook his head. "I keep it in the safe in my apartment. But I have my US driver's license." He leaned back and pulled a clip of money and cards from his pocket, then extracted a card with his photo on it and handed it to the policeman. Mari also handed over her identification.

The official looked at it, then waved Max's driver's license around and began shouting at her. He ranted for five minutes or so about foreigners not being allowed in the tunnels any longer. Then he pointed at Max's camera and demanded the photo card.

Mari sighed. Max wasn't going to like it. "He wants your memory card from your camera."

Max looked at her and shook his head. "Hell no. Tell him I won't publish the photos, but I'm keeping my card. I have other stuff on there I need."

Mari tried negotiating with the officer, emphasizing that Max was just a tourist, that no photos would be put online. But the officer was adamant and refused to budge. Finally he gave her the ultimatum, then crossed his arms over his chest and waited.

"He says you can give him the card, or we can both go to the precinct office to talk to his commanding officer."

Max hesitated, then threw his hands up and cursed. "Fine. I don't want to make trouble for you, Mari, so I'll give this sucker what he wants. But I'm not happy about it."

He flipped the camera over and hit a button to release the card, then pulled it out and gave it to her. Mari handed it up to the officer. He slid it into his shirt pocket, then pointed his finger at them one more time, and walked away.

Mari turned to Max. "And that, Sir Max, ends your short tour of Beijing's Underground City."

Max let himself into his apartment and stood in the doorway looking around. Already he missed being with Mari and listening to the musical sound of her voice as she did her best to be a thorough guide, reciting history and facts with the skill of a professional. He'd been sad to see her walk away and reminded himself he had no right to be—she was already taken. And he had no right to be craving the attention of anyone anyway.

He went to the kitchen counter and emptied his pockets. He was still ticked off about the memory card. But he'd bluffed on one thing— it was a new card, so all he'd lost were the photos of the tunnels. And it wasn't the first time he'd been shut down since he'd come to China. Without Mari as a guide, he'd already figured out that to find any kind of story was almost impossible. Hell—getting any leads, including addresses or names, was like applying to be included in a state secret. It was just so hard to establish any kind of contacts or gain introductions to the people he'd like to interview. If he followed procedures, he'd wait days to get permission to interview anyone—even a sweeper on the street was too afraid to talk to him.

Old fears never died, he supposed. Back in the day, the people would most likely be punished for saying anything that could be twisted and construed to be against the government—they were even made to do self-criticisms, claiming themselves to be of bad character if discovered to be anything less than loyal to the communist party.

Max felt that, despite decades of struggles, not much had changed in China. He'd even been asked to leave the area last week when he'd come upon a skirmish between a policeman and a man peddling fruit. Max sensed there was some sort of power struggle, or even sidewalk blackmail going on. But just like with the underground tunnels, he'd been given a choice to either disappear or be detained. Once he'd understood what the official was saying, he'd gotten out of there quickly. More than one journalist had been detained or jailed and charged with illegal activity for simply interviewing everyday people. With all he had going on, he didn't want to follow in their footsteps. And really, he was here for more than a story—he was here to fulfill a personal journey. Doing so from a jail cell wouldn't work.

So far he'd clicked along, trying to do what he thought it was *she* wanted. That enigmatic force that pushed him. But he still felt the heavy burden of guilt. Of failure. His shoulders sagged, and he shook off the façade of being confident and strong, glad Mari couldn't see him now, see the excuse for a man he really was. His stomach growled, alerting him to the fact he hadn't had dinner. He went to the small kitchen cove, opened the cabinet under the sink, and pulled out a bottle.

He held it up to his eyes and sighed in disgust when he saw the amber liquid was already half gone. When he'd drunk it, he had no idea. He turned to reach for a glass but then let his hand fall. Who was he kidding? He didn't need a glass. He was a pro. Closing his eyes, he brought the bottle to his lips, and within seconds, it was empty.

But it wasn't enough.

The flames licked at his memory, threatening to engulf him in visions he didn't want to see. He reached for his wallet, wanting to see her face, then remembered he didn't have it any longer. But he didn't need it—she was still there, smiling at him. Haunting him. Begging him for something he couldn't quite grasp. What did she want of him?

He slid down the cabinet until he was sitting on the floor, the stained linoleum squares of yellow beaming up at him in a garish reminder of his pathetic life. He was alone in a cheap room in a country where no one knew him or cared whether he lived or not. To be honest, even if he had been on his home turf, no one would care about his existence or even notice if he never emerged into the light of day. Once again, he struggled with the thought of ending it—craving the permanent blackness that beckoned to him when he was alone.

He leaned back until he could reach into his pocket, then pulled out the folded piece of paper. He opened it and scanned through to the bottom, reading the words until they blurred together. He couldn't leave China yet. He still had a few things to do. And then maybe when he'd done it all, she would stop calling out to him. Beseeching him for something he couldn't figure out. Or at the least, maybe she'd stop haunting his every thought, day and night.

But for now, he had a remedy. Short term, but it'd do the trick. On all fours, he crawled over to the opposite cabinets and opened the one that held the few pot and pans. Reaching toward the back, he pulled out another bottle he'd hidden from himself. He laughed—*as if he had any willpower.* Hiding it was a joke.

He sat back down and pried the cap off, then took a long drink of the Chinese *bai jiu.* He coughed and his eyes filled with tears. It tasted like kerosene, but he knew only a small amount was needed to make him sleep, and hopefully he'd go down enough to outrun the dreams he knew awaited him. He'd refused to close his eyes the night before, holding out until he'd finally nodded off sitting up. Then she'd come. Like he knew she would.

The first cramp hit his stomach, and he thought again of food, but he discarded the warning. He didn't deserve food. Or comfort. Or compassion.

Another drink, longer this time. Then a gasp for air. Outside, a flash of lightning lit the room, and then a roll of thunder followed. Perfect. A storm to accompany his misery.

Then the fire in his belly reassured him that the pain he'd feel later still wouldn't be penance enough. And thinking about it, he welcomed the darkness once more and lifted the bottle again.

Chapter Twelve

It wasn't worse than the throbbing of her leg, but An Ni's back was hurting. If she could just turn to sleep on her side, maybe it would stop. She tried to roll over, and a groan of pain made her eyes open wide. It was dark. And windy. And really, really cold. *But who was groaning?* It sounded like some kind of wild animal. She turned her head, slowly because it was stiff, and she saw Mei squatting beside her, rocking back and forth. Her eyes were closed as if she was praying, but her mouth wasn't moving.

"Mei?" An Ni called out weakly.

The little girl rushed to her side. "An Ni, you're awake finally! I was so scared."

The relief in her voice made An Ni use her elbows to prop herself up to look around. Her entire body hurt, worse than she ever remembered in her life. Beside her she saw her homemade crutches, neatly stacked and appearing to still be in good shape. The sight of them made her remember that she'd been up on them—briefly. Through her pain, she felt a flash of pride that she'd made something that had worked. It fled quickly and was replaced with more confusion. "Where are we, and what was making all those awful noises?"

She could see the glint of one of Mei's eyes staring down at her, a ray of moonlight illuminating part of her face.

"That was you, An Ni."

An Ni moved again, and an involuntary groan escaped her. So it *was* her. Her leg throbbed and felt hot all the way from her toes to her hip. It was getting worse. She pushed herself to a sitting position and reached down to run her hands down her pant leg. When she didn't feel any protruding bones, she let out a long breath of relief. She was sure her leg was broken, but maybe it was only a small break.

"Where are we?" When she looked around, it looked the same but different than where they'd been before she'd fallen asleep. Though now that she was waking up, she didn't think she'd purposely fallen asleep.

"We're just a little way from where we were. You fell and went to sleep when you tried to walk." Her voice wavered. "I think a storm is coming, An Ni."

She must have fainted. An Ni could see she'd really caused Mei to be afraid, and she swore under her breath. Then she remembered that only the bad boys used words like that, and she felt ashamed of herself. Mei needed her to be mature. She didn't need another hot-tempered bully around. They'd left those behind—hopefully for good. But she needed to get Mei out of the woods, especially before the rain started.

"Mei, we've got to get to that shelter. Let's try it again. Come on and help me."

Mei stood. "*Hao le*, I've already moved our food there. I hope the rats don't eat it."

"What else is in there?" An Ni moved slightly. She knew she was stalling, but she was afraid to put any weight on her leg. She also felt pressure in her bladder. She needed to pee.

"I barely looked because it's scary in there, but I saw I some old papers and rags. Some kind of little stove—a really short one that sits on three legs. A stool to sit on. No bed."

"Well, at least it's got a roof and a door. Did it have a lock on the inside?"

In the dim light, she could barely see Mei shrug her shoulders, but it didn't matter. They wouldn't stay there long anyway. Just long enough to get out of the brisk night air and figure out what to do. The wind picked up, howling around her ears, spurring her to move.

She took several deep breaths, then reached for one of her crutches. "Come here, Mei. First you have to help me use the bathroom."

"What bathroom?"

"You know what I mean. If I can get up, and you can help me with my buttons and getting these pants down, I'll just lean back a little and pee standing up, and hope it doesn't get all over me. There's no way I can squat."

Mei picked up the other crutch and came closer. An Ni draped an arm around her shoulders. Then, using the crutch on the other side, An Ni stood and kept her bad leg outstretched and away from the ground. *Do not fade out; do not fade out,* she coached herself as a wave of nausea hit her.

"You did it, An Ni, you're standing," Mei said encouragingly, wobbling under An Ni's weight. "Here, take this one."

An Ni ignored the sudden swirling brown and green of the trees and focused only on the other homemade crutch. She grabbed it and put it under her other arm, letting Mei ease out. She felt unsteady, and she wasn't sure the branches would hold, but at least from a standing position she could see the shelter. Mei was right, it wasn't that far away. She could make it. She just had to be tough.

· "Come on, Mei. Let's do this," she said under her breath. Mei leaned over and helped her with her buttons, then helped her ease her pants down just enough. An Ni leaned back in a sort of standing up squat, then let it go.

Her pee was hot coming out—so very hot that it surprised An Ni, and she jumped a little. She wondered if that meant she had a fever. A fever was one thing Tianbing was always afraid of, because he didn't want the entire gang of kids sick at one time.

She cringed when some of her pee came back on her and ran down the inside of her pant leg, but it couldn't be helped. Finally, she was done, and Mei helped her put everything back together and buttoned her up.

"Ready?" Mei asked.

An Ni took a deep breath and took one step, awkwardly gripping the crutch branches with her armpits as she concentrated on keeping her leg from touching the ground. When she didn't fall, she took another tiny step. She looked up and could tell they were getting closer. Not much, but just a little.

Mei walked just behind her, keeping her tiny hands on the small of An Ni's back, as though she'd be able to help her if she fell again. An Ni thought for a second how lucky she was the girl hadn't run off with the boys but instead had stayed with her. If she'd been alone, she would've lain next to the tracks forever, or at least until she'd died.

A gust of wind threatened to make her fall, but she steadied herself, then took another step. Through her jacket, she felt the roughness of the branches she used as crutches and thought they'd slice her armpit open. But she breathed out, then breathed in, and took another. Her foot throbbed. Or maybe it was her knee. Or somewhere between. She really couldn't tell now.

"I have to sit, Mei. Help me." She couldn't go on.

"No, An Ni. If you sit, you'll go back to sleep. Come on," Mei scolded.

An Ni was taken aback. She'd never heard the meek little girl use such a stern voice. Mei pushed her slightly on her back, encouraging her to take another step.

So she did.

Slowly, one step at a time, they spent the next hour traversing what would have normally taken them five minutes or so. Finally though, they were right outside the small shack. Mei pushed open the door, and An Ni wrinkled her nose at the stale smell that wafted out. The shack obviously hadn't been used in ages. That was good, in a way—but who knew what could be hiding in it?

"We've got two steps, and then we'll be in," Mei said.

An Ni looked at those two steps and thought they might as well be mountains. She couldn't possibly get up them while standing. Without saying a word, she threw her crutches down and, with her leg extended, used the door frame of the shack to lower herself to the step.

"What are you doing, An Ni?"

An Ni turned until she could plant both palms on the dirty floor, then she turned her body so that one knee bent on the floor supported her weight. Letting her bad leg flop behind her, she used her other three appendages to drag herself into the shack.

Once in, Mei shut the door, muffling the sound of the winds. Then she sank to the floor, sighing loudly. "I'm tired."

An Ni couldn't answer. She didn't have enough breath to respond. She panted, sounding like a stray dog, until she could finally relax against the wall she'd crawled to. She looked down at her feet, and her eyes widened at what she saw.

The sneaker on her right foot looked as if it were trying to split open at the seams. Her foot was swelling—and swelling really bad. "I think I should try to get my shoe off, Mei."

Mei crawled over and looked at it, and the moonlight that shone through the small window illuminated her grimace. "Eww, An Ni. I can't do it."

An Ni tried to reach the shoe, but the effort made the dizziness return. She stopped. Still, the pain remained. "I'm trying to remember when Kuan broke his leg, if Tianbing took his shoe off," An Ni said, thinking hard.

"Who is Kuan?"

"Just a boy who used to be in our gang. He fell, and Tianbing wouldn't take him to the hospital. I saw them make the homemade crutches—that's how I knew how to do it." She decided she'd keep the shoe on. Anything to keep from touching her leg again.

"Where's Kuan now?"

An Ni shrugged. She didn't know. Where were all the kids who'd come and gone since she'd been with Tianbing? It was a mystery. Traded? Dead? Could be either one.

"Did Kuan remember his family?" Mei asked.

"If he did, he never spoke of them," An Ni answered. She felt sorry for Mei and knew the girl thought about her own parents all the time. Her abduction was still fresh, but An Ni also knew the memories would fade with time until Mei wouldn't even remember their faces. "Listen, Mei, let's try to take stock of what we have."

An Ni looked around. The room was small. A metal slab attached to the wall under the window looked as though it was supposed to be a desk. Under it, a three-legged wooden stool. To the right of the window was a row of built-in cabinets.

"Did you look in there?" she asked, leaning toward the lowest handle. With the effort came the blackness, and the last thing An Ni saw was Mei's stricken face.

An Ni awoke again. This time the peeled and stained ceiling immediately told her where she was. It was cold, but she couldn't feel the wind howling around her ears any longer. She reached down to feel a heavy, coarse piece of material draped over her. She didn't know how long she'd been out, but it only felt like seconds. She slowly eased herself up until she was sitting. Her leg still ached, reminding her of their predicament. *Their* predicament—at least she wasn't alone, even if it was only a seven-year-old with her. But where was Mei? It felt like her heart went to her throat until she spotted a rumpled bundle on top of the desk.

"Mei," she croaked out.

The little girl sat up and rubbed at her eyes.

"You went to sleep again, An Ni. And you were panting like you were running. Please stop doing that." Mei threw aside a small piece of something and swung her legs over, then hopped down from the desk. "I'm sorry; I didn't want to lie on the floor. I kept hearing something scurry around."

An Ni looked around, squinting as she searched the dark corners of the room for any stray visitors. She couldn't see anything. She tried to swallow, but her mouth was so dry, she almost choked. It felt as if she'd swallowed a bucket of sand. She reached down and held up a corner of the material draped on her, then looked at Mei.

"Rice sacks. I found them in the cupboard. At least a dozen, and one even has some old rice in it. They make good blankets."

An Ni nodded, pleased with Mei for thinking smart. The rice sacks were huge, probably at one time holding thirty pounds or more of raw rice. Someone using the shack had gone through a lot of rice, that much was sure.

"Water?" An Ni asked weakly.

Mei went to the lowest cupboard, opened it, and brought out a dented tin bowl. "There's only a bowl but no water."

An Ni thought. *Why would there be rice if they didn't have water? And someone probably used the shack for days or weeks at a time.* "Mei, go outside and look beside the shack; see if there's a pump out there."

Mei looked her way, and though An Ni couldn't see her face clearly, she felt the reluctance.

"I promise I'll stay awake, and if you don't come right back, I'll come out there."

Mei snorted, telling An Ni she had her doubts about that, but she went. The door obviously had a lock, as An Ni could see when Mei reached up and turned it to the left, then pulled open the door. She stepped out and disappeared from view.

An Ni sat up, ignoring the flash of pain, and listened, hoping to hear Mei holler out something positive. She tried to swallow again, pushing the lump of pain down her throat. But it was hard. She knew she needed water badly.

Suddenly she heard a rusty-sounding creaking, then a swoosh. Mei had found water!

It ran for a moment, then there was another creak and it stopped.

Mei appeared in the doorway. "Here, An Ni. It was muddy at first, but then it turned clear." She held the bowl out, balancing it carefully with both hands.

"You first, Mei. You need to drink, too." An Ni could almost taste the wetness on her tongue, but Mei was probably thirsty, too.

"I already drank some out there," Mei said, gently placing the bowl in An Ni's hands. "It tasted kind of weird, but it was okay."

An Ni lifted the bowl to her lips and drank quickly, surprised at how much her hands shook. As she drank, she tried to think how long it'd been since she fell off the train. *One day and night? Two?* She didn't know, and Mei probably didn't, either.

Her stomach growled, and Mei went to the corner, picked up two of the plastic food trays, and gave one to An Ni, then dropped down to squat on the floor with the other in her hand.

"*Xie xie*, but maybe we should share one. We don't know how long we'll be here and need to be careful and ration the food." An Ni pulled the plastic back and used her finger to mix the chunks of meat into the compartment that held the rice. Then she lifted the tray to her nose and inhaled deeply.

"Is it still okay?" Mei asked. She set the tray she held down on the floor in front of her.

An Ni nodded. "That's a benefit to it being so cold—our food will stay good longer." She handed the tray to Mei. "Eat half of everything."

Mei took it, and using her fingers as a scoop, she ate quickly. An Ni realized she'd probably been hungry for hours, but after months of being the youngest in the group and waiting for approval to perform any function whatsoever, she'd waited for An Ni.

Finally, the little girl handed the tray back to An Ni. "Here, your turn."

An Ni ate so quickly, she didn't even taste the food. Once again, she felt thankful Mei had grabbed it so that they'd have something. Mei was a smart girl—much smarter even than the older boys in their group.

"What're we going to do, An Ni?"

"Somersaults?"

Mei gave her a strange look, letting An Ni know her joke fell flat. With a last swipe at the tray, An Ni set it aside. "I'm not sure, but Mei, next time if I'm asleep and you're hungry—just eat. You don't have to wait for me to tell you what to do."

"I'm cold." Mei grabbed one of the rice sacks An Ni had lain with and wrapped it around her shoulders.

"In the morning, we need to try to get back to the train station. Maybe someone will set their cigarettes down and we can swipe a lighter, then we can bring it back and make a fire in the corner over there." An Ni didn't know how she'd ever make it there, but it was the closest place to find people, and she had to give Mei some hope. In their different sleeping areas on the streets, they'd usually have a fire, even if only in a barrel. On cold nights, Tianbing or whoever was in charge would sometimes start one for them to stand around, then later to sleep by.

An Ni looked up when she heard Mei making a strange noise. "Mei? What are you doing?" She squinted, trying to see her face more clearly in the dim moonlight.

Mei didn't answer, except for a small sniffle.

"Are you crying? Oh, *bu ku le*. Come here."

An Ni scooted back until she was leaning against the wall and held her arm out. Mei came to her and snuggled in, bumping against An Ni's leg. Clenching her teeth together, An Ni breathed slowly until the sharp pain subsided back into a low throbbing. When she reached down, her hand moved over a bulge in her pocket. Then she remembered.

"Oh, I have something, Mei."

She dug in the pocket and came out with the wallet she'd found in the seat of the train. She'd forgotten all about it.

"Where did you get that?" Mei asked, sounding bored. Coming up with random wallets wasn't anything new.

"On the train. But look what I found in it." She opened the wallet and pulled out the paper with the white man's face on it. She set that aside, then plucked the photo of the little girl from the inside fold, then set the wallet down beside her. She held the photo where Mei could see.

Mei reached for it, then held it up, squinting in the dark. "Who is it?"

"I don't know. But she looks like she's happy. Like maybe she lives in a warm house and has a Mama and Baba, and probably goes to school."

Mei was quiet and An Ni could just see her imagination in motion, wondering what it would be like to be part of a real family again—to have someone to feed and protect you.

"I wonder what her name is," Mei said softly.

"I don't know what this says, but it's probably right here." An Ni took the photo from Mei and turned it over, then traced the letters with her finger. She'd learned the English alphabet early in school, in her old life. She couldn't put together words, but she did know her letters.

"I'm scared, An Ni. What if Tianbing comes to find us?"

An Ni squeezed her in and pulled the rice sack over them both. She wished they had something to lie on top of to separate them from the cold floor. She'd also thought many times of the boys leading Tianbing to the train, and then them hunting until they found her and Mei. It terrified her, but she wouldn't let Mei know that. "Don't worry. He won't come. But would it help if I told you a story?"

She felt Mei nod beside her.

"*Hao le.* You hold the picture." She handed it to Mei. "Have you ever heard of Guanyin?"

Mei gazed at An Ni's face and mumbled she hadn't.

"Guanyin is the goddess of compassion and protection. She was named Miao Shan and was the third daughter of a king, and she was the only one who defied him when he picked a rich suitor for her to marry."

"Why didn't she want to marry a rich man?" Mei asked.

"Because she wanted to be with someone who was kind and helped others. None of the men her father chose fit what she felt the gods wanted for her. So to punish her defiance, the king sent her to a monastery and ordered that the monks make her work hard on a barren part of the grounds around his palace. His daughters weren't accustomed to physical labor, so he thought he'd break her of her defiance. Soon, she attracted the help of animals who were drawn to her gentle spirit. Within months, the land she worked looked like a garden of paradise, even in winter. What her father thought would break her actually made her very content."

"Then what?"

An Ni smiled. Mei knew that couldn't be all to the story. "Then her father became sick, and the healer told him he'd try to save him. He went out into the kingdom to find all he needed to make his magic concoction. When he'd made it and gave it to the king to drink, it saved his life. The king wanted to know what was in the tonic, and the healer told him it was the ground-up arms and eyes of a saint."

An Ni glanced at Mei in the dark and could tell she was entranced by the tale.

"Once completely recovered, the king asked to be taken to the saint so he might thank him properly. After a day of travel, he was taken to the monastery and found the saint was actually his own daughter, Miao Shan."

"She didn't have any arms or eyes?"

An Ni shook her head. "No, but she didn't mind. She'd given them out of love for her father, without a thought for herself. Her father was overcome with gratitude and a realization that she really was special. He went to bow down at her feet, but when he looked up, she'd disappeared."

"Where did she go?" Mei asked.

"It is said that she reappeared later in the clouds, with a thousand arms and eyes in each hand. The people named her Guanyin, god of compassion and mercy. Her many arms are to support those in need, and her eyes are to help her find them. In homes all over China, there are statues of her, and people light candles to show their respect and beckon her into their lives."

"Maybe Guanyin is looking at us right now. Maybe it's this girl." Mei handed An Ni the photo and turned it over.

An Ni held the picture to her chest, then snuggled Mei closer. "I think she is, Mei. We have our very own Guanyin, and that means she won't let anything else bad happen to us. So go to sleep, and don't be afraid. Tomorrow, we'll try to make a plan."

Chapter Thirteen

Finally Mari felt cold enough that she headed home. Even with all of her procrastinating, she was still only going to be a little over an hour later than usual. And this morning Bolin hadn't even asked how she was going to pay their bills, so she hadn't volunteered that she'd be working with Max again. Not only did his silence make her feel that he didn't care, but her own reluctance to volunteer the information felt devious, as if she were lying, even though she wasn't.

She knew she lingered mostly because she didn't want to be questioned by Bolin. And if she was being honest with herself, she didn't even want to see him. After a day spent with Max, someone who appeared to enjoy her conversation and company, going back to her life and what her marriage had become felt more depressing than she could bear. It was past dinnertime, but what of it? Bolin probably wouldn't eat anyway. She also wanted to walk a few streets to see if she could spot An Ni. The night before, she'd dreamed of her, and that told Mari that fate intended for them to be more than a passing meeting.

She picked up her pace. She'd go in and make Bolin get up and act like a man. She couldn't take it anymore, him lying around like he was. She just had to get stronger, even meaner. For his own good, and for the good of their marriage.

She opened the bag and ate the rest of the tiny buns she'd picked up that morning and carried in her bag all day as she waited for her appetite to kick in. She thought of An Ni as she swallowed. She'd held on to a few just in case she ran into the girl, but walking up and down the streets hadn't done any good. The girl had moved on, obviously. Now Mari felt more guilt. She should've done something that very night, instead of walking away.

It wasn't as if she hadn't seen plenty of street children, before and after meeting An Ni. It was just something about her—that one little girl—that pulled at Mari and wouldn't allow her to forget her face.

Finally at her apartment building, Mari raced up the stairs and past the many other doors, not wanting to peek in or talk to anyone. She fumbled with her keys, then burst in.

The scene before her made her stop in her tracks.

Bolin was sitting at the table, calmly eating celery sticks.

"Mari, come sit down," he said and waved her over.

Mari was at a loss for words. Bolin was awake and off the couch? Could this mean he'd turned a corner? She set her bag down by the door and took off her jacket. She hung it on the coat tree then went to the table, pulled a chair out, and sat down.

"Bolin."

"Mari." He smiled, raising an eyebrow.

A smile! Mari couldn't believe it. He was still disheveled, and still wearing the same baggy and musty clothes from the day before, but he was up. And he was smiling. It was a victory, as far as she was concerned.

"I'm glad you're up. Let me fix you some real dinner." Mari stood quickly.

Bolin raised his hand to stop her. "No, please. We can worry about dinner later. First, though, I'd like to get cleaned up. Would you help me?"

Mari nodded. "Of course. Let me go get you some clothes ready, and you can take a shower."

Bolin pushed the dish of celery away and stood. He held on to the table for support, and when he swayed a little, Mari rushed over to him.

"Here, let me help you. I know your back is hurting." She wouldn't mention that he was probably dizzy from the pills combined with a lack of nutrition. They both knew it. Neither had to say it.

Together they shuffled to the bathroom, and Bolin leaned on the doorframe while Mari got out a towel and the soap. She was cautiously optimistic that his interest in washing his body was a turning point, but she carefully hid her emotions while moving around the bathroom.

She turned to him. "There's a towel and the soap. Want to call me when you're done?"

Bolin stared at her for a moment, then came into the bathroom. He leaned on the sink. "I don't think I can do it, Mari."

What was he talking about? "Do what?"

"Shower. Can you help me?"

He was right. He didn't have the strength to even shower. "Sit down there on the toilet, and let me go get out of these clothes. I'll help you."

In their bedroom, she changed quickly into a short nightgown. It would get wet, but it'd be easy to change out of when they finished. She looked at their bed, and a longing came over her, a longing that Bolin would sleep there tonight. With her. Even to simply hold her and help her feel less alone. She pulled down the covers and plumped the pillows, then went to the closet and got Bolin a clean set of pajamas and underwear.

She went back to the bathroom. Bolin was standing at the mirror, leaning in and staring at his reflection, a puzzled look on his face. He looked up when Mari came in and set the clothes on the counter beside the sink.

"I don't want pajamas. I want real clothes. Bring my lucky shirt, and can you find my belt?"

Mari was taken aback. Bolin hadn't worn real clothes in weeks, maybe months. But instead of arguing, she picked up the clothes and went back to the bedroom. She exchanged them for pants and his red shirt he used to love to wear on their occasional nights out to dinner, then returned to the bathroom.

"Are we going out?" she asked as she set the new clothes down.

Bolin shrugged. "First let's get through the shower, and then we'll see how I feel."

Mari was all for that, and she turned on the water. He stood and let his pajama bottoms drop from his skinny frame, then peeled off his shirt. Mari didn't comment that he wasn't wearing underwear. She didn't want to nag when he was finally coming out of his daze. When the water was just hot enough, she turned to him and smiled, then slipped out of her nightgown. Why get clothes wet when not needed?

Bolin smiled back weakly. "I wish. But, Mari, I barely have the strength to do this. It'd be better if you put that back on."

Mari felt her face burn with shame, and she slipped the gown back over her head and let it drop. She hadn't really meant she wanted to do anything—she just thought it'd be easier to help him shower without dealing with her own garments getting wet.

Bolin came over to the corner and stepped up on the small step, then leaned against the shower wall. He only stood for a moment, then he crouched down in a squat and covered his knees, reminding Mari of a child cowering in the corner after being scolded.

Mari began spraying him with the hot water, hoping it would bring him comfort. When he was finally soaked, she turned off the water and set the sprayer down. She picked up the soap and started to cover his back with a smooth coating of bubbles.

He held out his hand. "I'll do that."

She turned away and fiddled with her hair while he washed his body. When he gave her the signal, she picked up the sprayer again, using it to rinse him off.

"Aren't you going to wash my hair?" Bolin mumbled.

"I'm going to do that in the kitchen, over the sink. I think you need a long and relaxing head massage, and I can't do it in here."

Bolin sighed visibly, and Mari felt a rush of pity for him. He didn't ask for much—he just wanted to be out of pain and left alone. How had they come to this? How had her once strong and robust husband shriveled into this smaller, weaker man? It broke her heart.

When she had him rinsed and smelling good, she turned off the water, then reached for his towel. He stood and took it from her, and she turned away to give him privacy. It felt weird to see him naked, as if they were strangers and not intimate partners any longer. Mari wondered if he felt it, too.

"Get dressed and come to the kitchen," she said. She picked up the bottle of shampoo and left the room.

In the kitchen, she pulled the kitchen chair up to the sink and draped towels over the back.

Bolin shuffled in. He looked so different with real clothes on. He wasn't wearing the belt he'd asked her to find, but he'd tucked his shirt into his pants and was wearing shoes. Mari was impressed.

He smiled sheepishly, looking as close to happy as he had in a long time. "Can you cut my hair, too?"

Mari nodded and felt her eyes fill. He was making an effort, and that made her heart soar. Maybe they'd be okay after all. She waved him over, unable to speak from the lump in her throat. She'd cut his hair and do so gladly. For months he'd looked like a beggar with his long, shaggy locks. She'd finally stopped bothering him about it, so the fact that he asked her didn't go unnoticed.

He came and sat in the chair and leaned back. "Do you think Chu Chu's happy, wherever he is?"

That came out of nowhere. So his camel was on his mind. Mari thought maybe he was more of a farmer's son than he thought. Only someone who'd grown up close to animals would have such a connection to a creature like their stubborn camel.

"Chu Chu is still young enough to work, and that makes him worth more than just the meat any thief could sell him for. I think he's probably being taken care of better than even we did. Don't worry about him, Bolin." Mari leaned over him and adjusted the water until it was hot. His hair was still wet from the shower, so she squeezed some shampoo onto it and began rubbing it in. Then gently, with his face resting against her chest, she massaged his head. She looked down to see him close his eyes, a look of rapture on his face, and it made her smile. "I'm so glad you're awake, Bolin."

He nodded, then was somber again. "Mari, I just want to say I'm not mad at you about the foreigner anymore. I know you had to do what you could to pay our bills. And I'm sorry for what I've put you through."

She kept her fingers moving and was glad he didn't see the tears as they started to rain down her face. When she could speak without her voice trembling, she said, "It's okay. Maybe now we can get back on track."

Bolin shook his head and reached out and lightly grabbed her wrist. She stopped moving for a moment, relishing the feel of his touch on her skin. His words were sad, but ironically, his voice wasn't. He sounded as if he'd finally made peace with the truth. "No, it's not okay. I wanted to do more for you. *Be* more for you. I just wanted to be able to prove to everyone that I'm not just a farmer's son. But I've failed."

Her fingers moved harder, pressing against his neck now. She'd wanted him to take accountability for his actions for such a long time, but now that he was, her heart broke for him.

"Never say that, Bolin. You haven't failed. It's not your fault you got hurt." She wouldn't mention it was his fault he got addicted to the pills. He was on an upturn, and she wouldn't ruin it by pointing out the obvious.

"No, but it is my fault that I can't overcome it. I'm weak, Mari. My father was right—I should've never left the countryside."

Mari stopped massaging and began rinsing the suds from his hair, using gentle, repeated motions to comfort him. She didn't know what to say. It was clear now that everything Bolin had ever done was to prove to his father that he could do it. His current circumstances were more about the father-son battle than they were about her marriage. He carried so much resentment against his father. How was she to help him through that? Her words were going nowhere, that much was clear.

"If you want, we can always go back," she said softly. Maybe the clean country air and simple life would return him to health, get his mind straight again, even help him break his addiction for good. And it could be possible that, to bridge the gulf between father and son, they needed to be pushed together. She was willing to do whatever it took, even to labor on a farm again.

"Going back would be my last resort. My father would love to see my defeat—see how I've lost face. But Mari, I need you to know this, you are the one bright moment in my life. No other man from our village has ever or will ever have a woman like you. It was me—I won you over when my father told me I couldn't. I won the pretty girl who laughed like music." A smile of satisfaction lit up his face.

Mari urged him to sit up, then wrapped the towel around his head. She went to get the scissors from the drawer on the other wall. When she turned, he was staring at his hands, and his expression had changed to one of sadness again.

"Look at these, Mari. Why did I ever think I could be a business-man? These are nothing but farmer's hands. He was right. My father said all I was good for was laboring in the fields."

She crossed the room and took the towel from his head. She would not let him feel sorry for himself anymore, but his moods, switching from happy to sad so fast, were starting to worry her. "He wasn't right, Bolin. And don't talk like that. You are going to be the man you want to be. You just have to get back out there. We can figure out a new business, and we can make it happen. You think like an entrepreneur, and sometimes entrepreneurs fail at many things before they find just the right formula for success. We've just got to figure out the next thing."

She started combing and cutting his hair, letting it drop around them onto the kitchen floor. They stopped talking as she moved around him, trimming even faster. As she worked, the distance that had grown between them over the last several months got smaller and smaller, until Mari finally felt comfortable enough to lean against him, to feel her body touching his once again.

Bolin looked up at her when she'd finished. He stared into her eyes, and Mari realized it was probably the first time in months he'd really looked at her. She felt self-conscious for a second, wishing she'd taken more time that day to make herself pretty.

"*Xie xie*, Mari."

"*Bu ke qi*. No thanks are needed. You're my husband. I don't mind doing things for you."

He grabbed her hand and kissed it. "No, I don't mean for the bath and haircut. I mean thank you for everything. You were the one who inspired me to try to be more, and you have been the only beacon of light in this long, drawn-out, dark nightmare. I couldn't ask for a better wife."

She was speechless. His gratitude was overwhelming and unexpected.

He hesitated once more, looking around their small home then back at her. "Mari, I don't think I'm strong enough to go out for a meal, but if you'll go get it, I'll make sure to be awake and ready to eat whatever you pick out—even if it's meat."

Mari laughed. She doubted he'd go that far. She stared at him for a minute, so glad to finally see him acting human. He looked so much better with his hair cut and his good clothes on. His face shone, and his eyes for once were bright and alert. Besides the husband she used to know, Mari recognized something else settling around her that she hadn't felt in such a long while.

Hope.

The gathering clouds in the city-lit night sky hurried Mari along. The wind howled around her ears, and she pulled her sweater closer. She'd tried to talk Bolin into letting her cook for him, but he'd insisted it would be easier for her to buy dinner. She'd hated to leave him when he was finally talking to her again, but before she'd left, he had crossed the room and held her in a tight hug. Just a few seconds of his warm embrace, but enough to remind her he was still a man—and not just any man, but *her* man. She didn't feel alone anymore. When she left the apartment, she'd sighed and felt the heaviness disappear. She'd practically floated down the stairs, feeling lighter than she had in months.

Ahead she saw a line of people in front of a small wheeled booth, stacked high with rows of bamboo steamers. The aroma of pork-stuffed *bāozi* reached Mari and made her stomach rumble. She closed the distance and waited her turn, eager for something hot and comforting to fill the emptiness in her body. In front of her, harried businessmen waited impatiently, tapping on their cell phones or smoking their cigarettes. Mari wondered if they were simply picking up a snack for the long commute home or if there were that many unmarried men eating street food for dinner. Or maybe like her, they hadn't been able to resist the temptation. She'd get pork-filled buns for her, and a few with the bok choy that Bolin loved. They didn't need anything fancy—she was sure he'd only eat a few bites anyway.

At the booth, a man and woman worked together to fill orders and take the money. Almost as if one, their movements were so in sync and graceful Mari knew they must have been together through many years. The woman was old enough to be Mari's grandmother, but her lined face held a look of contentment, even as she worked in the crisp fall night. She wore a colorful scarf around her head, and a few gray hairs mingled in with the dark, proof of her earned wisdom. Mari watched, captivated. She enjoyed knowing a partnership like theirs existed, that it could happen even in a world with so much stress and pressure. But then, she'd known by her own Baba and Mama that love—real, true love—was possible. They'd both have been disappointed in her to know she had almost ruined her chance with her own marriage, that it had come close to a full-on failure. But at least now it was turning around.

Finally she made it to the counter, and the woman asked her what she wanted. Mari thought of the generous fee Max had paid her and decided to splurge, ordering a half dozen of each of the buns, her mouth already watering at the thought of what she knew would be spicy and juicy meat, something that normally Bolin would frown deeply upon in his obsession to prove he was nothing like his farming family.

The woman bagged the food and reached out to take Mari's money. When their hands touched, a slight shock started in Mari's fingers and shot up her arm. The woman dropped the bag, but clasped Mari's hand and stared into her eyes.

"You're about to go through a hardship that will make you question everything you think you are, but stay strong through the storm, and you'll find your peace."

Mari tried to pull away, but the woman held her hand firmly. "*Dui bu qi*, I don't understand," she apologized, still gently attempting to pull free. *Was the woman some kind of gypsy?*

"Ruyu, stop telling fortunes and get those customers taken care of," the cook hollered out gruffly, but with an underlying affection that even Mari picked up.

The woman dropped her hand, then picked up the bag of buns and handed them to Mari. "Keep your money—you'll need it more than I."

With the bag of buns in her one hand and her money still in the other, Mari moved away. She wondered what the woman had meant, but then she almost laughed. There could be no greater hardship than the one she'd been living for the last few months with her husband out of work, addicted to painkillers, and their only source of livelihood stolen out from under them. They might lose everything. Actually, it was starting to look fairly definite that, though her life had been close to crumbling just hours before, they might just make it.

Too late, she felt like calling behind her to the gypsy woman. *I already lived that prediction, and I'm coming out on the other side!* She moved faster, anxious to return to Bolin and move past this crisis once and for all.

She walked along the several blocks and marveled at how everything on the streets looked brighter, less depressing, now that she was in a better state of mind. On a whim she ducked into a small shop and looked at their selection of cheaper wines. She argued with herself for a few moments, debating whether to even buy wine, considering his problems with addiction, but finally the impatient store clerk pushed her to hurry, and she picked one and paid. She quickly tucked it under her arm, banishing the flush of guilt as she rushed out to the street again. Bolin would love it and tonight was a celebration. *A new start.*

Finally she arrived at their building. She climbed the stairs to their apartment and barely felt winded. Her weariness had disappeared with Bolin's transformation. Now she was so light on her feet she nearly skipped down the hall to their door. When she unlocked it and threw it open, she was disappointed to find the living room and kitchen empty.

"Bolin, I'm back. Sorry it took so long," she called out as she took the bags to the kitchen, then wiggled out of her sweater and hung it on her peg just inside the door. If she hurried, she could surprise him before he came back out. She crossed the room and pulled her red linen tablecloth from the drawer under the television. She spread it over the small table.

From the coffee table, she picked up the two candles and put them at each end of the kitchen table, then grabbed Bolin's lighter from the counter and lit them. Next, she pulled a large bowl from the cabinet and arranged the steamed buns in it, taking care to keep the meat-filled ones to one side. She pulled out two small plates and set the table, adding the ceramic chopsticks she'd received from Widow Zu for her wedding. The intricately painted tangled vines climbing the sticks like a trellis made them her favorite. That, along with the memory of Widow Zu's blessing when she'd given them to her, made them more than just eating utensils. The old woman hadn't wanted to see her go, but she'd promised Mari she'd look out for her Mama and Baba for as long as she could. Widow Zu might be old, but she was still holding on.

Mari brought the buns to the table and stood back, then remembered one more thing she needed to add.

Carefully, she reached into the cabinet over the sink and brought down their wedding glasses, then she set them at each place on the table. She didn't have a wine holder, so she used the bottle itself as a centerpiece. Bolin would be surprised. They hadn't had wine since the last New Year was brought in, and he so loved to believe they were of a class that could afford wine if they wanted—even though they both knew they weren't. Anyway, Mari didn't much care for it, but since he did, she'd act as though it was the best thing to ever touch her lips.

"Bolin?" she called. He sure was being quiet.

She went to the sink and washed her hands, then turned down the hall. She'd just go see what was taking him so long. She was sure he hadn't gone to their bedroom to sleep. He hadn't slept in there for months.

"Bolin? What are you doing?" She didn't want to intrude on him in the bathroom, so she approached it slowly and waited on him to answer. When he didn't, she pushed the door open and looked around.

He wasn't there.

That meant he was in their bedroom. She felt her cheeks flush. Had he really made that much of a recovery? Maybe they wouldn't need the wine after all. She went to the door and peered around it, fully expecting to see him stretched out on the bed that had lately become just her own.

All she saw was what appeared to be all his clothes, pulled from the closet and stacked over his pillow. Her heart fell. He was leaving her? What other explanation could there be? And where was he now? Her eyes were drawn to a piece of paper on the top of the pile. She picked it up and studied it.

The writing was in Bolin's simple, barely legible characters. It read, *Thank you for letting me hear your music.* One simple line—a few words that confused Mari even more. Thanking her sounded as though he was pleased with her.

But if so, why the clothes?

She walked over to the closet to see what was left, and she peeked in.

She froze. She couldn't really be seeing the horrendous sight her eyes were reporting to her brain. It just couldn't be real.

Her knees gave way, and she dropped to the floor, one hand over her mouth and the other holding her stomach. It was real. She shouldn't have left him. She rocked back and forth as an agonized scream filled the room—a sound she didn't recognize and was too traumatized to understand came from her own lungs.

Above her, Bolin swung from the top bar of the closet, his belt around his neck so tight that his eyes bulged and his tongue protruded.

Mari reached up and put her hands in her hair, yanking as hard as she could as she rocked.

Her husband was dead. She could wail and pull her hair out all she wanted, but there was no bringing him back. She only knew one thing. Bolin wasn't the failure—she was.

Chapter Fourteen

An Ni felt as if she were floating. Moving through warm clouds on the colorful scarf of a fortune-teller she'd once met when walking the streets. The woman had looked down at her and offered her something most didn't: a smile filled with kindness. An Ni hadn't wanted to talk to her—the other kids had always warned to never look a fortune-teller in the eye, or they could curse your soul. But locking eyes had been something she couldn't tear herself away from, and the woman had finally smiled, breaking the intensity of the moment.

Then she said, "Don't worry, little one. You'll know a family's love one day."

That was when An Ni knew she was a fake. And she'd been right. A few years had passed, and An Ni had known nothing that could even come close to that prediction. As a matter of fact, she'd known only the opposite of love. She wished she could see the woman again and declare her a fraud, even demand she pay up on her prediction or stop fooling innocent little kids who were dumb enough to cling to the hope of something that would never come true.

It was too warm. That was An Ni's first waking thought as she struggled to open her eyes. Then she remembered where she was and knew it shouldn't be warm. She bolted upright, and the streak of agony that traveled through her leg threw her back down again, making her scream.

"An Ni, what's wrong?" Mei was at her side in an instant, crouching down to peer into An Ni's face.

An Ni twisted her body until she was on her side. "Why is it warm in here?"

Mei's face was bathed in the morning light that shone through the small window, and she smiled in a proud way, then pointed. "I made a fire."

An Ni sat up again, this time slowly, and looked at the corner of the shack. In the small, portable stovetop, she could see a small fire going. "But how?"

Mei stood up and crossed her arms, her expression stubborn. "I told you, I'm not a baby. I went back to the train station when the sun came up, and I hung around and watched until I saw a man hand his wife a pack of cigarettes and a lighter to put in her bag. I waited for a long time until she finally set the bag on the chair beside her and closed her eyes."

"Mei! You could've been caught, then what would you have done?" An Ni was glad Mei had made a fire, but the thought of her being caught stealing and taken in by the *chengguan* terrified her. And the train station was some gang's turf, too. It was a miracle that Mei wasn't snatched up by an official or a criminal. Either of which would mean a horrible outcome for the small girl.

"But I didn't get caught. I stayed close to a woman and her child, pretending I was with them. I took her wallet out and set it on the chair under her jacket, then I took the whole bag, An Ni. She's got some other stuff in it, too."

An Ni couldn't even think of what other items might be there, for her leg throbbed so badly it felt as if it were about to explode. "My leg, Mei. It hurts. I mean—it hurts really badly."

Mei ran over to the desktop and grabbed something, then brought it back to An Ni. "She had this medicine in her bag, but I don't know what it is." She handed the small bottle over.

An Ni examined it. It looked like something bought in the local supermarket, and she couldn't read the characters, but she opened the top. Inside were five pink pills.

"It might be sleeping medicine," she mumbled. "I don't want to go back to sleep and leave you alone anymore."

"But it might help your leg."

Another streak of pain ran through her leg, making An Ni's decision easy. She shook two of the pills into her hand. "Get me some water, please, Mei. How long have we been here?"

Mei shrugged as she scrambled to get the cup from the desk and brought it to An Ni. It was already full. "Two or three days? I'm not sure. I got water this morning when the rain stopped. And it's muddy out there. It rained all night." She pointed at her shoes, lined up neatly beside the door.

An Ni threw the pills into her mouth and chased them down with the water, saying a prayer that they wouldn't kill her.

Next, she scooted herself closer to the fire to get a better look.

"What are you burning?"

"It took me a long time to get a fire and I think I might have used the lighter all up. First I tried to just burn leaves, but I think they were too wet. They smoked up the room and went out too fast. So then I tore parts of an old newspaper from the desk drawer and tucked it in around sticks I found under the fullest trees. They were drier. Did I do good?"

An Ni nodded. She was surprised she'd slept through all of it. And it was actually a really good little fire. Mei had made somewhat of a teepee in the bottom of the iron stove with twigs and bigger sticks, giving room for the fire to get the air it needed. Mei was proving to be the best partner in crime that An Ni could have hoped for.

"I'm not hungry, but I think I should eat," An Ni said. "Did you already eat something?"

Mei nodded and went back to the desk. An Ni could see she'd taken the photo of the little girl—their Guanyin—and propped it against the window, then made a tiny shrine of leaves and rocks around it. Mei plucked something off the shelf and came back.

She handed An Ni an apple. "I was saving this for you. It was in the purse."

An Ni almost smiled through her pain. Mei loved apples. Whenever one of the boys came back with their pockets bulging from hitting a fruit stand, the little girl begged and pleaded for just a taste of their bounty—especially when there were apples. Sometimes they even allowed her a bite or two. But this time she'd resisted and left it alone. As An Ni looked around, she realized that Mei had been busy. "No, Mei. You eat it." She handed it back. "You deserve it. I can't believe everything you've done while I was asleep."

The corners of the shack looked swept; all the leaves and trash were gone. Even the window looked as if someone had polished it, removing enough grime to let more light in. Under the desk, Mei had folded and stacked all the extra rice sacks. On top of the desk, other than their shrine to Guanyin, she'd put their remaining food trays, as well as lined up a variety of objects An Ni didn't recognize, and a fire-red flower stood wilting in a dirty water bottle.

"We'll share." Mei took the apple and bit into it, then a huge smile lit up her face. She handed it back to An Ni.

An Ni took a bite. It was sweet and juicy. She rolled the bite around in her mouth, savoring the flavor and the moistness on her tongue. The food trays from the train were okay—but they couldn't compare to the taste of the apple.

"It's so good, Mei," she mumbled with her mouth full. And it was. It was probably the best thing she'd ever tasted.

Mei nodded. "My Mama always cut apples up for my breakfast. Red ones, green ones—she even made me fried apples sometimes. My family called me *píngguǒ zǐ*."

An Ni smiled back at her. She could see the sadness in Mei's eyes when she talked about her family's nickname for her: Apple Seed. It just wasn't fair that she'd been snatched from them. But that was then, and this was now. They had to figure out what to do. Already An Ni's head was spinning as she thought through options. Should they try to stay there, or try to get somewhere else? But if they went to where people were, who would help them? Her gut told her no one. And if they went for help, there was a good chance that they'd be separated.

Mei stopped chewing for a moment and wrinkled her nose. "Except when I had a runny nose, then she made me eat persimmons."

An Ni smiled at her. Everyone thought eating persimmons in winter would keep away or get rid of a head cold. Not that she'd ever tried it. Fruit was getting harder to steal, as stand owners were much more wary when kids of her kind came around. Usually only the boys were successful in lifting anything, and they'd never go for persimmons.

"If the boys come back for us, don't tell them my nickname," Mei said.

"I won't, Mei." An Ni hoped they didn't come back. She didn't want Mei to land back in the hands of Tianbing, and he had so many friends who were *chengguan*. It wasn't fair. They had no one they could trust. And if Mei went back to Tianbing, she'd be beaten or worse.

An Ni shivered, even though she was warm. She just couldn't let Mei go back. Her leg needed to heal, and heal fast. Their only hope was to hop a train and hide until they were far, far away from Beijing and Tianbing. Maybe if they got far enough away, she could find someone to take Mei in as their daughter. She'd even offer herself as a housemaid, a farmhand in a village, or whatever it took, as long as she could do this one thing for Mei—give her something that An Ni had never had.

A chance.

Somehow the hours slipped by in a haze until day turned into night and back into day again. She must've fallen asleep again for when she looked around, the scene in their little shack had changed again. If An Ni hadn't been hurting so much—and hadn't been so groggy that she could barely focus—she'd have bust a gut laughing at what she'd opened her eyes to see. Mei had found an old, dented tin bucket somewhere, and she'd filled it with water. In the purse she'd gotten at the train station, she'd found a small bottle of hand lotion and was using it as soap to wash her clothes with. Now she bent over the bucket while wrapped in a rice sack with her shoestring tied around her waist. Her hair hung stringy around her head, hiding her face. Her bare feet looked cold, her toes bent to clutch at the floor around her to give her balance as she worked.

"You look like one of those old ladies that washes clothes at the canal. How'd you get that rice sack over your head?" An Ni asked. She reached up and felt behind her own head, pulling out a small plastic bag stuffed with leaves and tied in a knot. Mei had made her a pillow. While An Ni was sleeping, Mei was making pillows and clothes? What was going on?

"I tore a hole and just pulled it over, then I punched arm holes through the sides." Mei scrubbed at her underwear, and An Ni noticed the two wet socks that lay over the edge of the bucket. "We need to get you out of your pants and underclothes, An Ni. I'll wash them for you. I already had a bath myself. Did those pills help you?"

An Ni shook her head. Her pants weren't going anywhere. If she tried that, she knew what she'd feel: excruciating streaks of pain. She'd just have to stay filthy. At least until the swelling went down and they could get out of there. "That's okay, I'll wait on the bath."

Mei looked up and nodded. "Give me a minute. How's your leg?"

An Ni sighed. Her leg no longer felt as though it was a part of her. Now it was the enemy—a hot, throbbing monster she couldn't run away from. "You don't want to know."

Mei went to the portable stove and used a rice sack as protection for her hands as she lifted a pot from the fire.

"There was a small pot under that last cabinet. I found some wild onions and made soup, An Ni," she said, bringing the pot closer.

When she knelt in front of An Ni, the smell of the soup surprised her by making her stomach growl. "What's in it?"

Mei put the pot wrapped in the material into An Ni's hands. "We only had one food tray left, and we've had it so long I was afraid to use the meat. So I put the green vegetables and rice in the pot, then the water and onions. It should last us a day or maybe two if we're careful."

An Ni was impressed. Mei knew how to analyze a situation and think of solutions. For her age, it was quite something. She wondered for a moment if it was because, like her, Mei was forced to be resourceful because of her life on the streets. An Ni sipped at the soup, taking just enough to ease the aching of her stomach. Then she set it down, and Mei picked up the pot and took it back to the stovetop.

An Ni leaned back and picked up the piece of paper that lay on the floor beside her. It was no longer folded as it had been when she'd pulled it from the wallet. Now it was smoothed out, the man's face looking up at her. An Ni felt a flash of guilt that she had his wallet and he didn't. But she hadn't stolen it—she'd only found it, so why should she feel bad? She traced the man's face. All the kids liked to laugh and point at the foreigners for their big noses, and this one's wasn't any different.

"*Da bizi,*" Mei mumbled, reading An Ni's mind.

"Yes, he has a big nose, but his eyes are nice." An Ni turned over the paper and saw a drawing that wasn't there the day before. "Did you do this?"

Mei nodded as she worked to wring the water out of her socks. She must've found a pen in the purse, and with it she'd drawn a fairly good picture of a busy street, complete with stick people, cars, and lots of bicycles. A line of shops lined up on one side of the page, and a little girl with pigtails that stuck straight out sat on an overturned bucket in front of one of the shops.

"Is this you?" She held the paper up and pointed at the little girl.

Mei nodded.

"Where are you?"

"My Ye Ye's store."

An Ni was taken aback. Mei had never mentioned a store before. She looked closer and saw a drawing of a big clock hanging in the window. "Does he sell clocks?"

Mei shrugged. "Sometimes, I guess. But mostly he fixes them. Before I started school, I used to stay with him while my parents worked. All day long, the clocks ticked, tocked, and chimed."

The girl in the drawing was eating something, and An Ni could guess what it was. "An apple?"

Mei smiled. "*Dui*, from the fruit stand next door."

She was right. In front of the store next to the clock shop, Mei had drawn a big display of crates holding fruits, with overflowing baskets hanging from hooks in front of the windows.

"Your grandfather own that store, too?"

Mei shook her head. "No, but the store owner let me call him uncle, and I could have anything I wanted from there. I ate apples every day when I stayed with my Ye Ye."

An Ni realized she must've slept for a long time again, because the drawing was full of details that would have taken a while. On the end of the street, she'd drawn a huge store, complete with a winding staircase on the outside and a giant teapot perched on the curved roof.

"What's this?" She held the page up to Mei and pointed.

"The market of old stuff."

"Do you remember the name of it? Or do you know what town it's from?" An Ni asked, already feeling a burst of hope that possibly

Mei knew where she came from. If she could only remember, maybe someone there would help them if they could make it there.

Mei shook her head. She didn't remember. Her face turned sad. "I'll never go home, will I, An Ni?"

"Don't say that, Mei. You never know what fate has in store for you." An Ni had an idea, but she didn't want to make any promises she couldn't keep. But if she could use the drawing to get Mei to talk more about her home and that street, maybe it would eventually trigger something useful. That was their answer—return Mei to her family, and maybe they'd be so thankful they'd let her stay and not send her back into the streets. She watched as Mei worked to wash the clothing. How had she learned such a hard task? If all she'd done before her street life was sit on barrels and eat fruit, she'd come a long way to become the girl bending over the bucket now. An Ni looked around and was astonished at how shy, quiet little Mei had turned into this new, brave girl. The fire still burned behind her in the small stove, but An Ni knew it wasn't easy to keep it up. With such a small container, it took constant tending. Mei had also opened the window just a crack to allow some ventilation, something An Ni was surprised she'd thought of. And more plastic bags were stuffed with leaves and pushed against the doorframe and into a few of the holes in the shack walls, blocking out the many drafts.

Mei was much smarter than she'd let on—but then, all the kids who spent any time on the streets were. They had to be. "You've done a great job in here, Mei."

Mei smiled. "I'm not done yet."

An Ni didn't like the sound of that.

"I'm going to get some fresh water and heat it over the fire, then wash *your* hair. And don't tell me no. If you won't let me have your clothes, I can at least clean your hair." Mei crossed her arms and shot An Ni a sassy look. "We're getting rid of the bugs, An Ni. I found a comb, and I worked for hours to get them out of my hair."

An Ni did laugh at that one. Her hair was the last thing on her mind, but if Mei thought she could help rid her of the relentless lice, An Ni was all for it. She sat up, ignoring the pain it took to do so, and peeled her jacket, then her shirt off. She tossed the shirt to Mei.

She covered herself with the bag she'd been using for a blanket. "Here, if I'm going to have good-smelling hair from your lotion, I can at least have a clean shirt, too. But get one of those other rice sacks and make me a neat dress like yours."

Mei dropped the garment she was scrubbing and jumped up. She giggled and went to the stack of rice sacks, picking through them to find one to make a dress with.

"Mei?" An Ni struggled to get her attention.

Mei looked up, her eyebrows coming together in curiosity.

"I really need to go outside before I wet all over your sort-of-clean floor." An Ni knew that would get her moving. She had a suspicion Mei liked their new home more than she let on, and An Ni couldn't blame her. At least in the little shack, it was warm—and most of all, it was safe from anyone threatening to harm them. It was hard to believe they were only about a mile from a busy train station with thousands of people wandering in and out. But here—in their first little home together—they were blessedly alone.

An Ni wished they could stay forever, too, but the truth was that time was running out. Her leg was not getting better, their food was getting low, and who knew how long they'd be able to keep a fire? And what if Tianbing caught on that the boys were keeping a secret and made them talk? He could possibly find them! The thought of him invading their new, little home sent a shiver up An Ni's spine. Mei wouldn't like it, but they'd need to move on soon.

Chapter Fifteen

Max tucked his arms low and raced up the several flights of stairs. Luckily he'd passed out with his phone beside him on the kitchen floor, or he'd have never heard it ringing. Even so, it had taken at least ten rings to wake him, but the call he'd gotten from Mari only an hour before had sounded urgent—her words nearly unintelligible. When he'd cleared his head enough to ask her to repeat herself, she'd urged him to come right away, then she'd given him her apartment number and hung up.

On her floor, he busted out of the stairwell and walked briskly past the other apartments to the end of the hall where she'd said hers was located. At the door, he paused and for a moment, wondered what he was getting into. Then he knocked gently.

She didn't come to the door.

Max turned the knob and found it unlocked. He pushed open the door and there she was, sitting at a small kitchen table, her head lying on her crossed arms as she cried. The table looked dressed up—candles and clean dinnerware. Even wine glasses. Was she upset because her husband hadn't shown up? The scene looked like a date gone bad. Or had he walked into a marital spat of some kind?

"Mari?" He stepped in.

She looked up at Max, appearing confused.

"What's wrong?" Max stayed near the door, in case her husband was there and came out charging.

Mari pointed down the hall. Her soft crying got louder, and Max crossed the room.

He came to stand beside her and put his hand on her shoulder. "What? Tell me. Did he hurt you?"

Mari nodded and pointed again. Whatever it was, she couldn't say it, but she obviously wanted him to go down that hall.

"Okay, okay. I'll go talk to him." He moved away from her and started down the short hall. He truly didn't want to get into the middle of a married couple's problems, especially when his language skills were elementary, at best. But he'd do what he could.

Behind him Mari's crying evolved into sobs—gut-wrenching sobs that made the hair stand up on his neck. Her husband must've really done a number on her, and now Max was more than eager to talk to him. No one should cause another human being to be in that much emotional turmoil.

He passed a small bathroom that was empty, then moved on to the next door. It was the bedroom and by the look of the pile of clothes, someone was moving out. *So that's why she's crying*, Max thought. But did she really have to get him into the middle of it? He stepped in and a flash of red from the closet caught his eye. He moved closer and peeked inside, then jumped back so hard and fast that he fell back on the bed.

"What the—!" He shivered all over and stood up, then stepped forward and took another look. He knew from his experience as a journalist that he shouldn't touch anything, but he wanted to make sure the guy wasn't still breathing. He leaned in, his hands close to his chest, and judged by the look of him that he was indeed dead.

Max turned and left the room, and as he walked toward Mari, he could see her watching for him, her eyes round as saucers, silently asking him if it was true. "He's dead, Mari. Is that your husband?"

She nodded, and the sobs began again.

"You have to call the police."

She looked up at him, and he could see she was shaking.

"And I have to get out of here, Mari. If a foreigner is here when they arrive, they'll assume I had something to do with it. It'll be nothing but trouble."

Mari shook her head. "No—please don't go. I don't want to be here alone with him."

Max reached down and took her hands. "I'll come back. I promise. Just get this part over with, and then I'll come back. Can you call a friend, or maybe your family to come?"

"I don't have any friends, but I'll call my father. He won't be able to get here probably until tomorrow, but he'll know what to do."

Max gently let go of her hands. "Good. Call him. But you also have to call the police now. They'll come and ask you some questions, and take away his body. You'll need someone to help you through making funeral arrangements. Can your father do that?"

Mari nodded, then stood.

Max couldn't believe how much she looked like a terrified little girl. She stood there shaking, her expression confused.

"Do you know why he did it?"

She nodded. "He's been hurting for a long time, and he thought he'd lost face with everyone. He just couldn't handle our problems. I think losing his camel was the last straw. He tricked me into going out and when I returned, that's how I found him." She started sobbing again, and Max pulled her into his chest, hugging her tightly. "I . . . should've . . . known—he wanted to be clean and have his hair cut. He was acting unusual, but I thought he'd jumped a hurdle and was coming out of his depression. I should've seen it. I shouldn't have left him."

"It's not your fault, Mari. You have to know that. Suicide has the reputation of being a selfish act, but I know it to be one of desperation. Still, it was his choice, and it is not your fault."

She nodded, but she didn't look convinced.

"Now I'm leaving. You call the police first, then your father. Do you want me to come back in a few hours?"

"Please," she said, her voice muffled.

He let her go and looked down at her. "I will. I promise."

With one final look, he left her there. It broke his heart to think she'd called him—practically a stranger—because she didn't have family or friends nearby who she could depend on. What sort of isolated life had she led? He picked up his pace and was thankful all the apartment doors were closed as he passed them. He sure didn't need the pressure of being considered a part of someone's death. He had enough to deal with on his own, but he knew that tonight, he'd stay clean. He needed to resist the temptation to drown out his troubles. For once, someone else needed him more than he needed the bottle. And he'd be damned if he'd let her down.

Sixteen hours later, Max was at Mari's kitchen table again, this time sitting as the minutes ticked by. He had come before the police left, as Mari had called him again and begged him to return, saying that they were scaring her. The police had questioned who he was, but after Mari told them he was her employer, they'd taken his name and passport information, a statement, then dropped the subject of his presence.

When they were satisfied that Mari had answered the same questions with the same responses at least fifteen times, they'd left.

Now Mari slept, finally succumbing to her exhaustion after several hours of questioning and after dealing with the coroner who took away her husband.

They'd carried him out in a bag on a stretcher, but Max could've strangled the little men when they paused in the living room and unzipped the plastic enough for Mari to see her husband one more time.

She'd gone to him, and Max had watched as she'd gently put her hand on his face, then apologized to him for the way their life together had ended. As if it were her fault! He'd wanted to say something but knew it wasn't his place. He just hoped when her family arrived, any minute now, that they'd be able to give her the comfort that he couldn't. After she'd told the dead man that she'd love him forever, she'd crumpled onto his body, sobbing until the orderly had peeled her off of it and pushed her away. Max had picked her up off the floor and guided her to her couch, and only then when her husband was gone had she finally closed her eyes.

Max heard a commotion in the hall that led to the door. He rose, moving quietly so as not to wake Mari. He went to the door and opened it.

An elderly man and woman stood there, and when they saw him at the door, they looked surprised and speechless.

"Lao Zheng?" Max held his hand out to the man, locking eyes and marveling at the air of authority and wisdom the man carried.

"Ni hao." The man grasped it and shook it before Max could remember that shaking hands wasn't really the custom to the older generation. He watched Zheng's eyebrows lift and felt that the intense look he gave Max meant he'd save his questions for after he got to his daughter, but that sooner or later, he'd find out why a foreigner was in his daughter's apartment.

Max broke the uncomfortable eye contact and turned to Mari's mother. He smiled at the woman, noticing the kindness etched into the lines of her face—just as he'd imagined when Mari had described her—and she moved past him and made her way into the apartment.

Max moved aside, allowing Mari's father to also join his wife. They went straight to the couch and the woman sat on the edge. Without saying a word to wake her, the woman waited until Mari opened her eyes, then she gathered her in her arms and Mari cried. Locked together, they rocked back and forth as Mari's father paced in front of them. The scene was so sad and so personal, Max had to turn away.

When he looked again, Mari had sat up, and her parents were on either side of her, their arms around her in a protective embrace.

"Baba, I've failed him," Mari whispered.

"Bushi, bushi," her father consoled.

"A few of your sisters will be here later today," Max made out from the murmurings of Mari's mother. He was impressed with his comprehension, but it was only because she spoke with a soft confidence, helping him to pick up the words.

He first felt a wave of relief that her people would be there to help her through this tragedy. Then, as he slipped quietly out the door, he felt the loneliness stalking him, whispering that it was coming for him once again.

Chapter Sixteen

Mari sat on the sofa, her Mama beside her clutching and rubbing her hand. Mari wasn't crying any longer—after days of tears, she was cried out and felt nothing but emptiness, her heart and soul hollow from the long hours of mourning. The verses the monk had chanted during the last two nights to ease Bolin's passage into heaven still echoed in her mind, the words jumbled but beating a hypnotic and welcome sound to fill the blankness that threatened to consume her. Her Mama had caught her pinching herself, and now tried to keep her occupied. What Mari didn't tell her was she was pinching only to see if everything was real—if *she* was real. Everything around her felt so bizarre.

Her Baba had helped her more than anyone, solemnly reminding her that Lao Tzu taught that "life and death are simply one thread, the same line viewed from different sides." If that was true, then her Bolin was only a breath's distance away, and he could see her at this very instant. She would not disappoint him by questioning his choices any longer, or by wailing or pulling out her hair, or pleading with the gods to return him to her. What was done was done, and there was no undoing it. She'd simply sit and watch—and wait for the torturous process of saying good-bye to be over so she could be mercifully alone again.

Across the room, in the kitchen where the table once stood, was the coffin that held him. The simple pine box looked precarious, balanced only on the two wooden stools, but her Baba had assured her it was fine. The table had been moved until it was at the head of the casket, and now it held photos, flowers, wreaths, and a pile of white envelopes. Mari didn't know who'd placed any of it there, or who had covered all the mirrors in the house or even hung the appropriate death lanterns at the front door. She felt removed from it all, and the last few days had gone by in a haze of people coming and going. She kept it hidden, but the envelopes were a huge source of irritation for her, as she knew it was money offered to help her, the widow. She should be relieved, as she didn't have the funds to pay for her own husband's departure from the physical world, but still the thought of accepting charity from anyone made her cringe.

A man stepped through the door and to the casket, then bowed three times before he moved on to look at the table of mementos. He picked up a piece of candy from the dish and popped it in his mouth, loudly sucking on it—to wash away bitterness, as the legend went.

Mari had never seen him before. She assumed he was another neighbor—one of those faceless individuals who'd never reached out with a thoughtful word or help of any kind when she needed it, but who was now drawn into her life by morbid curiosity. She secretly wished they'd all just leave her alone, but her Mama told her it was only proper to allow some sort of wake for Bolin, and Mari should prepare herself for Bolin's parents to bring some of the old village traditions with them to put their son to rest.

Other people—more that Mari didn't recognize—stood around the room. Some had spent the night in the parking lot, playing cards in the moonlight as a way to stay awake and guard the body against evil spirits. They'd even tied Bolin's feet together, to make it harder for the corpse to move if it were possessed by ghosts. Mari thought they were too late on that one—as an evil spirit must have taken over Bolin before he died. The man she'd married had been a gentle, compassionate soul, not someone who would or even could do something so horrific to himself and his wife.

Mari pulled her hand away from her mother.

"*Nuer*, are you okay?"

"I'm fine, Mama. I just want to look at him again." Both her Mama and Baba had been wonderful. They'd taken over and organized everything. Her Baba was now down in the parking lot, making sure that those who lingered and burned paper offerings in the barrel set up for Bolin acted courteously and followed tradition. Neither of them had said anything negative about Bolin and how he'd died. They'd simply showed up and been there for her, making her eat and sleep and taking up her slack.

Her sisters Linnea and Daisy were there, too. Mari was so glad to see them—especially Daisy, as they were closest in age. Daisy hadn't changed at all since the last time Mari had seen her. She still flitted around like a carefree hummingbird, taking care of everyone. She was simply the same laid-back and forgiving person she always was—her eyes wide and knowing, void of any accusations and full of forgiveness.

Mari reached up and felt the silky waves of her own hair. Daisy had tenderly braided it the night before after running her fingers through it, over and over, to soothe her enough to finally fall asleep. For a moment, Mari had felt ashamed of the envy that had arisen when she'd learned Daisy was going to have a baby. With her naturally feathery touch and calming words, her sister deserved that position much more than she ever could.

It was nice to have family around her. While Daisy provided comfort to everyone, Linnea, always the more structured one, kept the small apartment neat and the banquet of food organized, arranging it accordingly and throwing out the scraps of food on dishes that had been picked over, replacing them with each new dish that arrived. With her ingrained ability to organize, she also didn't hesitate to move people around and out the door when needed, even convincing some of the neighborhood elders to do their crooning for the dead from down the hall instead of beside the body, minimizing the chaos in the room.

Mari was thankful for both of her sisters. She walked over to the casket, and two women she didn't know, dressed in black and whispering to each other, moved over.

He looked serene. That was her first thought. Then she wondered how the undertaker had managed to take the look of horror she'd found him with and transform it to this expression of peace. Mari had insisted that the red shirt be removed, as red symbolized happiness, and now Bolin wore white silk pants and a shirt—longevity clothes, as they called them in the old days. She knew Bolin's father was a traditional man, and it wasn't so much to please him, but instead a means to try not to offend when he would already be reeling from the disgrace of his son's suicide. Even in a city as big as Beijing, they'd be observing Bolin's death as much like a village as they possibly could. A gesture for his family, for it mattered not at all to Mari.

The door opened again, and Mari turned, ready to ask them to go away and give her a moment with her husband, but then she saw Max.

"You came," she said quietly as he closed the door behind him.

He nodded. "You asked me to. That's all you needed to do."

She gestured toward Bolin. "Well, he looks better than the last time you saw him."

Silence settled around them as she let Max take in the scene, knowing it was all unfamiliar to him. She assumed he'd never been a part of a death in China.

He looked at Mari, a spark of panic in his eyes. "Mari, I'm so sorry." His eyes darted to the couch where her Mama now sat talking to another elderly lady, someone else Mari didn't know. "And I can't stay long. I just don't know what to do here, and I don't want to embarrass you in any way."

Mari smiled a little. He was trying so hard, and he'd shown up—the only foreigner in the place. She had to give him credit for that. "You don't have to go. I'll talk you through it."

He looked relieved. And she was glad to have something to do, other than sit or stand around, accepting empty condolences.

"Stand at his head and bow three times for respect," she said.

Max followed her instructions, pausing to gaze down at Bolin before he bowed. Mari appreciated that he looked genuinely sad, even though they'd never met.

"Now go to the table and eat a piece of candy," Mari said.

He looked so confused, but he did as he was told. He stood at the table, sucking on the candy as he studied the long, white ribbons attached to the wreaths. He picked up one ribbon and squinted at the Chinese characters written along it.

"Those are condolences," Mari said.

"How long will the mourning last?"

"In the old times, it could be well over forty days. Now it's more like a week."

Max turned to her, his eyes wide with surprise.

"But in Bolin's case—because of the circumstances—we'll only mourn for another day before his body is processed, then his bones will be given to his parents."

"What will they do with them?"

Outside in the hall, a woman wailed loudly, making Mari turn quickly toward the noise. The howling was so heartfelt and agonized that Mari knew instantly who it was.

Bolin's parents had arrived.

For the first time that day, Mari felt some emotion. But it wasn't sadness—it was foreboding that came creeping down on her and settled around her shoulders. It was time to face his parents, and other than a firing squad, Mari couldn't imagine what could be worse.

Chapter Seventeen

Max followed the procession down the street. Somewhere, they'd picked up fifty or more mourners who waited outside the building that held the incinerator, and now they emerged as one, most wearing white paper hats that Bolin's mother had brought with her from her village and handed out. At the front of the line, walking beside her husband, the woman now clutched a small, red, fabric bag that carried her son's bones. When Mari began to go over the entire protocol and what would happen with Max the day before, she was just explaining that Bolin's bones would be picked out of the ashes and buried on his family's land. They never resumed the conversation after his parents had made their dramatic appearance, and things had gotten tense for a few moments.

Max had seen Mari visibly wince at the screams of her mother-in-law as she'd gotten closer and closer to the apartment. She'd stood there, frozen in place, watching the door as if she expected the devil himself to bust through it. Max had felt uncomfortable, but he'd stayed rooted to the spot, unwilling to leave her when she looked so frightened.

Mari had jumped as the door opened, and a man and woman stood there. The woman, still wailing, looked around her husband at the casket, then shrieked and fell to the floor. The man had left her there and came to stand over his son.

"Lao Yhong." Mari had acknowledged him with a slight bow, then she'd gone to help the woman. Mari's mother also came from the couch, and the two of them lifted her up and led her to a chair, though her head kept turning back to keep her eyes on her son. Max had watched them as they'd interacted around the coffin, and he could see they were avoiding touching their son. The mother had reached out only once, but her husband pushed her back, barking at her in a dialect that Max couldn't understand. He assumed because it was not a natural death, they probably had some sort of cultural rule that their son couldn't be touched. Max wished again that his language skills were better—he'd have loved to have understood everything that was happening. He'd also thought that maybe this subject—the high rate of suicide in China and the impact on the survivors—could possibly be the story his boss wanted him to write. However, the idea had quickly left his thoughts when he'd looked up at the ravaged face of Mari standing over her husband's body; he couldn't prey on her tragedy. Mari had asked him to come as her friend, and he wouldn't sully that gesture, even if they never met again.

Now he walked slowly in the procession, just behind the four men who carried the three-feet-high paper palanquin balanced on four poles. He struggled to keep his eyes on Mari as she weaved around pedestrians and obstacles on their march back to her home. Max was glad that she was surrounded by her family, her parents on either side of her and her sisters directly behind. He watched her walk, her arms clutching the small wooden box of her husband's ashes, her eyes fixed on the pavement in front of her. She was suffering—he hoped that was clear to her husband's family so they'd stop their indifferent treatment and offer her the condolences she deserved. Yes, it was their son, but he'd been Mari's husband for more than a decade. Couldn't they drum up an ounce of compassion for their son's widow? Something told him that after the services were over, Mari would never see or hear from her husband's people again.

He continued with them and, as they passed various small shops and businesses, people emerged from the buildings and stood silently, watching them. Small children ran in and out of the procession, thinking it some sort of parade, most not understanding the somber atmosphere. Many curious bystanders stopped short when they spotted Max in the crowd of mourners, staring or pointing at him in their confusion or shock that a foreigner would be a part of such an event. Max kept a humble but reassuring expression fixed on his face, avoiding eye contact, for he didn't want to take any of the attention off the dead; he just wanted to blend in to show his support of Mari.

As they neared the parking lot of the apartment building, Max jumped when a series of fireworks were launched behind him. Ahead he could see that the small fire that had been kept going for days was now being teased even higher, the flames flicking hungrily. The procession moved in closer, wrapping two or three deep around the barrel as they watched first the paper palanquin being tossed in and burned, then other paper offerings of fake money and household goods—even a paper-cut car was tossed in and shriveled into ashes. Max had heard about the tradition and knew the offerings were sent up to help the deceased in the afterworld, yet he was surprised that so many people cared what happened to the young man who'd taken his own life.

Max felt a wave of sadness, but it didn't have much to do with Mari's husband's passing. He didn't know the man, and yes, it was disheartening that life hadn't gone his way, but Max also thought it cowardly for him to leave such a mess for Mari to sort out. When she'd called to ask him to come today, she'd told him that her parents had talked her into going home with them for a while, at least until she could figure out what to do next. She would be leaving with them the next evening on the night train, and he didn't even know whether he'd get to say good-bye to her or not.

He strained to see her through the crowd, but too many people stood between them, and Max didn't feel comfortable moving in any closer. So with hands stuffed into his jacket to ward off the cold, he waited, hoping for a chance to talk to Mari for a moment to show her he'd come.

When everyone was finally in the parking lot, Mari's father-in-law held the lit joss stick high in the air, signaling for silence. His grim face and hunched posture made him appear as if he carried the weight of the world on his shoulders. He walked to the barrel and tossed the stick in. When a flurry of sparks shot up, the crowd erupted into a loud blend of voices and more exploding fireworks.

The father stared stone-faced at the ground for a moment longer, shaking his head, then turned and went inside the building. His wife followed, then Mari and her family. Everyone else dispersed slowly, until Max found himself standing alone.

Again.

Chapter Eighteen

An Ni wiped the sweat off her brow with the back of her hand. She was too hot. She tried to lift her head to look for Mei, but the effort made her dizzy, so she lay back again. She heard something clacking together, then realized it was her own teeth. Around her face, her hair stuck to her head in sticky wisps, arguing the logic that it had been washed only the night before.

"Mei?" she called out weakly.

Mei was up in a second, throwing the empty rice sack off so she could lean over An Ni. She'd changed back into her regular clothes, and the faded pink of her jacket reminded An Ni that she was just a little girl—one burdened with the job of taking care of her. An Ni could only see the outline of her face, lit by the small fire behind her, and An Ni was sorry that she'd put them in such an impossible position, but she was glad to know she wasn't alone.

"What is it, An Ni?"

An Ni struggled to speak. Her throat felt parched and dry. She gave it another try. "Water?"

Mei went to the desk and retrieved the tin bowl she'd filled with water before they'd gone to bed. An Ni used her elbows to prop herself up enough that she wouldn't spill the water, then Mei held it to her lips, letting her sip it slowly.

"My leg, Mei. It feels even more puffed up, and it's burning hot."

Mei set the bowl down on the floor. "But your teeth were chattering. I thought you were cold?"

"I'm cold. And hot. I don't know, Mei, but my leg hurts farther up."

The last time Mei had helped her a few steps out the door to relieve her bladder, An Ni had noticed the skin just over her knee and spreading up her thigh was redder than it had been. Now she suspected it was even worse. It throbbed so bad that An Ni had to grind her teeth together to keep from screaming out. She didn't want to scare Mei, but it was hard to keep control.

"What do you want me to do?" Mei asked, her voice shaking.

"Help me outside and let me pee. While my pants are down, I'll try to take a look." She rolled over and bent her good leg, supporting herself on it along with her two arms.

Mei brought her the crutches, and An Ni attempted to stand. She couldn't. She was too weak and her leg hurt too much.

"I'm going to have to crawl, Mei. When I get to the door, I'll sit on the top step, and you can pull my pants down, then I'll hold myself off the step with my arms and go." An Ni was embarrassed, but Mei scrambled around, moving things out of the way and opening the door. A freezing cold gust of wind blew in, threatening to put out their fire. An Ni shivered again but started crawling.

"I'm sorry. I wish I could help," Mei said.

An Ni spoke through her clenched teeth. "You are helping. Don't worry."

A few more feet, and she made it to the door. She rested a moment, then stretched her good leg out and rolled over onto her backside. She took a moment to scratch at her head, realizing the war against the lice hadn't been won after all. Carefully she brought her legs around, almost screaming when she had to move the bad one, until they were both dangling over the ground in front of the shack.

"Now, help me get my pants down enough."

Mei moved in front of her, and once An Ni unbuttoned the top, she pulled gently.

With the first tug, An Ni couldn't help it—she screamed once and threw her hand over her mouth.

"*Dui bu qi*, An Ni!" Mei called out, letting go of the pants.

"No, Mei, don't be sorry. Keep going. I need to see it." An Ni started breathing in through her nose and out of her mouth, concentrating on staying calm.

Mei tugged again and this time the pants came down quickly, along with her underwear.

"*Hao le*, let me pee first," An Ni said, though the steady and hot stream was already forcing its way out of her body. The moonlight shone down on her, illuminating the dark red blotch that had climbed even higher on her leg.

Releasing her bladder burned like fire, but An Ni didn't want to alarm Mei any more than she already was, so she didn't say anything about it. When she finished, she leaned back against the doorframe and helped Mei tug her pants back up. Jiggling her legs was excruciating, even more so now that she'd seen the color of her skin. She felt light-headed, feverish.

"Let me turn back over and crawl in, and bring me the last two pills," she said. She turned to the side and stretched her hurt leg out, then before she could warn Mei, she spewed vomit all over their floor.

Exhausted from the effort, she dropped to her stomach and lay limply with her cheek flat against the wood planks, her eyes only centimeters from the chunks she'd sent flying out of her mouth. She just couldn't go any farther. She couldn't even fake it for Mei. She was done. Beaten down by fate once again.

The wind caught their fire again, and Mei scampered over her and into the shack. When An Ni heard her groan, she opened one eye to more darkness and watched Mei scramble to throw things on the fire, afraid to let it fizzle out.

An Ni tried to move again. She at least had to get in and shut the door to keep the wind out. She struggled onto her knee, supporting herself with her arm, and moved a few feet until she was out of the door. Mei came around and shut it, and An Ni dropped to her pallet, dragging along a trail of vomit as she moved.

"I'm so sorry, Mei." It was An Ni's fault. The wind almost blowing out the fire, the clean floor ruined—all of it. Everything was her fault. With her distress came more pain—this time in shooting streaks up her thigh, much higher than where she'd thought the break was.

"You're really sick, An Ni." Mei leaned over her and put her small, cool hand to An Ni's forehead. Her touch felt so smooth and soothing—An Ni wished she'd just leave her hand there. She started to tell her that, but then she felt her body being lifted, and she just let herself go, releasing her hold on the here and now, and embracing the possibility of a forever of nothing. As she faded away, she thought she heard Mei calling her name.

Chapter Nineteen

Max paced the floor in his apartment, staring at the frazzled piece of paper in his hand. He hadn't found a story, but as for what was on the paper—the real reason for his trip to China—he'd done almost all of it. Or at least the things that he understood. So why did he still feel the same bitter turmoil rolling in his gut? He tried to think, but his concentration was broken by the thought of Mari on her way to the train station. He'd waited and waited for her to call, hoping they'd meet once more. But when the day had come and gone, and the hour drew close for the night train he knew they'd be boarding, he'd realized she was leaving without saying good-bye. And that felt wrong.

He looked at his watch. There was no chance he could make it across town and to the station before Mari and her parents pulled out. Or was there? He looked at the paper again, scanning with his finger down to the last item. Could Mari hold the key to fulfilling it and allowing him to put it behind him? What if he never knew and he had to live with the same restlessness forever? He couldn't. He knew that leaving this elusive task undone would be his downfall—he'd finally succumb to the demons that chased him, hot on his trail, enticing him with the oblivion that only the burning liquid poured down his throat could bring. He blinked hard and saw her face, that sad expression that had darkened her features the last time he'd seen her months ago. If she could see him now, what would she think? He knew what she'd think. She'd be disgusted.

He stuffed the paper back into his pocket and grabbed his phone from the table. He at least had to try. Her parents might think him crazy, but he just had to say good-bye. He ran out the door, not even bothering to take the time to lock it. He could only pray a taxi was waiting at the curb, hoping for a patron. Then traffic needed to cooperate. But he knew that only if the stars aligned just right could he have a chance in hell of making it before it was too late. And if he was basing his luck on everything else in his life . . . she'd be gone before he got there.

Mari stared out the window, watching Beijing fly by in a blur as they moved closer to the train station. Her parents sat on either side of her in the taxi, doing their best to show their support as the car moved away from the only home Mari had known for the past ten years. The finality of her leaving added to her depression over the end of this part of her life, though she'd have to return if and when the apartment sold, to pack up her things. Conversation was stilted—a little chitchat here and there, interspersed in the stretches of silence as the driver weaved in and out of traffic.

"I hope all is well at home," her Mama said as she fiddled with the clasp on her purse.

"Mama, I'm sure all is fine, or they would've called."

"Yes, you're probably right." Mama pulled a tissue from her bag and blew her nose. "It was a fine ceremony for Bolin, wasn't it?"

Mari nodded, not sure what to say. It was all too soon. Too final. Words couldn't really match up to the thoughts that swirled in her mind about everything.

"It was a fine showing," her father answered, taking up her slack. "His parents obviously brought some family and friends from their village. And even your neighbors pitched in at the end there, giving his street procession the respectability he deserved."

Mari snorted. He didn't know that not a single one of those people had ever spoken to her before Bolin's death. They'd only come out of curiosity. Or maybe she was being too harsh? But what did it matter, after all? She'd never see them again.

"And your friend—the foreigner—he came. What does he do?" Mari's father asked.

"He's a photojournalist," Mari answered, her mind wandering back to the last time they'd spoken. She wondered what Max thought of her, since she hadn't called him to say good-bye. He knew she was leaving, but time had flown since the day before when he'd walked in the funeral procession, and she hadn't had a chance to call him. It wasn't as if she wanted or needed to see him—she just felt bothered by the fact that they didn't have any finality. She almost felt as though she was leaving a job undone. Something niggled at her, telling her that Max hadn't found what he was seeking in China and still searched for that elusive thing, whatever it was. And she only wished she could've helped him to find it.

"A very respectable profession," her Mama murmured.

"But a difficult one in China," her Baba added. "If he's looking to be published in China's papers, he'll hit more than a few brick walls. Censorship is still strong, despite information the government feeds to the rest of the world."

"What do you mean, Baba?" Mari was thankful for the conversation on any topic other than Bolin.

"Well, you can put it this way: I still remember back in the late seventies when it got out that one of the upper staff members of the most famous paper in China, *the People's Daily*, said lies in their newspapers were like rat droppings in clear soup—both apparent and appalling. He was not proud of his position but could do nothing about it."

"But that was decades ago, Benfu," her Mama said.

Her Baba snorted in derision. "Don't let them fool you, Calla Lily. Not much has changed since then, other than the fact that now the government has a full-time battle on their hands as they try to police the Internet, even with their many filters. They print what they want to print, or twist a story into what they need it to be. But I'll say this— their obsession with censoring everything has become much harder with the inception of the World Wide Web."

Mari didn't answer. Her father's dislike for the Communist Party and their many ways of controlling China's people was a sore spot that ran long and deep. He'd lived through many a trial brought on by poor leadership, and he had a right to the opinions he held. Her Baba was an intelligent man, and one of the things she loved about him was that he wasn't afraid to have intelligent daughters. He'd taught them one of the most important tools in life: to think for themselves. For the daughters who hungered for history—like Linnea—he had fed them everything he knew, from both sides of an issue. But for those who didn't have a thirst for it, he didn't try to shove it down their throats. But now that Mari was older, he was much more transparent with his views than he'd ever been before.

The driver slammed on his brakes, closing the subject abruptly as he narrowly missed a motorcycle carrying a man, woman, and their child. Her Mama gasped, throwing her hand to her heart.

The rest of the ride to the train station was quiet. Mari stayed immersed in her own thoughts of mortality, brought on by Bolin's funeral and the near-miss of an entire family in one split second. Mari knew human life was fleeting. And at this stage in it, she didn't even know if it was worth fighting for. She looked over her Mama's head, wishing she could reach the window, to lean her head against it, and let the coolness of the glass soothe her. Sitting between her parents was supposed to bring her comfort, but she longed for solitude. Or at least for someone who could truly identify with her deep sadness.

The driver pulled up to the curb, and her Baba paid him, then went to the trunk and lifted all their bags out, setting them on the walkway. Mari looked around, feeling claustrophobic from the sudden onslaught of people. It felt as if all of Beijing was packed into and around the station, and her first instinct was to bolt. She looked up, seeing another red-sky night, and though she wouldn't miss the pollution of Beijing, she would miss the dreamlike backdrop it created on rare occasions.

But she needed to return to her childhood home. At least to retreat for a while, to try to put the pieces of herself together again. Still, she felt as if she were forgetting something. A feeling she couldn't quite place pulled her to keep looking behind her.

"Guo lai." Her Mama beckoned her to join them. She and her Baba had moved quite a few feet ahead and waited for her to catch up.

She let out a long, mournful sigh. "I'm coming, Mama." She picked up one of her bags and looped the strap around her shoulder, then grabbed the handle of her rolling suitcase. With one last look behind her, she moved toward her parents. As she drew closer, she kept her face down.

She felt her father's arm slip around her shoulders. *"Nuer,* what is it? Why more tears? Is this not what you want to do?"

Mari looked up, ashamed that the dam had broken again. "That's just it, Baba. I don't know. I feel like it's not worth it anymore. No matter what I choose to do, it'll be wrong. I feel so tired. And used up—as if I have nothing left to offer anyone."

Her Mama set her bag on the sidewalk, then moved in to grab her hand. "Oh, Mari, don't even think like that. This will pass, child. You are so overcome with grief that you can't see anything clearly right now. Give it time."

Mari didn't see how time would change anything. Bolin was dead. She was broke. She'd lost everything.

Her Baba reached up and wiped a tear that hung at her chin. The rough planes of his hands brought back a memory of him holding her as a child, when she'd cried her heart out after he'd told her that they would be her new family. *Her forever family.* But back then, her tears were of relief that her life of hardship would be behind her. No one ever told her that it could come back around again, this time as an adult.

"Listen to me, Mari. We all have a purpose. You just haven't found yours yet. Think of the last few days as a lesson—one of many. You'll also be connected to many others on your journey to find what fulfills you, but you'll have to be patient. Be strong. And Mari—be watchful. You'll find it. I promise."

Mari considered what he had to say. She'd never known her Baba to be wrong. He was a wise man, so maybe it was true, and she hadn't yet found what it was she was meant to be. A few weeks or months back under their roof might be just what she needed.

"Mari!"

Mari whipped around.

It was Max, getting out of a taxi only feet from where theirs had let them off. He waved at her, then bent down and threw a few bills at the driver. Mari was confused. What was he doing there?

"Mama, Baba, I'll meet you inside," she said, waving them along. Her cheeks flamed, but she needed to say a real good-bye to Max, and she wanted it to be private.

He jogged to catch up with her, then he stood there, smiling hesitantly at her.

"Are you going somewhere?" Mari asked.

He shook his head and the smile disappeared. "No, I—I—oh hell, this sounds so ridiculous. I didn't want you to leave without a proper good-bye."

Mari felt a weight lifted from her. It wasn't like her sadness about Bolin had disappeared, but something about the fact that someone other than her family saw her as worthy, even for a moment, made her feel human again.

"*Xie xie*, Max. I hope you will find what you are searching for in China." She wasn't sure what else to say. It wasn't as if they knew each other that well, but still, they'd shared something, even if she couldn't define it and didn't know where to go with it.

He shook his head sadly. "I don't know if I ever—" He was abruptly cut off by the wailing of a little girl, a street child that suddenly appeared between them.

"*Bang wo, bang wo, da bizi,*" she pleaded, pulling on Max's shirt.

He looked down, bewildered, then back up. "Mari? What's this?"

"She's a beggar—probably homeless. They're thick here at the train station," Mari said, already digging in her purse. It was clear the girl didn't belong to anyone. Besides her stringy hair, her pants were much too short, and her soiled pink jacket was too ragged for even a poor village mother to allow their child to wear. She was alone, and it tore at Mari's heartstrings. She didn't have much, but she'd share what she could.

Max held his hand up. "No, let me, Mari. Poor kid."

"She called you Big Nose," Mari let out a little laugh, then watched as Max pulled his money clip from his pocket and pulled off a one hundred—renminbi bill, then held it in front of the wailing girl. She was then shocked after the girl slapped it from his hand and attempted to pull him along behind her.

"*Bang wode jie jie,*" the girl stammered, and Mari tried to understand her.

"Your sister needs help?" she asked, trying to detach the little fingers from Max's jacket. She knelt and picked up the bill that had fluttered to the ground, and quickly stuffed it in Max's pocket.

The girl nodded, her eyes huge with fear. Mari thought she looked as if she were beyond panic and closing in on hysteria. "I think she's telling the truth. Something's very wrong."

"What can we do?" Max asked, looking around for the sister. He ran his hand through his hair, making it stand on end.

Mari turned, and though she saw other pitiful boys hanging around for handouts, she didn't see another girl, other than the few who were attached to families. They'd have to follow. She turned the other way and saw that her Baba and Mama were still standing just outside the station doors, waiting for her. Her Baba obviously hadn't trusted her to be alone with the foreigner. He raised his eyebrows at her, too far away to hear what was going on but able to see that something was happening.

"Wait here, Max. *Deng yi xia*," she told the girl to wait a moment, then picked up her bag and quickly ran, dragging her luggage until she reached her parents.

"Mama, Baba, something is really wrong with that little girl. She's asking for help for her sister. I'm sorry—but I'll only be a minute."

Her Baba reached out and took her luggage, setting it beside theirs, then nodded. "Go. We'll wait."

"Oh dear," her Mama said, squinting to get a closer look at the little girl.

Mari turned and ran back to where the girl stood, still pulling on Max to make him move. "*Hao le*, where is she?"

Mari was already out of breath, and from what the little girl was yelling at her, they weren't even close yet. She and Max had followed her away from the station, across the parking lot, then down a dirt road that ran parallel with the tracks, leading farther from the bright lights.

For a moment, she wondered if it was a ploy to get them away from the station, and she hoped the girl wasn't that good of an actress. Street gangs were smart—and sending children as decoys wasn't too unethical for them.

Her heart pounded in her chest, and her lungs felt as if they'd burst. How much farther? She remembered that she'd barely eaten anything in the days since Bolin's death. She was weak, and she was slowing them down. A few steps ahead, the girl ran with Max, keeping a firm hold on his shirt, refusing to be separated from him.

"Wait," Mari called out. They didn't hear her, and the girl continued to lead them along the wide span of grass that fell between the tracks and thick trees.

"*Ta bing le,*" Mari heard her say, and she stepped up her pace, the threat of a sick child making her forget her own weakness.

The little girl stopped short when a shack no bigger than a toolshed came into view. Instantly they saw the heavy plume of black smoke billowing from it. It only took seconds to register, then the little girl's mouth opened, and she let out a shrill cry of anguish.

"Noooo . . ." she wailed, then let go of Max's shirt and took off, running for the engulfed structure. The girl was intent on reaching it, and Mari had no doubt she was going in when she got there.

"Oh no, I think her sister's in there! Catch her, Max!"

Max looked back at her, his eyes wide with disbelief, then he took off after the little girl, scooping her up just before she reached the inferno. Mari let out a sigh of relief; the girl had been only seconds away from running through what once must have been the door.

Mari caught up to Max as he struggled to keep the girl in his arms. She kicked, screamed, and scratched like a cornered cat as Mari rushed to try to calm her.

"You can't go in there. *Dui bu qi*—I'm sorry; I'm sorry," she chanted, rubbing the girl's hands as Max held her with both arms to stop her thrashing. He held on, she had to give him credit. He was confused, yet he was following his instincts.

"An Ni, An Ni," the girl wept, huge tears making tracks down her dirty, red cheeks.

Max froze and looked at Mari. "What is she saying?"

The girl nodded, her sobs racking her small body as she pointed at the blaze. "An Ni," she choked out again.

The name rang a bell with Mari, but it couldn't be the same girl. Then she saw it also meant something to Max. For a moment, he looked dumbstruck. Then the blank look was replaced with one of determination.

"Hold her," he shouted.

Mari almost dropped the girl when Max shoved her into her arms, then took off toward the shack. He was like a wild man, screaming the child's name as if he knew her. He got to the door and kicked through a few boards that had fallen and lay blocking the entrance. She watched as he dropped to his knees and then disappeared into the black smoke.

She felt sick. Max was going to die in there.

And all because of her.

He'd never be there if it wasn't for coming to say good-bye to her. She screamed for him to come out and just when she thought she couldn't hold on to the child any longer, the girl stopped thrashing in her arms, and remained silent and waiting with her for Max to emerge.

Seconds ticked by, but they felt like hours. Finally, he fell out of the door, holding his mouth and hacking, bent over at the waist. "It's too late. I can't find her."

The little girl started to sob again, and Max fell to the ground on his knees, holding his head in his hands.

"Max, are you hurt?" Mari set the girl on her feet and went to Max, dropping to the ground beside him. Between his coughs, tears ran down his face and he sobbed.

"I couldn't save her. I didn't make it. I let her down," he cried.

Mari reached out and stroked his head. "Max, we tried. I'm so sorry." She felt her heart fall. Did death just follow her around? What was wrong with her? Was she cursed?

Even over the little girl crying, Max was louder. He was inconsolable, and Mari didn't understand the emotion coming from him. Yes, it was sad—tragic even—but he didn't know the child, making his reaction seem to her a little extreme.

"Max—"

Suddenly the girl shrieked and pointed behind them. Mari turned, and her next words froze on her tongue.

Scooting along on her butt from out of the trees was An Ni, the girl Mari'd met on the sidewalk near her home weeks before. The girl moved slowly, a large bag looped around her neck, but it was really her, and she was alive.

But she looked sick. And hurt.

And just like on the first night they'd met, An Ni looked at Mari, her eyes wide with fright. Mari jumped to her feet and ran to her, with the little girl and Max hot on her heels. When she got to her, An Ni reached for her, and Mari dropped to her knees, gathering the girl close to her.

"You came," An Ni whispered. "I knew it was you all along. You came."

Chapter Twenty

The taxi pulled up to the hospital building. Max climbed out of the car, picked An Ni up off the seat, and gently cradling her in his arms, he turned to rush her inside. In the lobby, he found himself in the center of what ironically mimicked a busy train station. The lobby of the hospital was huge, with windows along several walls and people shuffling around. It was utter chaos. He turned first to the left, then to the right, confused about which way to go.

Mari tapped his shoulder rapidly. "Take her over there and sit down; I'll go talk to the admitting clerk."

Mari went one way while he headed toward the few rows of tattered plastic seats. When they got there, he gently placed An Ni into one and helped her prop her hurt leg on another. He sat down beside her. Through the black smudges on her face, he could see she was pale, and though the night was crisp and cool and she was barely dressed for it, beads of sweat glistened on her forehead. He could tell she was in pain, but she was taking it like a little warrior—not surprising, considering she'd gotten herself out of the burning shack and into the protection of the woods, all by herself with a probable broken leg. The thought of all she'd dealt with alone sickened him.

He also still hadn't explained to Mari why he'd lost his mind back in those woods, and as embarrassing as it was, he didn't relish having that conversation any time soon.

He looked at his watch. Almost midnight. It had taken them too much precious time to separate the girls, convincing the littlest one—Mei, she'd called herself—that An Ni would be fine with him and Mari, while she went on with Mari's parents to the apartment.

Mari's father had gathered the little girl in his arms, and his strong, confident, and caring presence had calmed Mei. He'd whispered to her that his daughter, Mari, was a big sister to many little girls and would care for An Ni like her own, and then Mei had settled down and agreed to go quietly. Once that was decided, An Ni was all for going to the hospital, confident that some sort of god—Guanyin, she'd called it—had directed Mari and even him into their path, giving her peace that they were with the right people.

Across the room, he could see Mari gesturing wildly as she spoke, pointing at him and the girl. She looked upset, then crossed the room and stood before him. Tears glistened in her eyes. "I'm very sorry, but the deposit is one thousand renminbi. I don't have near enough to pay it. Please tell me you do."

"A deposit? Don't they treat her and then tell us what the bill is?"

Mari shook her head. "It doesn't work like that here. They set an initial deposit, then we pay from it as we go for each procedure. When she's discharged, if there's anything left, you'll get it back. If you can pay now, I'll find a way to repay you. I've told them she's my niece from out of town and I don't have her *hukou* with me. That's why they set the deposit so high."

Max stood and dug into his pocket, pulling out his money clip and quickly peeling off ten bills and handing them over. "No, you won't give this back, Mari. I'm paying for this, and I never want you to mention it again." He didn't care what it cost; he just wished they'd hurry and give the girl something for her pain. Mari turned on her heels and stomped back to the window, and he returned his attention to the girl's little face.

She was staring up at him, a funny expression forming.

"Ni hao?" he said, feeling more awkward than he'd ever felt in his life.

"Ni?" she asked softly.

He knew what *ni* meant—it was the word for *you*. But he didn't know why she was saying it. *She must be in shock*, he thought, then nodded to satisfy her. "Yes, it's me."

The little girl wiggled around, each movement bringing a different expression of discontent to her face, until she finally got her hand to her pocket and carefully pulled out a piece of paper. She handed it to him and he took it, then looked back at her.

"What's this?" She couldn't understand his words, but he felt sure she knew what he was asking.

"Ni," she answered softly.

The paper was worn and looked as if it had been kicked around on the streets one time too many, but he began unfolding it, careful to avoid ripping it in case it meant something special to her.

When it was completely unfolded and he could see what it was, he was so surprised he almost dropped it.

It was the copy of his passport that he'd lost along with his wallet almost a month before.

He looked back at her, and she nodded her head emphatically. *"Ni. Da Bizi."*

How did she have the copy? What the hell was going on? And why did she keep calling him Big Nose?

Before he could work it out in his head, Mari returned along with two male nurses pushing a stretcher. She waved at the two of them. "Now we go to the X-ray department."

One of the nurses reached for An Ni, and she resisted, shrinking back against the seat. Her expression changed to fear, and Max stood up, waving at them to step back.

"Let me," he said. He quickly folded the paper and stuffed it into his pocket, then picked up the girl and moved her to the stretcher. He wouldn't worry about the paper now—they'd have plenty of time later to find out when and where she'd lifted his wallet from him, and how they'd tracked him to the train station.

As the nurses wheeled her away, the girl reached for his hand. Max felt a lump move into his throat as he gave it to her, and he walked beside the stretcher. For the first time in over a year, he felt needed, and he also felt he was where he was supposed to be. And those feelings were something he'd trade everything he'd ever owned to hold on to for a moment longer.

Six hours, three bags of fluids, two bags of antibiotics, a cast, and too many vials of lost blood from one skinny little girl later, they were on their way back to Mari's apartment. An Ni slept between them, her head leaning on Max's shoulder, her arm snaked through the straps of the purse that she'd dragged with her out of the shack.

At the hospital, he'd had to once again dig deep into his pockets. He wasn't proud of it, but he'd greased the doctor's palm when it came time to get him to release An Ni. The stubborn girl had already told Mari in no uncertain terms that she wasn't leaving Mei overnight, and she'd hop out of the hospital if she had to. Max believed that she had the nerve to try it, too, even if she didn't know where Mari's apartment was. The kid was just resourceful enough that she might be able to find it.

The doctor almost wouldn't yield. But An Ni's leg wasn't too bad. He'd even been impressed that, as swollen as it was, the actual break wasn't worse. He called it a *stable fracture of the fibula*, which meant that the bones, though broken, were still aligned—the best way to break a bone, in his book. However, she'd originally had a lot of open scrapes from her fall, and they'd never been cleaned. The doctor concluded that she'd contracted osteomyelitis—a bone infection—either from the tissue wounds or even through her bloodstream from the urinary tract infection he'd also diagnosed—which, from what Mari explained, was the most serious issue at hand. He'd pumped her up with antibiotics, and her body temperature finally came down to normal. However, the hospital policy was they couldn't give prescriptions for most drugs. So in addition to keeping her casted leg propped for the next several weeks, she'd have to be brought back to the hospital daily for intravenous antibiotics.

Surgery wasn't completely off the board, either, but the doctor was open to trying noninvasive measures first. But bottom line was that An Ni was going to need several weeks to completely heal. Already the idea of the girls traveling to Wuxi with Mari was out of the question.

He looked down at An Ni's face. In sleep she was more childlike. The tough mask she'd worn for the last several hours dissolved, transforming her back into the young girl she really was. Her eyelashes fluttered a few times, and she jerked in her sleep. Max wondered what dreams haunted her. With the life she'd led, there were probably more bad memories than good that she ran from when she closed her eyes.

A few feet away, Mari stared out the window. It was early morning, and the streets were starting to show some activity—the early risers already out, bundled up as they wove bicycles in and around each other, business owners opening up shop, and cars and trucks starting to hog the road.

"Mari?"

Mari looked over An Ni's head, meeting his eyes.

"If you can keep her with you for a while, I'll come every day and take her back and forth to the hospital, until she's released from care."

Mari gave him a small smile, though she didn't answer.

He felt sorry for her. She was exhausted, and she was still processing the last several hours and the reality that she'd almost left Beijing to return to her hometown as a widow, but now was going back to the apartment she'd shared with her husband, where she'd be caring for two children until they could figure out a plan. He agreed it was mind-boggling, but her silence was frightening. Surely she wasn't thinking of giving the girls over to the authorities? They'd talked for most of those hours as they sat waiting for An Ni, and she'd confided in him some serious horror stories about her early street life, crooked authorities, and the broken—or basically nonexistent—foster care system. While it wasn't his decision, he felt strongly about helping to care for An Ni, even if he had to extend his visa to make sure it happened. Hell, even if he had to bring both her and the little one to his own rundown apartment, he'd do it! Of course, that wouldn't look appropriate, and he'd probably end up in jail.

He stared out the window. Now the morning light washed over the streets and buildings, flooding in through the glass to rest on his face and arm. With the sudden warmth, he realized something. For the first time in a very long time, he'd gotten through the night without drinking.

He realized something else, too. Somehow, someway, he had to figure out what was the best way for him to help An Ni. There were so many coincidences that had brought him to the girl . . . he knew now that this was the last task. And he wouldn't walk away until he knew for sure this time that he'd succeeded.

Chapter Twenty-One

Mari went to the stove and pulled the teakettle from the red-hot burner. She took it to the table and filled the four cups there, breathing deeply the scent of the dark tea leaves as they steeped. She set out a pack of dried rice cakes and put down a few napkins. There wasn't much to choose from, but she felt relieved she hadn't subleased the apartment. Once again, her Baba had been right when he'd warned her not to make any hasty decisions. Though it was sparse, at least they'd had a place to bring the girls.

Now her feet were planted in the exact place where, only days ago, her husband's body had lain for everyone to see. She'd thought she wouldn't have to return there until several weeks or more had passed to give her time to digest everything. Yet here she was.

Yes, he's really gone.

Her breath caught in her throat, and she felt a wave of dizziness.

"*Zuo xia*, Mari," her Mama urged, gesturing at the chair.

She dropped into the empty chair. She was tired—more tired than she'd ever been in her life, it seemed. They'd returned, and Max had carried An Ni up all the stairs and into the apartment. The girl had barely stirred except for a moment to ask where Mei was, then had settled back into sleep when he'd laid her down right beside the sleeping little girl in Mari's bed.

"They'll probably sleep until noon," Max said, then brought the cup to his lips and sipped cautiously. "Poor kids—they've been through hell. Can you imagine living out there in those woods alone?"

Mari's Baba was quiet. When they'd returned, her Mama was sleeping in the bed beside Mei and he'd been snoring on the couch, but both had gotten right up. Her Baba asked all about the care the hospital had given An Ni, and what it cost, then he'd slipped into one of his contemplative moods, letting her Mama take over the conversation. He'd barely acknowledged Max, and Mari couldn't tell if he approved of her friendship with him or not.

Finally, he cleared his throat. "Mari, we've got to make some decisions about those girls."

She nodded. Her parents needed to get back to Wuxi—she'd interrupted their lives enough with the troubles of her own. She knew they worried about Mari's younger sisters, even though Widow Zu had promised to look after them. And as attached as Maggi Mei and Jasmine had always been to her Mama and Baba, she knew it was rough for them to be apart.

One quick peek at Max told her he didn't understand her Baba's local dialect, but he refrained from asking what was said. "*Zhi dao*, I know. An Ni can't travel, though." She quickly translated her words to English for Max's sake.

"Then you must stay here until she can. I'll stay, too," her Mama said softly.

Mari shook her head quickly. "*Bushi*, Mama. You have to go back with Baba. You're needed at home. I've got this—and Max has promised to help."

Max looked up, hearing his name. Mari told him what was being said, and he nodded in agreement. "Of course I'll do all I can to help. I can make a few calls and get my boss in the States to work on extending my visa."

"We could take the little one with us. But what worries me is that legally we can't just take them out of the province without approval. What if we're stopped and asked for her *hukou* registration?" her Baba asked.

Her Mama looked frightened. "*Aiya*, they might accuse us of child trafficking if we can't prove she's ours."

"From what I gathered from An Ni last night, she won't agree to be separated anyway. I'll just have to take care of them both until we figure something out," Mari said. Taking the girls on the train was risky—it was common for the conductors or security to conduct random identification checks. Mari wouldn't tell her parents, but she really didn't know how she'd afford to feed the girls. Her parents didn't yet know the extent of her situation. She'd finally told them about the camel, but she'd made it out as if everything was fine because she'd been working as a tour guide to Max. And Mari was a little ashamed, but she'd built that up to be much more than it actually was. The truth was, after paying for Bolin's funeral and then the rent for the upcoming month, she was broke. Again.

She'd just have to find a job immediately. The girls would be fine staying home alone—they were street children, after all. They'd learned to survive thus far; a few weeks in the shelter of her apartment would feel like paradise to them.

"I wonder if either of them knows where their families are?" her Baba asked.

"An Ni doesn't. I asked her last night. She doesn't remember them at all. I don't know about Mei. She mentioned the man I met weeks ago—the leader of the street gang."

"*Liáng shàng jūn zǐ,*" her Baba muttered.

"What is that?" Max asked, straining to follow along.

"*Liáng shàng jūn zǐ* means *thief*. It literally translates to *man on the roof beam*. We were talking about the one in charge of the street gang An Ni and Mei were a part of."

Mari watched as Max's expression changed from curious to fiercely determined as he strained to understand. She'd described to him how street gangs worked the night before, and the roles and pecking orders of those in charge of the helpless ones.

"What was his name?" Max asked.

"He goes by Tianbing to the kids," Mari said. "But it doesn't matter—he can't be touched. Believe me, he's just another gofer. He reports to others much higher up than him."

"Maybe, but he's the one standing those two girls out there on the corner day and night," Max said, gesturing toward the bedroom. "He should have to answer for that."

No one said anything, and Mari didn't translate. Her Mama and Baba were bright enough to know that Max was simply venting about the man who'd been the girls' captor.

Mari waited, letting Max calm down. She'd learned a lot in the last few weeks, and one thing stood out—Americans were very openly emotional people. And he had a lot to learn in China, especially that bringing down someone involved in the gangs was next to impossible.

Finally Max let out a long sigh, shrugged his shoulders, then put both hands on the table. "So what have you all decided?"

Mari spoke more confidently than she felt. "The girls will stay here until An Ni is well enough to travel. Then if we can't find where they came from to return them to their families, we'll have to rent a car to get them to Wuxi."

Chapter Twenty-Two

Max blinked his eyes rapidly, trying to clear away the bleariness from being awake so long. He'd been up and down streets for hours since he'd left Mari's apartment. She'd told him that she'd first met An Ni close to her home, and she didn't know it and probably wouldn't approve of it, but Max was determined to find that spot. After he'd stopped by his own place for his camera bag, he'd begun his search.

So far, it had netted nothing. Ahead he saw two young boys squatting against a wall, looking bored as they slung a rock back and forth between them. He approached them, his friendliest smile fixed on his face.

"*Ni hao,*" he called out, and he waved at the two.

They looked up and returned his greeting with probably the only word of English they knew. "Hello!"

He laughed and came closer, then focused his attention on the boy that sported a jagged scar on his face. He hoped he got his words right.

"Tianbing *laoban*?" He asked if they knew the man who An Ni claimed was their boss.

The smiles disappeared from the boys' faces, and they jumped up, suddenly afraid and needing to look busy, revealing to Max that they probably knew him.

They held up their hands, shaking their heads *no* as they backed away.

"Wait! *Wo*—um—*wo gei ta qian*," he hoped his words were at least close to right and the boys would understand that he wanted to give Tianbing money. That was all they were interested in, after all.

It worked. The boys stopped. The bigger one, at least a head taller than the other, seemed to struggle with himself. Max knew he wasn't sure if he'd be in trouble for pointing out where the man was, or more trouble for letting someone go when they claimed to want to give his boss man some money.

Max decided to make it an easier decision. He pulled out a fifty-renminbi bill and leaned over and held it out.

"Tianbing?" he asked, pushing the bill into the boy's hand and closing his fingers around it.

The boy squeezed the money and looked at the younger boy, who just shrugged his shoulders. Finally the bigger boy pointed behind Max.

Max turned around and saw a noodle shop across the street. In the corner of the building, sitting at a booth looking out the window, he spotted a man.

Tianbing. It had to be.

The boys took off running, and Max waited for traffic to give him enough of a lull to step out into the crosswalk. He kept his eye on the window, watching to make sure Tianbing didn't slip out unnoticed. As Max drew closer, he went back over his plan in his head. Just before entering the shop, he changed his mind and ducked into the shadow of the alley. It wasn't long before Tianbing made his way out into the street and scanned the sidewalk. For a second, Max considered that with only a few steps, he could wrap his hands around the man's neck and squeeze until he'd rid the world of one more piece of trash. But then Max would be just like him, using violence to get his way. So instead he snapped a few photos, then waited.

Tianbing turned west and began walking, looking up and down alleys and seeming to pay attention to street corners. Max followed him for close to half an hour before finally, Tianbing sauntered up to a small boy who lay flat on his stomach, rolling around on what appeared to be a modified skateboard, wider but with more wheels. In front of him, the boy nodded at a ceramic bowl used for begging from pedestrians as they walked by. Shockingly, the boy didn't have any legs at all.

Max watched as Tianbing crouched down in front of the boy, who tensed up. The crude man picked up the bowl, plucked the few bills out of it and waved them in front of the boy, taunting him. Max stayed back in the crowd, clicking his shutter as fast as possible—though what he really wanted to do was intercede with his fist.

When Tianbing stood and began walking again, Max straightened his shoulders and got in behind him, careful to keep plenty of people between them. Max was tired—so much so that he felt he could huddle in the corner of the alley and sleep forever. But he'd stay with the man, and in a few hours, he would have exactly what he needed.

Mari laughed out loud at Mei's antics. It was just after noon, and the little girl was dressed in Mari's own tattered pink bathrobe. She had tied it high above her waist, the hem hanging to the floor, covering her feet as she danced around the room. She'd declared herself *Huo Chengjun*, the empress from the Han Dynasty and the subject of the bedtime story Mari had told them the night before. Mei had been enamored when she'd gotten to the part about the empress continually rewarding her servants with gifts of wealth. That someone in power had deigned to care about the lowest in her household had surprised Mei, prompting her to ask a half-dozen questions before Mari could get her to finally close her eyes. Once again, as Mari dug deep in her memory for more of the story, she realized what a gift she'd had in being raised by her Mama and Baba. Because of them, she had stories in abundance stored up—she'd just never had anyone to tell them to.

Now Mei was wide awake and full of sass. She'd already taken a shower, washed her hair, and stood ready to take on the day. The only downer so far was that Mari had nothing suitable to clothe the girl in. If she could talk An Ni out of her clothes and into a gown like Mei, she'd take both of their sets of clothing down to the laundry.

Despite her weariness, Mari had to smile. It was astonishing how having the two girls in the house had turned it from a somber, cold, and depressing environment into what felt like a bright, cozy home that she barely recognized. She wished that Bolin could be a part of it—to feel the warmth, and experience the life it now held.

Mei giggled brightly again. Instead of a formal empress, she reminded Mari of the fictional fairies she'd read in legends of long ago. She was a cheerful little thing—unrestrainedly happy at her and An Ni's new circumstances.

"I can make soup for lunch," Mei said, then jumped up on the couch beside An Ni.

An Ni flinched. "Not your soup—please."

Mari could see that even several hours of sleep in a soft, warm bed hadn't given the girl much relief from the pain of her leg. At one point when An Ni had cried out in her sleep, Mari had almost relented and given the girl one of Bolin's pain pills, but then stopped herself. The doctor had said An Ni was too young for pain medication given orally, and since they were seeing him that afternoon for more antibiotics, An Ni would hopefully get something for relief then. Mari wasn't sure why, but she felt an almost magnetic pull to An Ni. She stared at her from across the room, trying to fathom what it was about her that captivated her so.

"I thought you liked my soup?" Mei asked, her lips forming a pout.

"I did. I'm teasing," An Ni reassured her. She scratched at her head.

Mari cleared her throat to get their attention. "Actually, my parents went to the store for my Mama to get stuff to make her Duck Soup with Four Gods—a legendary health soup. They should be back anytime, but how about something small for now?"

Both girls nodded, and Mari headed to the kitchen. She pulled two bowls of instant noodles from her cupboard, then set some water on to boil. Her Mama had awakened with one thought in mind: that the girls needed medicinal soup to help restore their depleted bodies. Mari thought that it was going to take a lot more than duck, yams, lotus seeds, and even gorgon fruit. Both Mei and An Ni were way too thin—they were gaunt, actually. And her Mama always comforted with food, so it was her contribution to their recovery. Her Baba had simply smiled at Mari over her Mama's head and winked, then put on his jacket to escort her to the street shops.

Mari still hadn't figured out what she was going to do. As she saw it, she didn't have many choices, though. The girls couldn't travel. They couldn't be thrown into the social services cesspool. And they sure weren't going back to the streets. That made the decision easy, but even though Max said he'd help, what if he didn't? And what if she couldn't find a job? How would she clothe and feed them?

Mei ran up to her and beckoned for her to bend down.

"Mei, no!" An Ni said from the couch.

Mari bent down, and Mei whispered in her ear. "We have head lice."

Mari stood up and looked at An Ni. The girl sat looking at the floor, her face scarlet with shame.

Mari reached down and hugged Mei close to her. "It's okay, Mei. It's nothing to be embarrassed about. I've had head lice before, and my Mama knows just how to get rid of it. We'll have you two fixed up in no time."

Mari looked around the room. In addition to all of their heads, the bedding, rugs, and even the couch would need to be treated. More expenses to figure out how to cover. She realized now why the gods hadn't seen fit to bless her with a child. All these years later, and she still wasn't prepared. She couldn't even imagine how parents going through hard times supported their children.

Maybe that was why I was abandoned.

Mari was taken aback by the suspicion that snuck up on her. She hadn't thought of her birth parents in many years. She'd purposely shut them out of her mind—and her heart. Baba and Mama were all she had room for, and the ones who hadn't wanted her didn't deserve any space she might have left over. But now, feeling so overwhelmed about the girls, she felt the first stirrings of mercy toward her birth parents. Her Baba said everything was a lesson. *Is this what fate is trying to teach me? To let go of my bitterness? Focus on compassion?* She'd thought she'd shown her humanity while taking care of her sick husband, but perhaps that wasn't enough. Perhaps to feel at peace, she had to also let go of all the repressed resentment she'd carried since she was a child?

Mei giggled again, bringing Mari back to the present. The kettle whistled, and Mari poured hot water into the plastic bowls, popped the chopsticks in, and carried them to the living room. She handed one to Mei and set the other on the small table beside the sofa so that An Ni could reach it. "Be careful, girls. It's really hot."

The girls dug in as if they were at the fanciest banquet in town instead of holding bowls of instant noodles. Mari smiled, watching them eat with gusto. The days in the shack must've been rough.

She heard a knock on the door and crossed the room. When she opened it, expecting her parents, she was pleasantly surprised to see Max standing there, juggling at least a half-dozen bulging plastic bags.

"*Ni hao.*" She moved aside so he could come in.

"Hi, Mari." He turned to the girls as he hurried to the table to set the bags down. "*Ni hao!*"

Mei giggled at him, and Mari saw An Ni trying to hide a smile behind the bowl she held to her mouth. Mari was sure the girls weren't used to foreigners—especially handsome ones, at that.

"Everything okay?" Max looked from her to the girls again.

Other than the fact I'm impoverished and the girls have head lice— what isn't okay? Mari thought. "*Dui,* everything is fine. What did you bring?" she asked.

Max started pulling things out of the bags and slinging them onto the floor in front of the couch. Girls' clothes—all pinks and reds, prissy and sparkly—soon littered the floor. On top of those, at least four pairs of new shoes.

"I'm not sure if I got the right sizes. I told the woman one girl was this tall,"—he held a hand up to just over his waistline—"and the other was this tall." He raised his hand to his chest.

Mei practically threw her empty noodle bowl into Mari's hands as she dived onto the floor and began finding the items that looked like her size. Mari's pink robe swallowed her, making her even more hilarious as she held each shirt, pants, or sweater up and exclaimed over it, or threw it to the couch to land beside An Ni.

An Ni picked each item up hesitantly, looked for a moment, then set it aside.

"Max, you shouldn't have done that," Mari whispered. But *aiya,* was she glad he did. She just couldn't bring herself to ask her parents to part with their limited funds to clothe the girls she'd brought home. It wouldn't be right. She'd been thinking of selling her television set to get some funds, but Max had come through. Now she could save the television for bigger things—like another month's rent.

He started unloading the other bags and setting grocery items on the table, then looked up at Mari. "I know you probably cleaned out your pantry because you were leaving, so I thought I'd help you fill it back up."

He set a huge bottle of the finest oil on the table next to a bag of rice. Soon there were piles of fruits, vegetables, and several different cuts of meats—*Oh, the meats!*—covering the surface. For a moment Mari thought of Bolin and his staunch vegetarian ways. Then she remembered he didn't have an opinion anymore. This was her kitchen. Her life. He'd chosen not to live it with her. And she'd be cooking *meat* for the girls!

Tears of gratitude and relief filled her eyes, and she looked down at the floor. Max came to her and put his hand on her shoulder. "Mari? Is this okay?"

She didn't answer. The lump in her throat prevented her from speaking.

"Oh man, I'm so sorry," Max muttered. "Did I break some kind of cultural code? Oh great, I'm an idiot. I am, aren't I? Just say it."

Mari shook her head, then met Max's eyes. He looked like a hurt little boy, wringing the empty bag between his hands. And he looked exhausted. "No, Max. I'm very thankful. You have no idea just how thankful. Don't worry—you did exactly the right thing."

A smile spread across his face, then he turned his attention to An Ni. "Figure out what you want to wear, Princess. You and I have a date with Doctor What's-His-Face."

An Ni looked at Mari questioningly.

Mari translated, "He said after you're dressed and get your belly full, he's taking you to the hospital to get your meds. We'll go when my parents return and can stay with Mei, *hao le?*"

An Ni nodded. Mari didn't think she mistrusted Max, but he was a foreigner, after all. Not to mention his Mandarin wasn't that great, so Mari could see how it could be awkward for An Ni to go with him alone.

While Max helped Mei fold up the new clothes, Mari went to the kitchen and began putting away the food. She piled all the fruit into the top tier of the three hanging baskets. Then she added the potatoes and onions to the bottom two. Everything else went into the cupboard and refrigerator, and when she'd put the last item in place, the door opened again and her parents were back.

Mari turned just in time to see her Baba's eyes flash with surprise when he saw Max on the couch. Mari's Mama smiled as usual, then crossed the room and laid her own bags on the table. It was obvious by their body language that they both knew the friendship between her and Max had risen to a new level—but just what that level was, Mari herself hadn't figured out.

"Now let's get this soup going, *nuer,*" her Mama said, and winked at Mari.

Chapter Twenty-three

An Ni ate slowly, savoring the broth of the delicious soup Mari's Mama had made again. It eased down her throat like a slow river of comfort while she watched everyone around the table. Even after two weeks of living in close quarters with them, she was still wary. Always on guard—that was what her life on the streets had taught her to be.

Mari had fretted over leaving her on the couch again, but since her cast was so big and awkward, it was just easier for her to stay there. And An Ni didn't mind—it gave her the opportunity to study them while they all gathered around the table.

An Ni wasn't sure what Max, as Mari said to call him, was saying, but she heard her name. Mari rose and brought over a steaming bowl of three or four dumplings, putting them on the table beside her. Mari's mother had said they needed some meat to go with the healthy soup, so she'd made dumplings. And not just street dumplings like An Ni had eaten once in a while when a vendor had been too busy looking the other way—but real home-cooked ones filled with spicy pork and so light they melted in her mouth. An Ni was grateful the old woman had declared she and Mari's father would stay until An Ni's cast was removed, though she'd never admit it.

"Xie xie," she told Mari, leaving out that she'd already had a half-dozen of the dumplings that the old woman had slipped her as she'd cooked them. Max smiled from the table, urging her to eat more.

An Ni listened as Mari's Baba asked questions and Max struggled to answer. Mari acted as a translator for most of it, but An Ni wished she'd just let Max try to say it all. His Chinese wasn't *that* bad, and it gave them all something to laugh at.

Mari turned to Max. "My father wants to know why a journalist would want to come to China?"

An Ni had wondered that herself when Mari had explained to her what Max did. She waited to see what answer he'd give the old man.

"China has only opened up to the rest of the world very recently, and it still harbors many stories that would be valuable for all to know," Max said.

"The written word is sacred to China," Mari's Baba began. "When for so many years the government forbade any sort of reading or writing, other than to study Mao's words . . . To finally have the same freedoms as the rest of the world is not something most Americans, who have only known free press and a flood of books and newspapers, would understand."

When Mari finished speaking for her Baba, Max nodded solemnly.

"I agree. That's why I'd love to hear your stories—even record them into history so that your descendants could have whatever wisdom you want to impart with your memories."

"I've held my memories and my stories close to my heart for so long, it'd take an ice pick to finally pry them loose," Mari's Baba said.

Mari's Mama put her spoon down. "In the old days, the written word was really honored. Now it's splashed all over the place—billboards, walls, bridges. Back when I was a girl, it was believed that it had so much power that sorcerers would write a few characters on a piece of paper and stick it to the front of houses to ward off evil."

Max looked captivated by her words, making An Ni wonder if he understood more Chinese than they all thought, possibly even all of what she said. An Ni brought another dumpling to her mouth as she watched the emotions play across his face. He intrigued her. He was always looking out for her, making sure she had enough to eat, or that she was comfortable and not in pain. Why was a foreigner so interested in *her*? And just the fact that she'd found his wallet in a random train car and then, weeks later, Mei had picked him out of the crowd to come help her at the shack was too bizarre to understand. It made An Ni wonder if their Guanyin had directed Mei to him. It was their Guanyin's photo, after all, that was found in his wallet.

An Ni was glad that when the ember had popped out of the fire, setting their shack ablaze, she'd been able to stand long enough to pick up the photo off the desk and stuff it into the stolen bag before falling back to the floor and crawling out and into the shelter of the trees. She'd been so scared but now she was thankful the stray spark hadn't jumped onto the rice bag when they'd both been sleeping. They probably both would have died from inhaling the thick smoke before they'd gotten out. Since then, no one knew it, but she'd used the big purse for other items. She wasn't going to be left back on the street with nothing. The bag was in the crack between the couch and the wall, and in the last few days, she'd added coins she'd found between the cushions of the couch, a warm, knitted hat for Mei, and even several packaged snacks that Mari's Baba had brought and laid on the table for them. She knew she was hoarding things that didn't belong to her, and that it was wrong. But she'd be at least a bit prepared when it was time to go.

She continued to eavesdrop on the conversation at the table, to them talking about her and her progress. She loved the sound of Mari's voice and could listen to it all day. All of them were kind to her, but it was Mari who made her feel protected and even wanted.

"The doctor said that based on her white blood cell count today, the infection is retreating nicely," Mari said.

Mari's Baba added his thoughts and concerns that maybe they should let her see another doctor for a second opinion to be sure. Mari's Mama patted her husband's hand as she nodded in agreement. An Ni watched them and the way they acted. If she'd ever known grandparents, she imagined they were just like those two. Always hovering over her and Mei, making sure they were warm enough and had enough to eat. But she didn't like the idea of seeing yet another doctor.

Going back and forth to the hospital with Mari and Max was interesting, but An Ni would be glad when it was over. Mari told her she'd only known Max for a few weeks, but to An Ni they seemed like really good friends. The first few times, Max had carried her from the taxi into the hospital again, and he hadn't even struggled. He was strong—and tall. When he'd come through the door with her in his arms, every person in the hospital waiting room had turned to stare, as if she were a movie star or something. Now she'd figured out how to walk on the cast, and she was able to get around by herself—with a little help, of course. But having a tall foreigner with her still brought her a lot of attention, even if he wasn't carrying her.

"And what about the surgery he said she might have to have?" Nai Nai, her new name for Mari's mother, asked.

"He thinks she'll be fine without the operation. The cast comes off in another two weeks, then he'll say for sure."

An Ni was glad to hear that. She needed to hurry and get healthy so that she could try to find Mei's family. An Ni knew from experience that nothing good ever lasted, so she wouldn't be able to count on Mari and Max—she needed to get a plan in place for Mei. It was her responsibility to take care of the girl, and she wouldn't trust anyone else to get her home.

Suddenly she remembered that Max had taken the paper that Mei had drawn her grandfather's store on. Max's photo was on the front of it, and she'd been so delirious with pain she hadn't realized she'd need to keep it. He'd also asked her about the other things that had been in his wallet, but An Ni had lied, telling him she'd thrown it all away.

"Mari?" she called out.

Mari turned to her to see what she needed, her chopsticks holding a dumpling in midair.

"I gave Max a piece of paper the first day in the hospital. Will you tell him I need it back?"

Mari conveyed her message, and Max turned to her. "But it's the copy of my passport. Why do you need it?"

After translating, Mari waited for her to explain.

An Ni tried to give a look of warning to Mei, but the girl was too deep in her dumplings to pay any attention. "Mei drew me a picture on it while we were in the shack, and I just want to keep it."

Mari told Max what she said, and he nodded, then dug in his pocket. An Ni was relieved he hadn't lost it. Who knew if Mei could draw the same details she'd drawn before?

He unfolded the paper and started to get up to bring it to her, but Mei saw it first.

"That's mine!" Mei jerked it out of his hand and held it up for everyone to see. "This is my Ye Ye's store."

An Ni sighed. This wasn't going as planned.

"Your Ye Ye?"

Max looked confused, and An Ni could see that he'd definitely understood at least part of her announcement. But she wasn't ready for anyone else to know the little bit she did. An Ni struggled to her feet, balancing on her good leg as she held the cast out. "Give me that, Mei."

Without saying a word, Mari's Baba held his hand out, and Mei obediently laid the paper in it. He studied it for a moment, then looked up. "Your grandfather owns a clock shop?"

Mei nodded. "*Dui le*. His shop has really old clocks. He calls me his *píngguǒ zǐ*."

"Do you know the name of it? Or what town it's in?" Mari asked, her voice escalating with excitement.

"*Bushi*, I don't know," Mei answered.

An Ni waited, holding her breath. If anyone recognized it, that would make her job even easier. But then on the other hand, they might take Mei there before An Ni was ready to say good-bye. For in her heart, she knew that Mei's family wouldn't take her in. Why would they, when she was a connection to the street gang that Mei had been forced into?

Max spoke, then Mari's Baba handed him the paper. He studied it.

"Is this a giant teapot sitting on the roof?" He pointed at the paper.

Mari translated the question to Mei. She nodded. An Ni felt like throwing a blanket over her head so she'd just stop.

Max looked up, a smile spreading across his face. "I know where this is."

Everyone started talking at once, confusing An Ni even more. "What did he say, Mari?"

"He said he knows where Mei's grandfather's store is."

An Ni didn't know what to feel. She sat back down on the couch, suddenly hungry no more.

Chapter Twenty-Four

Max looked over at Mari as the taxi driver swerved around yet another pack of bicycles in the street. Mari looked lost in thought as she stared out the window. As for him, he was feeling victorious. He'd finally broken through his writer's block, and after five straight nights of nothing stronger than lots of coffee, his fingers zoomed across the keys of his laptop, putting together his first story in a long time. Just as the sun peeked over the horizon and streamed into his apartment, he'd finished it and sent it off. He'd probably know by the next morning if it had passed muster.

His sudden new routine was also going well. He'd made good on his promise, helping Mari with An Ni every day to make sure she got the care she needed to recover. Mari was quiet most of the time. She was still grieving, he could tell, but around the girls, she put on a bright face and worked hard to make their days interesting. He'd watched the two girls flourish in such a short time. No longer did they seem like two wise old ladies stuffed into children's bodies—now they played often, Mei especially enjoying the dolls and other toys he'd brought them. An Ni loved the different board games and cards, even whipping his tail in most every challenge he threw down. Max was lucky that he'd been able to extend his stay and his rental, but he really only slept there. The girls and even Mari begged him to stay late, then return early each morning. Finally, he felt needed. And the best part about it was that after that first night, he'd poured out all the bottles he'd stashed in his room and suitcase, and he hadn't touched a drop. Even though he wasn't still completely at peace, Mari and the girls were good for him. Or maybe they were simply good for each other. Whichever it was—it made him feel like living again.

When they returned from yet another hospital visit, Mari's mother urged them to go out and leave the girls for a few hours. Max was glad for the interruption in their routine, for he knew Mari needed to get out, and she also needed to be doing something important to keep her mind from her recent tragedy. He hoped that their afternoon away would serve both purposes.

After a lengthy taxi ride, they climbed out, and Max led Mari down the street, his hand on her arm to help guide her around the many obstacles of food stands, standard and electric bicycles, tables displaying small antiques, and the packs of people everywhere. He and Mari moved under a canopy of strung red lanterns that swayed in the wind like a red sea, most likely leading them to the most profitable part of the busy street. If he remembered correctly, it was also where the teapot on the rooftop was located.

He gave Mari's arm a playful nudge. "So it's my turn to be the tour guide. This is Liulichang, the antique market I told you about. My daughter read about this place, and she was obsessed with Beijing's crickets and the elaborate handheld palaces you can buy here to house them in. I came to check it out when I first got to China."

"Did she have crickets?"

Max laughed softly. "The first time she figured out that our local boating store kept a bin of crickets to sell for fishing bait, she climbed out of my truck and waltzed over there, then lifted the lid and let them all out. I had to pay for two hundred and thirty-seven crickets, yet only took one home. She named it Freedom, and I told her it'd die—but just to prove me wrong, that stubborn thing lived for months. When it died, I felt so sorry for her that I snuck a new one into its place before she figured it out."

Mari smiled. "Did you buy her a bamboo cricket palace when you were here?"

Max pointed at an old man feeding a red, twisted candy on a stick to a toddler in his arms. Both of them were a sticky mess—and he paused for a moment and took a picture. "No, I just came to witness a cricket fight. Now that was an experience."

Mari cringed. "I guess you saw they can get dicey. Sometimes the crickets are allowed to fight to the death. But this *is* a nice market."

Mari paused to look at a row of calligraphy brushes on display. "I can't believe Bolin and I never made it to this part of town. All we ever did was work. And now he's gone."

Max didn't reply. He wouldn't have a clue how to, so he held his tongue. Secretly he might not respect the life her husband had built for them, but he'd respect the man's memory.

They continued on and passed small shops of books, paintings, and even puppets on their way to the middle of the antique market where Max believed the area Mei had drawn would be found. It would be like finding a needle in a haystack, especially because Mei didn't know her family name or even the name of her grandfather's store. He and Mari discussed it, and that was another reason they'd come without Mei—they didn't want the little girl to be too disappointed if they found nothing. He patted his shirt pocket inside his jacket, making sure the photographs were still there.

"I'm still a little worried about An Ni," he said, narrowly avoiding a small boy who walked into his path.

"Because of her leg?"

"No. Well, that, too, though you said the doctor says she's healing fine. But didn't you think she acted upset that we were coming here without her? I can't get a feel for if she wants us to find Mei's family, or if she's afraid we might."

Mari shook her head. "I don't know, either. For the last few days she's followed me everywhere in the apartment, afraid for me to disappear. I think that as close as she and Mei are, An Ni is afraid of losing her. But if things go right and by some miracle we find Mei's family, I'm hoping they'll also take in An Ni."

Max was quiet. He didn't know if he liked that idea. Mari didn't know enough of his story to understand it, but finding An Ni was a miracle—and not something he was ready to let go of yet. Helping her and Mei made him feel that perhaps he'd finally completed all the tasks set out for him, yet that elusive something he sought still felt an arm's length away. He also wasn't ready for Mari to leave for Wuxi again. Crazy, but after so many months of isolating himself to the point that no one in his life ever called or made an effort to see him anymore, Mari and the girls made him feel ready to be a part of humanity again. He didn't want to lose that.

Not to mention, photographing the girls this morning would easily be one of his favorite moments in China. While Mei loved posing for the camera and had given him many shots to choose from, An Ni was resistant, only allowing one photo. Knowing he only had one shot at it, Max had thought he'd really need to set up the perfect pose, but before he'd had time to think it over, he'd looked through his lens to see her framed in the window, a shadow cast across her face. He'd snapped her right then, with the unprotected emotion glimpsed in her dark eyes for that instant, before she'd hidden it again. The girls were opposites—where Mei was loud and cheerful, An Ni was always quiet and pensive. Max felt that the older girl had led a tumultuous life, even more than she'd admitted to.

But the photos in his pocket only featured Mei, and Max hoped that with them he'd find someone close to her or her family, someone who could help them bring the little girl home. He thought of his own daughter, and his gut tightened. If she'd ever been abducted, he would've moved heaven and earth to find her. He couldn't imagine what Mei's parents were going through, and it was his duty to at least try to reunite them. He wished he could do the same for An Ni.

"Has An Ni told you if she remembers her parents or where she was before the street life?" Max asked, keeping his eye out for any kind of watch shop.

They passed a large stand of buttons—hundreds and hundreds of red buttons sporting the proud profile of Chairman Mao. Max was amazed that the people still collected Mao memorabilia, even after so many were now coming out and calling him a destroyer of their country.

"No, she won't talk about it. She either doesn't remember, or it's too painful to go back there in her mind. Yesterday while we waited for the nurse to start her antibiotics, she spent the hour asking me about Bolin and why we didn't have any children . . ."

Max thought he heard a catch in her voice as she trailed off to nothing. "She's getting very attached to you."

Mari nodded. "She's growing attached to all of us. I tried to explain to her yesterday that our situation couldn't stay the same. I don't even have a way to support myself right now. If it weren't for you and my parents—we'd all be in trouble. And on that note, thank you, Max."

Max felt his face redden. He stopped at a table of small souvenirs and browsed through key chains and tidy rows of miniature terra-cotta soldiers until the shop owner came flapping out of the door, ready to make a deal. Max moved on, Mari right behind him. "You're welcome, Mari. It's nothing, really. I'm glad to help."

They went around a small bend in the street and Max saw the giant teapot sitting precariously on the rooftop of the china shop, beckoning in shoppers to browse the thousands of porcelain bowls, plates, and exquisite tea sets. He stopped and pointed. "So there it is. And if Mei's drawing is really accurate to her memories, then her grandfather's shop should be somewhere within view of that teapot."

They both turned first one way, then the other, visibly scouring the many shops on both sides of the streets.

"I don't see a clock shop," Mari said.

"And I don't see a fruit stand." Max sighed. It wasn't going to be as easy as he'd hoped. Shops changed hands all the time. People came and went. Who knew—the grandfather could've died or even shut down his business in the last few months. But it was their only hope to find Mei's family, so they had to keep looking.

"Come on. It's going to be a long day." He plucked one of the photos from his pocket and handed it to Mari. "You start on that side of the street, and I'll start on this side. Ask everyone you can about the shop and if they know Mei. Someone here has to know something."

Three hours later, Mari felt as though her feet were on fire. They'd walked up and down the street several times, even a few side roads, showing the photo of Mei and asking around until Mari's throat was dry and parched. She finally caught Max's attention from across the street and waved him over.

He waited for a lull in the traffic of electric bikes and pedestrians, then took a chair opposite her at the small bistro table she'd snagged.

"I'm beat," she said.

Max waved a waitress over and told her to bring two cold Cokes. The waitress nodded and scurried away.

"Me, too," Max agreed.

"Has anyone at all recognized Mei or known of an antique clock shop?"

"Most everyone I talked to acted as if they couldn't understand my Chinese. Even when I pointed at my watch, they simply told me the time or tried to send me to one of the vendors that sold knock-off watches," Max said.

Mari set the photo of Mei down on the table and leaned back in her chair. "We may have to come back another day. I'm getting worried about the girls." She didn't mention that she also felt tired to the bone. Even though she'd been eating more lately, with all of Max's grocery store trips filling up her pantry, she still wasn't sleeping. Nightmares of Bolin hanging from the closet made her afraid to close her eyes, and when she finally did, it was only for short periods at a time.

The waitress returned and set two cans of Coke on the table. Max reached for one, and Mari caught his grimace that it wasn't cold. She looked at the young girl that waited for the money and smiled, then asked her to bring them two cups of ice.

The girl nodded, walking away quickly as she worked to push a stray hair back into her ponytail. She looked a bit harried, and for a second, Mari felt bad for asking her to do more work. But then she remembered how Max tipped and knew the girl would be rewarded for the extra effort.

"I forgot it's not easy to get cold drinks here," Max said.

Mari shrugged. "Not at these small places. It takes too much electricity to make ice, and anyway, warm liquids are much better for your system than cold. But I'll admit, I enjoy a cold drink when I'm overheated."

It was a nice day—the sun shone brightly overhead and made Mari sweat from all the trekking around. A cold Coke sounded wonderful to Mari. A nap did, too, but she doubted she'd be so lucky.

"What if we don't find anyone? Are your parents prepared to take the girls to their home?"

Mari hesitated. "They will—but it would put them in a bad position to take the girls out of this jurisdiction. If caught, I'd be subjecting them to some possible serious charges. I'm not ready to give up on finding Mei's family and seeing if they'll take them both."

Max nodded, and Mari was thankful he didn't tell her how hopeless it all was. She wasn't stupid—she knew the chances of ever reuniting either girl with her family were tiny.

The waitress returned and set the two plastic cups of ice down on the table. "Thirty renminbi," she said.

Mari didn't even attempt to pay for her own. She'd spent enough time with Max to know he'd never allow it. He'd proven to be very old-fashioned and believed he should open doors and pay for things—even though they were both clear that being together was nothing romantic.

As he dug for his money clip in his front jeans pocket, the waitress looked down at Mei's photo lying on the table. "Your daughter?" she asked Mari.

Mari shook her head. "No, we're looking for her family. She was found after wandering away from them. Do you recognize her?"

The waitress picked up the photo and studied it, looked interested for just a second, then set it back down. "*Dui bu qi*, I don't recognize her." She took the outstretched fifty-renminbi bill, and Max waved away her offer of change. "Do you have a family name, or know what they do?"

Mari felt a wave of disappointment. She'd thought the girl recognized Mei. "We only know that her grandfather had a small clock shop. He either sold them or repaired them—we aren't really sure."

"Do you know of any clock shops?" Max asked in what Mari thought was pretty good Mandarin.

"*Dui,*" the girl answered. "There's a clock shop in the Liulichang West Alley, just a half mile from here."

Mari and Max both sat up straighter.

"Mari, you ask her again. She probably thinks I want to buy a watch and is going to tell us about some street thug."

"No, she's talking about a real shop," Mari said, then turned back to the girl and asked for more directions.

When she'd gotten as much detail as they could from the waitress, Mari urged Max to carry his Coke and continue their search. She picked hers up, too, and they took off in the direction of the waitresses instructions. After they'd snaked through the crowd for another fifteen minutes, they finally turned the corner onto Xijie Road, and Mari jabbed Max in the arm, unable to contain her excitement. "I don't see the clock shop but look—there's a fruit stand!" She pointed at the small store. It was barely more than four feet wide, but it looked cozy, with baskets hanging in front of the window and overflowing with fruits and vegetables. Under them were stacks of crates, each holding a different color or variety of freshly farmed food.

"It has to be close," Max said, and Mari could hear he was just as excited.

Mari suddenly saw another fruit stand on the other side, then one farther down the street. She sighed. "Ah, Max, I now see three different fruit stands."

He nodded. "I do, too, but don't get discouraged. Let's just keep looking."

They came upon two old men sitting on overturned crates, playing a game of cards atop the crate between them. Max took her empty Coke can from her, and threw it along with his in the trash bin beside the men, giving him and Mari a reason to move in closer.

Mari pulled the photo from her pocket and showed it to them both. "Have you ever seen this little girl?"

They looked only for an instant, then one of them bellowed at Mari that the girl looked like every other little girl he'd ever seen.

She had to laugh to herself, then Max joined her when she told him what the old man said.

"Half blind maybe?" Max said.

"No, they're just cranky old men—set in their ways. They choose not to see girls as individuals. To some of the elderly in China, a female child is still just a hindrance to the family tree."

They walked a little ways more before Max spoke up.

"They do realize, don't they, that they wouldn't be here if not for some little girl who grew up to be their mother?"

Mari laughed again. She should've told them that. "Well, they aren't all like that."

They walked another half a block, showing Mei's photo around and asking about a clock shop.

Finally, an old woman sweeping the walkway in front of her cigarette store brightened when Mari showed her the photo. "I think I've seen her before," she said. "Who is she?"

"I'm not sure. That's why we are asking around. We're trying to find her family," Mari said.

The old woman pointed a bit farther down the alley. "Ask Lao Feng Ji in that clock shop at the end of the lane. He lost a granddaughter last year. That might not be her, but you should at least ask. The officials said she's long gone, though."

Mari looked up at Max, and their gazes held. She smiled. The woman had said *clock shop*. It had to be him. They'd found it.

The woman went back to sweeping, and Mari led the way, practically skipping to the end of the street where, almost at the very corner, a tiny shop with many clocks in the window waited.

Max held the door, and Mari entered with him behind her.

The shop was dim, and Mari's eyes took a moment to adjust. She realized there were no sounds of ticking.

"It's too quiet in here," she said. Mei had talked about how she loved to listen to the clocks, but in this room, all was silent.

Max grunted a response just as she spotted the old man.

He was at the back of the room behind the counter, hunched over a scarred, wooden desk. With a headlamp strapped to his close-cropped white hair and rounded bifocal glasses perched on his nose, he used a large magnifying glass to examine a pocket watch he held in his hands. He was thin, a much smaller man than her own Baba, but he also looked older. He wore the bland clothes favored by the older generation: faded blue Mao-style jacket and matching pants—clothes meant to make a man blend in with everyone around him, clothes that, for some back in Mao's time, helped them disappear into a crowd to avoid being targeted for any sort of unfounded transgressions that a person could be accused of.

"Be with you in a minute," he muttered.

Mari could wait. She could wait there for a year, if that was what it took. She looked around, taking inventory of the many old and new clocks on the walls. Cuckoo clocks were among the many types, and Mari felt on edge that a silly bird might pop out at any moment and make her jump in fright.

Max nudged her. "All the clocks are stopped at three fifteen."

She looked closer. He was right. Every clock—even the cuckoo clocks—read three fifteen. Mari wondered what that was all about.

"I've never seen clocks with Chinese numbers on them," Max said.

In modern China, most clocks sported Roman numerals or just plain numbers like the rest of the world used. But here, in this man's small shop, it was like stepping back into another era.

The man finally stood, and bringing the bronze-colored pocket watch with him, he approached the counter. He looked up at Mari and Max, barely mustering what would pass as a pleasant look. The deep crags and wrinkles in his face gave him an air of a scholar, and Mari straightened with respect.

"*Hao,*" the man greeted them.

Mari wanted to see what his first reaction would be. That would tell her so much more than any amount of conversation. Without saying a word, she pulled the photo of Mei from her pocket and slapped it down on the table.

He peered down at the photo, surprised at first, then his expression changed to disbelief. He pushed his bifocals up higher on his nose and picked up the photo, bringing it closer to his face.

"Maelyn?" he asked, then he looked up at Mari, his face paled as if he'd seen a ghost.

Mari looked at Max. That was surprisingly close to the nickname, Mei, that the girl had adopted. She turned back to the old man. "Do you know her?"

The old man swallowed hard, then backed up until he was leaning against an old stool behind his counter. He still clutched the photo, studying it.

"Does he know her or not?"

"*Laoren*, please. Do you know the girl?" Mari asked again.

The old man's eyes filled with tears. He spoke low and gravely, barely loud enough for them to hear. Mari leaned down and strained to catch his words.

"Does the bumblebee know a flower? Does the moon know its stars? Of course I know this girl—she is the child of my heart, my little *píngguǒ zǐ*. If you know where she is, you'd fulfill an old man's final wish and return her to me."

Until that second, Mari hadn't realized she was holding her breath. Now she let it out. She smiled reassuringly at the man, nodding. She had to swallow back tears herself, but finally she was able to speak.

"If you can hold on for one more day, we'll bring her tomorrow."

Mari was drained, and yet she owed it to her parents to stay awake until the girls went to sleep, so that she could explain to them what she'd found. It had taken two long bedtime stories filled with legends of dragons and a foreign princess thrown in for good measure before Mei had finally dropped off to sleep. An Ni had been easy. From what her

Mama said, An Ni had been on high alert all day, intuiting that something was going on. When Mari had returned as if she'd done nothing but a day of shopping, An Ni hadn't fought an early bedtime one bit.

"So after two hours of talking to him, I feel pretty sure it's the right family. I promised I'd take Mei there tomorrow." She held her cup up to her Mama and let her add a dab of honey to her tea. A day out in the pollution wreaked havoc on her throat.

"But he hasn't really proven he is her family," her Baba argued from his place on the borrowed cot. He'd set it up next to the couch where Mari's Mama had slept since they'd come. Mari would crawl in with the girls again, and it made her feel bad that her parents had such uncomfortable sleeping accommodations.

"Tell us what makes you so sure, Mari," her Mama said.

"He had other photos. Lots of them. It's definitely her. He admitted to me that when Mei was born, he was disappointed she was a girl. But he said when his son started leaving her at the store with him while they worked, that she lit up the place, bringing life where before there was none."

"What did he say about how she disappeared?" her Baba asked.

"He feels responsible. Listen to this—he somehow has made every clock and watch in the store stop at three fifteen, the exact time that someone saw Mei snatched from his doorstep almost a year before. She was thrown into a white van and never seen again. He said his life stopped at that moment and couldn't begin again until Mei was returned." Mari took a long drink from the tea, letting the warmth fill her up.

"It's a shame that the local police didn't do more to find her—especially when she was literally only a few kilometers away," Baba said. They'd already discussed and discarded the possibility of involving authorities in the handoff, as they'd all agreed that any official involvement would simply muddy the waters. The police had done nothing thus far, so Mari had no reason to believe they'd be any more helpful now that the major work was complete.

"*Dui le*, and from the rumors over the years, usually the children who are taken are immediately routed to a province too far away to be found. Lucky for us, they hadn't yet sent Mei away," Mama said.

"Lucky for her family," Mari agreed.

"Will we go to their home, or are you taking her back to the shop?"

"Back to the shop. The old man says that her journey must come full circle to be settled in her mind and keep away a lifetime of bad memories. So she'll return to where she last saw her family, but they'll all be there this time. And my hope is that they'll take An Ni in as well. I spoke to Mei's grandfather about it, and he was going to talk to his son and daughter-in-law tonight."

"How do you think An Ni will feel about that?" her Mama asked. "The girl has been through a lot. Much more than I think any of us know. She doesn't even remember her family, she told me."

"I don't think she wants to be separated from Mei, so I hope she'll be okay with it," Mari said. "And the family should feel grateful that An Ni has kept Mei safe so long. If they are, they'll allow her to stay."

"With that little bossy thing, I'm not sure that it wasn't the other way around—Mei taking care of An Ni," her Baba said from the other side of the room, his voice getting more drowsy-sounding by the second.

Mari would have to agree. Mei was very protective of An Ni, making sure she got the same amount of food as everyone else, constantly asking her if she was comfortable. It looked to Mari like a role reversal, with Mei taking the big-sister attitude while An Ni recovered.

Mari felt her eyelids getting heavy. It had been a long day, physically and emotionally. She was drained.

"Max is coming for us at nine o'clock," she said. "We'll talk to the girls when he gets here. I think his presence makes An Ni calmer."

Her Mama stood and came around her chair, slipping her arm around her shoulders. "You did well, *nuer*. Now go on and get some sleep. Tomorrow will be a good day, but also very difficult for all of us. Saying good-bye to the girls is going to take all of our strength."

Mari knew she was right. She didn't even want to think of that moment. After only a few weeks, the girls were like family.

She stood and kissed her Mama good-night, then crossed the room and did the same to her already dozing Baba. In sleep, he looked so much smaller, and she realized how much he'd aged in her time away from Wuxi. Both of her parents were nearing the twilight of their lives, she'd known that. Still, no matter how far they had to travel, if they were needed, they'd be there. Mari wished she'd called on them earlier, before her life had crumbled and Bolin had decided to bail on her.

"Good night, Baba," she whispered, then headed down the hall to crawl in beside the two warm, little girls.

Chapter Twenty-Five

The next morning, Mari bustled around the kitchen, helping her Mama throw together their last meal as a family. Max had called and said he was only minutes away. He'd also said he'd splurged and rented a van for the day so that they could all ride together and not have to take separate taxis to Feng Ji's shop.

Mei ran through the hallway and stood beaming at them. "Am I pretty?"

Mari's Mama was first to answer. "Of course you're pretty, child. You were pretty even before your long shower and without An Ni having braided your hair—but she sure did a good job."

Mari had told Mei to take extra care—that it was going to be a special day. Mei still had no idea how special, and wouldn't until they arrived. Mari had tossed and turned most of the night and decided not to tell her. She wanted—no, she needed—to see Mei's first reaction to the family to be sure she was doing the right thing by leaving her with them.

But her mind was still on An Ni.

They heard heavy footsteps coming down the hall outside the apartment.

"That's Max," Mari said. The fact that she could recognize his footsteps didn't occur to her, but the spark of gladness his arrival brought did.

Mei ran for the door. Max always brought the girls something, and the little one had come to rely on those treats and gifts. She could barely contain her excitement and threw open the door to reveal Max to them, smiling from ear to ear as he held onto two tiny cricket cages made from bamboo, both elaborately designed to look like mini pagodas.

"Crickets?" Mei looked confused first, then a smile lit across her face as she stood aside to let him come in.

Max went straight to the table and set the cages down. "Yes, crickets. I want the girls to feel what it's like to help something gain its freedom—when the time comes, they can be the ones to let these creatures go. But listen, Mari. I need you to turn on the news."

"The news?"

"Yes, the news. Your television gets the news, right?"

Now Mari joined Mei in the confusion. Max wasn't acting like himself. He seemed overly excited. Had he seen an accident on the way over? Or was there some event happening that she didn't know about?

"What's going on, Mari?" her Baba asked from the couch.

"He wants to turn on the news."

Her Baba rose and went to the television, switching it on. He went back to the couch, and Max joined him, scooting in beside An Ni.

Mari observed them as they watched the news go by—reporters talking about the price of oil, upcoming bans on fireworks for the New Year festivals, and the dispute with the Japanese over tiny islands in the East China Sea. She marveled that her Baba looked so comfortable with a *waiguoren* so near. Finally, Max gestured to her.

"Come over here, Mari. Mei, *guo lai*," he called to them. "Mari, please translate."

Mari nodded. Max talked, pausing every few seconds for Mari to translate. "We all know the issue of children living on the streets, whether voluntarily or under duress, is huge here. And I know I am only one person,"—he paused—"but I believe that every small gesture can leave ripples that can turn into bigger changes later."

Mari was still confused, but she finished translating the words and then turned back to Max.

"Remember I told you that I was here in China looking for a story to write?"

She nodded.

"It wasn't the only reason I was here. There was something bigger—something more important. But I was also here to do a job, so I tried writing several different stories about things I'd seen. I was so frustrated because I kept hitting a wall, what we call *writer's block*. But, by meeting An Ni and Mei, I realized that they represent many children—kids who may never go home or even know what it means to have a family."

Mari translated, watching her Baba's face. He was definitely interested in what Max had to say.

"And someone should have to pay for what they took from these girls."

Her Baba nodded. Finally she was seeing a connection between the men.

Max took a deep breath and continued. "So I decided to write their story, and that decision made me realize something else. I hadn't been able to write anything worth sending before because I hadn't found anything that made me feel passionate enough. Until An Ni and Mei."

He stopped for a moment, and Mari saw him struggle to maintain his composure. He pointed at the girls. When he spoke again, his voice was shaky.

"These two little girls made me feel again. And that's what my words were missing before—emotion. But with the knowledge of what's happened with An Ni and Mei, I felt outraged. I sat down and with their faces in my mind, I let the tragedy of their lost innocence pour out of my fingers and onto the page. Then I sent it over to my boss—not thinking there was any way he'd accept it, mind you."

"He accepted it?" Mari stopped translating to ask. She felt a sense of pride for him. Getting to know him over the last few weeks, she'd sensed he needed something to lift him up and give him a new zest for life. She hoped this was it.

Her Baba asked a question. "But why are we watching our news if he sent it to his boss in the States? We don't get international news channels here."

Max waited for Mari, then smiled. "That's just it, Mari. He published my article without even asking for any changes. He said he didn't want even one word touched. It went viral on our news website, then the media picked it up. My boss called me at four o'clock this morning to tell me that it was being aired on BBC, and he thinks probably from there, it will be picked up by at least a few Chinese stations. He—well, both of us—feel the government will want to address it, and spin it to their benefit, before it tarnishes their reputation."

She told her parents what he'd said. Her Mama looked worried.

"Mama, what's wrong?"

Her Mama beckoned her closer, and Mari leaned in to her, listening to her whispered question. She looked back at Max. "You didn't submit photos of the girls, did you, Max?"

The girls were quiet, watching and listening.

Max shook his head. "No, of course not."

"Then what will they show?" She couldn't imagine what footage would be included. Just the streets?

"Wait, there it is." Max pointed.

Mari held her hand up for all to be quiet. As they watched, a pretty, young newscaster sitting at a desk told of China's problem with children forced to live on the streets and the gangs that recruited them.

She rattled off statistics like a robot. "The *United Daily News* reports that over one million children in China are homeless and live on the streets, begging or stealing to eat."

Suddenly, Mari saw a photo flash up of the two young boys whom she'd talked to briefly when she'd tried to find An Ni. In the photo, they were tossing a rock back and forth as they squatted in an alleyway. Their clothes were filthy, their hair disheveled, and their faces gaunt. But even with the obvious bad shape their bodies were in, the boys wore defiant expressions. Mari knew those looks—the kids were hardened by their circumstances.

"There's Li Xi and Guo Ji!" Mei shouted, pointing at the television. An Ni sat up straighter on the couch and leaned forward, a look of surprise on her face at seeing someone she knew on television.

"Max, how . . ." Mari felt her words trail off to silence in her confusion.

"I did some research," Max answered. More photos were shown, of children holding out tin cups on the corners, others squatting against walls. Mei and An Ni shrieked each time someone they knew flashed by.

The newscaster continued. "In 2012, a zero-tolerance policy toward child trafficking was implemented by the Ministry of Civil Affairs. Working with the Ministry of Public Security, they have successfully arrested hundreds of suspects and sent thousands of children home."

Mari's father cleared his throat and interrupted. "More misrepresentation by our friendly national censors. They probably sent home only a fraction of that number with their measly efforts."

"Listen, m'love," her Mama gently scolded, laying her hand on her husband's arm.

The newscaster's face never changed; it remained frozen in a grimace of professionalism. "China does not forbid begging by minors, but the law can be applied when someone is caught organizing disabled people or minors under the age of fourteen, with threat of violence or coercion—"

Mari watched, forgetting to translate for Max as the screen to the right of the newscaster turned from still-shot photos to a video. In it, three policemen walked a man to the squad car, his arms behind him, hands tied together with a plastic tie.

". . . and are working every day to abolish organized trafficking rings."

The camera cut to a close-up of the man, an expression of rage across his face.

"That's Tianbing," Mei said, and Mari turned, seeing both girls shrink back against the couch. Even safe in her living room, they were terrified of him, as if he would come through the screen and take them back.

An Ni looked frozen in fear.

Max leaned over and put his arm around An Ni. Mari's Mama held her hands out toward Mei, and the girl stood and went to her, cuddling into the warm, safe space between Mari's parents, a feeling Mari had known since the day her Baba had taken her in under his roof.

"Girls, they've taken Tianbing to jail. He can't hurt you anymore." Mari said it to ease their minds, but she also felt as though the words spoken out loud benefited everyone.

"He'll never give up who he works for," her Baba said. "He's just a small fish in a big ocean of corruption."

Max nodded. He'd understood.

"I agree, Lao Zheng, but it starts with the small fish. That's one less piece of trash combing the streets, snatching China's children. And maybe we can't put them all away, but we can start with one," Max said.

Her Baba mumbled in agreement. "I'm glad they got the cowardly piece of pig manure."

Mari got up, crossed the room, and turned off the television.

Max stood, too, and went to the table. He picked up the bamboo cages and gave them to Mei and An Ni. "A sign of your freedom," he said. He put them in the girls' laps, then bent down and hugged them.

Mari felt her heart swell with gratitude. It was perfect. He'd known the girls needed something symbolic to hold on to, to celebrate the fact that the man who'd made their life hell wouldn't be able to touch them any longer. It was a momentous victory.

And Mei's day was only going to get better. Mari hoped the same for An Ni, though she had to admit she felt torn . . . and hesitant that she was doing the right thing. Mari's stomach shifted nervously. *Butterflies—that was what it was, but was that a good omen or bad?*

She needed to put the thought aside for now, because it was time to eat breakfast and then be on their way. There was no doubting one fact: it would be a day to remember, especially for a little girl who thought she'd never go home again.

Scrambled eggs with tomatoes, sticky rice breakfast balls, and even fragrant jasmine tea filled the senses with the aroma of comfort and family. It was as close to perfect as Mari could imagine, considering she was still mourning her husband. But even the flittering image of him hanging in the closet that never quite retreated from her thoughts couldn't ruin the anticipation the day brought.

Mei was going home. And that was a place that many of the lost children of China never found again. Mari could barely contain her nervous excitement—her thoughts were everywhere at once, never finding a solid idea to cling to. She was thankful that Max was there to anchor her. With the girls and her parents gathered around the table, eating and occupied with banter back and forth, she beckoned for him to follow her outside. They crossed the room and quietly slipped into the hallway.

"It's going to be a big day," Mari said. She led Max to the end of the hall and they went into the stairwell. She sat down on the top stair and patted for him to join her.

"Huge," Max agreed.

"I just wanted to talk to you about what's happening after we leave Mei and An Ni. My parents have talked me into going home with them for a while, just to get my head together."

Max nodded. Mari couldn't tell whether he was sad to hear she was leaving or not.

"You think An Ni will agree to stay with Mei?" Max asked.

"I hope so. It's her only chance at having a family again."

The quiet felt so loud between them that Mari was uncomfortable. She felt they both had more to say, but neither wanted to speak the words.

"I'll be headed back to the States, too," he said, breaking the silence.

Mari hesitated. She needed to stop being so culturally correct. There were some things that didn't need to be left unsaid. At least she could get out part of it. "Max, I want to thank you."

He looked confused. "Thank me? For what?"

"For being my friend."

He smiled at her. "You don't need to thank me for that, Mari. It goes both ways. Because of you, I've learned so much about myself. But what will you do now? Are you sure you want to leave Beijing?"

"Just for a short time. Then I'll be back. I need time to mourn my husband, but then I'll be on my own. I need to learn to live without him. I need to learn to live without anyone. I don't really remember much of my life before my Baba found me, so basically I went from being loved and sheltered by him and Mama, to being supported by Bolin."

"So you've never been on your own?"

She shook her head. It was embarrassing, but it was true. "No, I haven't. But it's time I learn how to stand on my own two feet."

"It looks to me, with your husband's troubles and even the loss of your business, that you were the one shouldering the responsibilities— and doing a fine job of it, if you ask me."

Mari shrugged. He didn't know how close she'd come to total ruin. "Maybe. But I always felt Bolin was there if I needed him. Until he wasn't. And I never want to feel so hopeless again. That means I need to figure this thing called life out and decide where I want it to lead."

Max took her hand and looked at her, his stare intense. "Me, too. Hopefully I'll see you again and I'll have become half the man I used to be. But for now, let's get these girls started on the right track again. What do you say?"

Mari would've liked to ask him more about what he meant, but he was right. They needed to get on the road. Mei's family was likely pacing the floor, waiting to be reunited with their spunky girl.

She stood. "*Hao le*, I'm ready."

Chapter Twenty-Six

As the van bumped along, Mari adjusted one of the ribbons she'd tied to Mei's braids. She knew she was being fidgety and nervous, but she couldn't help it. What if somehow they were wrong? Or what if Mei didn't want to stay? And what would they say about An Ni? So many questions swirled in her mind as the driver Max had hired weaved in and out of traffic. She sat between the girls, and she couldn't stop touching them—squeezing their hands, playing with their hair, anything to get one last memory in before they were gone.

But she could barely look at An Ni. The pain she got in her heart from just thinking about saying good-bye to her was overwhelming. Mei was going back to her family, but An Ni—she was simply being transferred to yet another place. Mari prayed it would be a good one. She suddenly wished it was a much longer ride to the Liulichang market.

"Don't forget your crickets," Mari said, looking at the two small cages sitting on the console between the driver and Max.

"But where are we going?" Mei asked for the third time. An Ni hadn't asked at all, and Mari felt guilty again that she hadn't prepared An Ni for what was about to take place.

"Somewhere special," her Mama said from the backseat, where she sat with Baba.

Mari had taken the girls down the street for a short walk while Max had loaded all their clothes and things into suitcases and then into the back of the van. Now Mari was second-guessing the entire surprise plan, wishing she'd sat them down and discussed what was about to take place, like her Baba had recommended. But Mari had stood her ground. Now she knew he was right. *Why do I always screw everything up?*

"Mei, I have something to tell you," she said.

Max turned in his seat and gave her a questioning look. "Mari?"

They'd determined together that Mei's reaction was important to knowing if they were right in leaving her with the family who would claim to be hers. But maybe Mari hadn't thought it through well enough. What if Mei got scared? What if there was a reason she'd been separated from them that they didn't know about?

Mari took a deep breath. "If we found your family, would you want to go home?"

First surprise, then a flash of joy replaced by wariness crossed Mei's face. "Why? Have you found them?"

Mari bit her lip, hesitating.

"Just tell us, Mari," An Ni said, her eyebrows coming together in a scowl.

Mei looked outside the windows. They were now on the main street near the antique market, literally blocks from the clock shop. All around them, people bustled back and forth, shopping or walking arm in arm. "This looks familiar," she said.

Mari felt a burst of hope that they were in the right place and doing the right thing. The driver turned down the side road, and then it was too late to say more—they were within sight. It would all unfold now. For good or not, they'd know Mei's fate in minutes.

As instructed, the driver pulled up to the curb a half block in front of the shop and turned off the motor. Mei stared out the window, and Mari watched her face carefully. She saw the exact second that Mei's face transformed with recognition and she bolted up from her seat.

"This is it—my Ye Ye's street!"

Max hopped out of the van and came to open the side door for them. Mari got a glimpse of An Ni's face and knew immediately that she was skeptical, despite the guarded expression that she'd perfected.

Mei climbed out of the van and stood looking up and down the street, holding her cricket cage close to her body. Mari could tell she knew the shop was close, but she wasn't sure in which direction. Mari stood aside as her Mama and Baba climbed out and stood with her. An Ni still sat in the van, looking around.

"An Ni, are you coming?" Mari asked.

An Ni shook her head. She looked afraid.

Mei suddenly pointed across the street to a giant teapot perched atop a building.

"Look, An Ni, the teapot!" She exclaimed.

An Ni didn't respond, but she lowered her head enough to see the teapot out the window.

Max gently nudged Mari aside and climbed into the van. He sat beside An Ni and spoke so quietly to her that Mari didn't catch what he said. But when he was finished, An Ni nodded and climbed out, with him following behind her.

"You forgot your cricket, An Ni." Mari pointed at the cage that still sat on the seat.

An Ni ignored her. Instead she nodded at Mei to come along, and the two of them made their way down the sidewalk. They went slowly, Mei taking care not to hurry An Ni because of the clumsiness of her cast and crutches. But An Ni had learned to maneuver well with the inconvenience, and with just a few looks back at Max to see that she was headed in the right direction, they continued on.

Mari and Max followed behind them, with her parents taking up the rear of the procession. Mari felt as though her heart was in her throat, and she concentrated on breathing in and out, hiding her anxiety.

"What did you tell An Ni?" Mari asked Max.

He leaned in and whispered, "I told her about Mei's grandfather and asked her if she wanted to be the one to lead Mei home. She said yes, because she promised the girl weeks ago when it was just the two of them that she'd help her get there someday."

Mari wished she'd thought of that. What an amazing gesture for Max to do for An Ni. He never ceased to surprise her. "Did you tell her about the family possibly taking her in?"

He shook his head. "No, because if they decide against it, I don't want her to be disappointed or feel any shame."

Hurrying their pace, they caught up to An Ni and Mei.

"Turn here, girls," Mari said when they came to the corner.

They continued down the narrow side street until the store came into view, mostly recognizable from the crowd gathering on the walkway in front of it. Mari could see Lao Feng Ji sitting on a short stool. What had to be his son and daughter-in-law were on either side of him, with at least a dozen other people behind them, all looking around. When finally the old man's eyes alighted on An Ni and Mei, he slowly rose and shielded the sun from his eyes with his hand, squinting to get a better look.

The girls drew closer, and the woman beside Feng Ji shrieked and broke from the crowd. It was obvious that she was Mei's mother. She carried herself in the same way and possessed the same stocky body and short but strong-looking legs. Even her rounded cheeks were like Mei's—bright, rosy splotches, looking like two ripe apples. "Maelyn!"

An Ni and Mei stopped in their tracks as the young woman ran toward them. Just before she reached them, Mei dropped An Ni's hand

and met the woman in the middle. The woman threw her arms open wide, and Mei hesitated.

Mari watched closely as Mei studied the woman's face, searching. "Mama?"

The young woman nodded. "It is you—my Maelyn!"

That was all it took for Mei to accept that it was for real. She set her cricket cage down on the sidewalk, then threw herself into the open arms and sobbed against her mother. As everyone watched, the two held each other and rocked back and forth. After an instant, a man joined them, and judging from his emotion and the way he threw his arms around both Mei and her mother, he was the father.

Mari felt her eyes well up. Max put his arm around her and squeezed. She knew what that silent gesture meant—they'd done it. There were millions more out there lost, but at least they'd reunited one child with her family. And it felt good. Then she noticed that An Ni still hadn't moved. She stood in the middle of the sidewalk, leaning on her crutches as she watched the scene around her. Mari moved up until she was beside her, then looked down and saw a smile playing across An Ni's face. She felt a sense of relief.

An Ni turned to Mari. "But how?"

"Max recognized the picture she drew, and we came and just started asking," Mari said.

An Ni shook her head. "They were this close all the time? It just can't be."

Max joined them. "It can and it is, An Ni."

Mari was proud that he'd caught their words and processed them, then answered so eloquently in Mandarin. His weeks of immersion with her family were paying off, and his vocabulary was soaring because of it.

"*Guo lai; guo lai,*" Lao Feng Ji called out to them, and Mari felt her Baba's hand on her back, urging her on.

"Let's go meet them, *nuer,*" he said.

Mari took An Ni's hand and then began walking, bringing her to Mei's family, which would hopefully be hers, too.

Max watched Mari and the girls from across the room. The three of them huddled together, Mei pointing out her favorite clocks and some family photos hung around the walls. Mei's mother and father sat together and watched their daughter, never taking their eyes from her as she chattered to An Ni and Mari.

Max had to smile at her excitement to share her memories. He supposed that she'd probably forgotten many things, but now, with it all suddenly in front of her, she was apparently washed in recollections. The entire last few hours were some he'd never forget in his lifetime. He'd mostly been a silent witness to the reunion, watching as the grandfather grabbed Mei and set her on his lap and then, as plump tears ran through the deep crags and wrinkles of his face, had begged her forgiveness for allowing her to be taken from them.

"My *píngguǒ zǐ,*" the old man had affectionately murmured as Mei had taken him through the shop and helped him start all of his clocks back. It was clear from her confident touch that she'd handled the clocks before, and it was all familiar to her. That gave Max another bit of reassurance that they'd returned her to her rightful place. Now the loud ticking of the clocks settled around them, bringing even more life to the tiny shop.

Max was pleased, too, that he hadn't gotten as lost in their language as he'd thought he would. He'd come a long way, and his daughter would be proud. He didn't understand everything, but facial expressions, gestures, and emotions conveyed what the scattered unknown words hadn't. Most of all, as a stranger and even a foreigner, he knew he was blessed to be allowed to be a part of the magic of the moment, and he was thankful. But now he worried about An Ni.

Earlier Mei's mother had gestured for Mari to join her outside, and she had beckoned him to come, too. Once away from the crowd, the woman thanked Mari again and promised her that An Ni definitely had a home with them. They hadn't told An Ni yet.

But their afternoon was wrapping up, and some family members had already left to go home, reminding Max that they needed to say their good-byes.

"Mari?" he called out.

Mari looked his way, and he tapped his watch. She nodded. It was their signal that it was time to tell An Ni. Mari gestured toward the staircase that ran along the far wall and Max stood to join them. He crossed the room, looking to see if Mari's parents had reemerged yet.

Mari's mother had disappeared with a few other older women, headed to clean up the dishes from the feast they'd prepared for Mei's arrival. Conveniently, her grandfather had a small kitchen in the back of the shop, as well as a small living area on the upper floor. Max had been surprised when family members started carrying out steaming dishes of vegetables, buns, and treats, laying them out all along the shop's glass counters. They'd eaten buffet style, with Mei and An Ni at the front of the line, symbolizing that they were the guests of honor.

Mari's father now sat outside with a few of the men—exchanging stories and anecdotes, no doubt. Max would've loved to sit with them and listen to their stories and memories, but something told him his foreign ears wouldn't be welcome, despite their attempt to be polite. So he'd stayed indoors, watching from his perch well out of the way.

Max saw Mari send Mei across the room to her parents, and she led An Ni to the old, wooden staircase. They took a seat on the last step, sitting side by side. Max joined them and climbed to the step over An Ni, then sat down.

"An Ni, we have some good news for you," Mari started.

Max nodded, silently giving Mari the go-ahead to do all the talking.

"*Shenme?*" An Ni asked what the news was.

"Mei's family wants you to live with them and stay in Mei's life." Mari held her hand, peering into her face as she gave her the news.

"Stay with Mei? And her family?" An Ni asked.

Mari nodded, smiling at An Ni. Max reached out and rubbed An Ni's back, encouraging her to take in the news.

But An Ni didn't smile. She looked confused. "But what about you?"

"What about me, An Ni?"

Max watched the two of them, something unspoken lingering in their words.

An Ni finally nodded. "*Hao le*, I'll stay with Mei," she somberly agreed.

Mari turned and looked at Max, her eyebrows rising together.

"Aren't you happy about staying with Mei, An Ni? Her family will be your family," Max said.

An Ni stared out over the shop, her eyes falling on Mei and her parents. "I'm happy enough. I just hope they can afford another daughter."

Mari hugged her close, and Max had to restrain himself from joining them. He felt so bad for An Ni. She was obviously confused and maybe feeling left out. Even though Mei's parents had agreed to take her in, they'd not shown much interest in her. *Fair enough*, thought Max. *After all, they're just getting back the daughter they thought lost to them forever. Who can blame them if they only have eyes for her?*

"An Ni, give them some time. Once they're over their relief at getting Mei back, they'll want to know more about you. They're so thankful for you keeping their daughter safe—I promise you that."

An Ni nodded, but Max wasn't so sure she was agreeing. Before they could question her more, Mei and her parents approached.

"You're getting ready to go home?" Mari asked, and they confirmed.

Max stood and helped An Ni to her feet. He put his arm around her for support, and they followed Mei and her parents to the door.

Mari knelt down and put her hands on each of Mei's shoulders. "Mei, I'll be in touch, but I want you to be a good girl, and be careful not to wander around alone. *Hao le?*"

Mei nodded. Her eyes filled with tears. Mari hugged her, then stepped back, making room for Max.

He took her place. "Mei, it was so nice to meet you, and I want to thank you for coming to me in the train station—thank you for trusting me. You were very brave, and you probably saved An Ni's life."

Mei smiled. Max looked at An Ni, and she looked away. Was she mad at him?

He stood and touched Mei's nose, made a small clicking sound. "Cute as a button."

With their good-byes said, they all went out the door. Mei's Ye Ye approached Mari and handed her a small wooden clock, the front of it exquisitely carved into the shape of a dragon. *"Xiao liwu."*

A small gift. Mari smiled and nodded. *"Xie xie."*

"You will come home with us?" Mei's mother asked An Ni, beckoning her to come closer.

Max watched as An Ni hesitated and readjusted her hold on her cricket cage, tightening the fingers on her hand that also wrapped around the grip of one of the crutches. He'd brought the cage to her when Mei began showing hers to her parents. He didn't want An Ni to leave hers behind and then regret it later. After he'd explained to them about setting the crickets free, they'd both appeared to look forward to doing it. Now he watched An Ni's face, trying to decipher what she was thinking. Finally, An Ni moved toward Mei and her parents.

The driver had brought the van down to the shop, and now there was nothing left to do but climb in and head back to Mari's apartment. Still, they lingered.

After a bit more conversation and talk of Mei and An Ni starting school, Mari turned to her Baba. "Are we ready to go?"

Max knew that leaving the girls behind was killing Mari, but she was holding up well. Either that or she was just bankrupt of emotion. They went to the van, and after they unloaded the suitcases and bags from the back, they climbed in, leaving the girls and Mei's parents standing at the curb, waving good-bye.

Mei looked so happy, flanked by both her parents. She smiled and waved, even blew kisses. But An Ni—she wore one of the saddest looks Max had ever seen. It broke his heart to have to remember her that way, so he waved once more and averted his eyes.

Mari kept her gaze on the back window, waving gently. When she turned just enough for Max to see her face, he saw that the emotion had broken through, and her cheeks were wet with tears.

"She asked me to keep her cricket safe," Mari said quietly. She held the cage on her lap.

"How do you feel?" he asked.

"Empty," she replied as she stared out the back window. "As though I'm leaving behind a piece of myself."

"Mari?" her Baba spoke to her from the middle seat where he and Mari's Mama sat, both of them amazingly composed.

Mari turned to him, finally taking her eyes from An Ni.

"Maybe you are," her Baba said softly.

Max watched Mari and saw the anguish in her eyes change to a spark of realization. She sat up straighter, turning to look behind her at An Ni again. Max followed her gaze and saw that Mei and her parents had gone back into the store, but An Ni had turned over a suitcase and sat perched atop it. She looked still as a statue, her proud chin in the air as she watched them drive away.

Max couldn't bear it—he had to stop looking. Already the haunting image would be burned into his memory forever.

"*Ting le*—stop, driver," Mari called out and stood, bracing herself against the seat.

The driver looked into the rearview mirror, questioning, yet he didn't slow down.

"My daughter said to stop this vehicle," Lao Zheng said, the authority in his voice causing the driver to hit his brakes too suddenly, thrusting Mari forward.

Max caught her and held her steady. "What are you doing?"

Mari smiled down at him. "I'm doing what I should've done the first second I ever saw An Ni. I'm going back, and this time, I'm doing what fate had in store for me all along—I'm bringing An Ni home."

He didn't respond, even though he saw that she hesitated as if she were waiting for him to try to talk her out of it. When he didn't, she pulled her shoulders back and took a deep breath. "For good, this time."

Chapter Twenty-Seven

Three weeks later, Mari and An Ni were in the backseat of a rented car, headed toward the main highway that would take them out of Beijing and to Wuxi for an extended stay. This time Mari knew she was doing the right thing. She wanted An Ni to have the chance to get to know the rest of her forever family, and the only way to do that was to plop her down right in the middle of them and let them love her to pieces. And now it didn't feel as if she were running from her problems. An Ni's cast was removed and she was doing so well with her leg. They'd spent some glorious weeks together, interspersed with Max's company as they visited sites around Beijing and even popped in to check on Mei a few times.

In those weeks, Mari still mourned, and many things reminded her of Bolin, but she thought he'd be happy to know that she'd started to laugh again. Maybe she didn't *laugh like music*—but at least with the new and intoxicating feelings of mothering An Ni, she felt her personality was returning to close to what it used to be, before life had beaten her down.

And An Ni wasn't like any other child Mari had ever known. She was sharp—even overly intelligent for her years. Together, as a team, they'd brainstormed several possible ways to make a living. Mari was sure she'd be able to succeed when they were ready, but it had taken the death of her husband and the dramatic meeting of her new daughter to realize family should always come first. She'd have the rest of her life to make a living—the details could wait.

"You're sure you want to leave Beijing without saying more to Max?" An Ni said, her voice low and quiet—and more grown up than Mari had heard in the entire time she'd known her.

"What do you mean?"

An Ni shrugged. "I don't know what I mean exactly. But I do know we were meant to find him and that he was meant to find us. Saying good-bye yesterday didn't feel right—it was as though we left something behind. Something unfinished."

Mari chuckled. Since the afternoon in front of Mei's family when Mari had asked An Ni to be her daughter, the girl had really come out of her shell. She'd turned a corner, and now she spoke her mind, instead of keeping it bottled up inside. Mari was glad—that told her that An Ni was comfortable with her.

And she had a point about Max. His coming into her life and helping her find An Ni had a supernatural feel to it. But that wasn't something she wanted An Ni to dwell on. Max had said his good-byes only the day before, keeping it short after he told them he was flying out the next day. Mari had been so sad to see him go, but knew he needed to get back to his real life.

An Ni nudged her. "Well?"

She smiled and nudged An Ni back. "Yes, it is sort of strange that first I saw and spoke to you on the street, then more than a month later, Mei finds Max and me in the train station and leads us to you. But there are such things as coincidences, An Ni. Even miracles. Sometimes—things are just unexplainable."

An Ni stared out the window, the bag she and Mei had shared when Mari and Max had found them still propped on her lap. At the last minute, Mei had shoved it into An Ni's arms, telling her she still needed protection. How a bag could protect a girl, Mari didn't know, but the scene was emotional enough without her questioning them.

An Ni turned back to her. "Oh, I know how it's explained."

"How?" Mari humored her. She leaned into An Ni as the driver took a turn too fast. Using the handle over her head, she pulled herself upright.

"Our Guanyin led Mei to him."

Mari was surprised she even knew what Guanyin was. "You have your own Guanyin?"

An Ni unzipped the purse and dug in it for a second, then her hand emerged with a photo. She handed it to Mari.

Mari held the photo, gazing down at the girl with deep brown eyes and an impish smile. She looked happy—satisfied, even. In her pink Hello Kitty shirt, she could've blended in with any of a million girls that Mari had seen in her life. "Who is this?"

"I found Max's wallet on the train, and this photo of a Chinese girl was in it. Mei was afraid because I kept slipping in and out of sleep, so I told her it was our Guanyin. I didn't really believe it at first, but now I do."

Then it hit Mari.

It was Max's daughter. The aura of happiness shining off the face and out of the photo made sense then, because she knew without a doubt in her mind that Max loved his daughter. And this girl—her look of contentment rivaled any she'd seen.

"An Ni! Why didn't you give him this photo like you gave him the paper? This is his daughter."

"His daughter is Chinese? How?" An Ni looked dumbfounded.

"She's adopted." Mari could see by the confusion on An Ni's face that she didn't understand Chinese children could be adopted by foreigners.

"There's a program for international adoption," Mari said. "Max and his wife were matched up with their daughter when she was just a baby. They flew to China and picked her up."

Mari didn't mention that Max and his wife were no longer together. She doubted that An Ni would understand divorce. She waited until her words sank in, then finally An Ni started to look as if she understood.

An Ni turned to Mari. "We have to give him this picture back."

Mari shook her head. "It's too late. He's already gone."

An Ni face filled with guilt, then crumpled.

Mari didn't know what to do. Max had already turned the keys in for his apartment. He was scheduled to fly out of China, and as far as she knew, he could be halfway to the airport.

"Please, Mari," An Ni pleaded. "She helped me to find you. I have to tell him."

Mari could feel her resolve slipping. "But I don't even know where to look."

That wasn't completely true. She had a gut feeling where she might find him. They could at least try one place. If she was wrong, they'd only be out a bit more money for the fare than she'd expected. And if she was right—well, she didn't know. But the look on An Ni's face told her she needed to try. She let her heart make the decision.

"Turn around," Mari said, tapping on the glass that separated the driver from her and An Ni.

The driver jerked his head to the side, barking out what amounted to him asking her if she was crazy. *"Ni shuo shenme?"*

"I said, turn around," she repeated. "I need to make another stop before we leave town. I forgot something important."

The driver shook his head no and kept going.

"I'm not paying you if you don't turn this car around," Mari said, then told him where she wanted him to reroute to.

He took his foot off the gas, cursing again as he looked for a place to turn around.

Mari looked over at An Ni and winked. The smile that lit up her face was worth any extra fare the driver might try to tack on. Even so, he kept up his long string of curse words, but he obediently pulled into the next parking lot and turned the car around. Within seconds, they were headed back in the direction they'd come from. In defiance, the driver lit up a dirty, brown cigarette, going back on his original promise to Mari not to smoke on the trip.

She decided she'd let him go as soon as he stopped—she wouldn't let An Ni breathe his poison all the way to Wuxi. But she'd let him get them to the next stop. They rode in silence, Mari sort of hoping Max would be there and sort of hoping he wouldn't. She didn't want him to think she was too forward, or that she didn't want to say good-bye. She did have her pride, after all.

Even if she *didn't* want to say good-bye.

Ten minutes later, the driver pulled the car up to the curb in front of the old *hutong*. Mari looked but didn't see Max anywhere.

"Come on. Let's go in. If he's here, he'll be this way." She hurried An Ni out of the car and onto the sidewalk. After telling the driver to open the trunk, she pulled their luggage out and then returned and tossed a bill into the front seat. As she backed away, she mumbled to him what he could do with his thick cloud of nicotine.

Then she led the way quietly, both of them lost in their own thoughts. As they walked up to the place she and Max had visited what felt like only days before, she saw him.

He knelt in the mulched beds between the two trees, on his knees with his shoulders hunched and his head bowed. Mari held her finger to her lips, signaling An Ni to be quiet. They softly approached, giving him time to finish doing whatever it was he was doing.

When they were just behind him and he still hadn't risen, Mari softly called out to him. "Max?"

He turned, and the look on his face struck straight to her heart. Gone was the easygoing smile she'd grown accustomed to, and in its place was a ravaged man. Tears ran down his face, and he rubbed at them, obviously embarrassed.

"Mari? An Ni?" He stood, clasping a small jar to his chest. "What are you doing here?"

Mari gave An Ni a small nudge. "Go give him the photo."

An Ni took a step forward, suddenly cautious in front of this new, vulnerable Max that neither of them had seen before. Mari watched her closely as she rummaged in the bag and brought out the photo. Then An Ni took another few steps until she was close enough to hand it to him.

"What's this?" He took it from her, and with one look, his silent tears turned into muffled sobs. He looked at An Ni. "You had this? All along?"

An Ni nodded.

Mari stepped forward and put her arm around her shoulders, giving her reassurance. "She said the photo was her and Mei's Guanyin— that she led Mei to you."

Max sat down abruptly between the trees. Suddenly he nodded, laughing through his tears. "Yep, that's her. My daughter—always trying to help people."

Mari sat down next to Max and pulled An Ni down, too. "Why are you crying, Max?"

Max pulled a tattered piece of paper from his pocket and unfolded it. He handed it to Mari. "This is a list she made a long time ago. She called it her *bucket list*, but every item on it is something she and I planned to do in China together."

Mari scanned the list, seeing things like the Great Wall and the antique market. Each item had a number and most of them had been checked off.

"Look at the last thing on the list," Max said.

Mari read down through the items, seeing tasks that she'd even helped Max to do, before her eyes came to rest on the last ones.

10. Watch a cricket fight

11. See my Finding Place

12. Help someone like me.

Now she understood his passion to see and do so much in China. And Max *had* helped someone like his daughter, at least in the coincidence that the girls were both Chinese and had been separated from their families. Still, Mari was confused. "But why didn't she come with you?"

Max looked down at the ground, then he met Mari's eyes. In them, she saw the deepest pool of sadness she'd ever seen in a person.

"She did." He held her photo to his heart and, with the other hand, held up the small, empty jar.

Mari didn't want to understand. She suddenly knew exactly why she couldn't meet his daughter face to face. But she wouldn't make him say it.

Max swiped at another tear. "These were her ashes—what was left of them. She always said that, when she died, she wanted part of her to be laid to rest in her homeland. Leukemia took her from me last year."

Mari looked at the jar, noticing the remnants of a fine brown powder smeared across the glass. She put her hand to her mouth, and she suddenly knew. All the sadness he'd been carrying, that something mysterious he'd kept hidden, the questions he'd evaded—all of it was his reticence to admit his daughter had died. She felt so stupid, so uncaring that she hadn't figured it out. Here he'd been helping her through her tragedy as he carried his own grief alone. Sadness overwhelmed her. "I'm so sorry, Max."

He shook his head. "Don't be. She led me to you two. When she was at her sickest, she made me promise to come to China and do the things on her list. I came, hoping that, once fulfilled, I'd find peace or I'd be able to end everything. But in the process I found something else I never expected. I found a friend in you, Mari. And I found you, An

Ni. Both of you have brought me out of the darkness and given me hope that I can go on in this world without her. And that—well, that's more than enough."

Mari fought to control her own tears as she watched Max stare down at the photo. Not having a child had always been hard for her, but having one, then *losing* your child—that was worse. Even unimaginable. "What was her name, Max?"

He looked up slowly, locking eyes with An Ni. Then he smiled, the lines around his eyes crinkling with true mirth, and there Mari thought she saw the first real spark of serenity she'd seen in him since the day they'd met. He straightened his shoulders, and as if a weight had been lifted, he suddenly appeared lighter.

"Well, girls, that's the best part of this whole crazy adventure. Her name was Annie."

Author's Note

Red Skies was inspired by an online article that made the news around the world when three young boys were found suffocated in a trash bin in China. Tragically, they were poisoned to death from the coal they burned in the enclosed bin in their attempt to stay warm. In my travels to several countries across Southeast Asia, I saw many a child holding out a cup, pulling on my clothes, or trying to sell me a simple flower for a coin. The anguished decision of whether to give or not to give always haunted me as I walked away, and many of those faces continue to linger in my mind.

In 2012, Dale Rutstein of UNICEF in China stated that up to 1.5 million children were thought to be fending for themselves across the country, but exact numbers are impossible to record. Why so many children are forced to live on the streets is contradicted regularly, but we know that some of them are abducted from their families, some are left behind by parents seeking work, and others are simply abandoned. Regardless of how they come to be street children in China, or Thailand, or even the United States of America—the plight of street children is a global issue and only getting bigger each moment of the day. If you'd like to help, there are now *volunteer vacations* where you can give a week or two of your time, but if you can't volunteer in person, donations and even helping to raise awareness is an important part of making a difference. It is my hope that the story of *Red Skies* will educate those who have never dreamed that such a problem affects the innocent—the children who like all of us, deserve a future. Readers, if you enjoyed this book, please consider posting a review on Amazon or Goodreads. And you can purchase my newest novel set in China, *The Palest Ink*, on Amazon, releasing fall 2015.

Acknowledgments

Many thanks to Kate Danley, Karen McQuestion, and G.M. Barlean, my team of author friends, who generously offer critiques, advice, and support while I am trudging through a story to find my voice. Thank you, Caroline Lynch, for your eagle eyes that gave me that final polish. Much appreciation to journalist Kit Gillet for his in-depth report on the underground tunnels of Beijing, found on the blog of Jonah M. Kessel, a cross-platform, freelance visual media specialist based in Beijing, China. Your descriptive words and astonishing photos helped me to create the scene when Mari and Max ventured into the historical underground tunnels of Beijing.

To my readers, including my Facebook and Twitter followers, with your ongoing support you have helped me to reach a long held dream of becoming a successful author. Many of you have shared your China memories with me—allowing me to include them in my stories to bring a level of emotion that could only be gained through real-life experiences. I also want to say thank you for posting such favorable reviews of my work on Amazon and Goodreads. Please know that all you do to help me in this adventure that is my life is very much appreciated, now and forever.

Lastly, to my husband, Ben, what more can I say other than the support you've given me from day one is the reason that I am now writing the acknowledgments to my eleventh book. I love writing—we all know that—but I love you more, m'love.

Glossary

Aiya (pronounced I-yah):	Expresses surprise or other sudden emotion
Bai jiu (Bye jee-oh)	Chinese liquor
Bang wo (Bong whoa)	Help me
Bāozi (Boww-zuh)	Steamed buns, usually with filling
Bu ku le (Boo koo luh)	Don't cry
Bushi (Boo-sher)	No/not
Chengguan (Chung-gwon)	Local Chinese urban-management officers
Chī le ma? (Chrr luh ma?)	Have you eaten?
Da bizi (Da bee-zuh)	Big nose
Deng yi xia (Dung ee sha)	Wait a minute
Dui (Dway)	Correct
Dui bu qi (Dway boo chee)	An apology
Gei wo qian (gay whoa chee an)	Give me money
Guo lai (Gwoh lie)	Come here
Hao le (How luh)	Okay
Hukou (Who-ko)	Chinese identification
Hutong (Who-tong)	Lane or residential area (neighborhood)
Jiǎozǐ (Joww-zuh)	Dumplings
Jie jie (Jay jay)	Big sister
Laoban (Loww-bon)	Boss
Laoren (Loww-run)	Form of title used for senior citizen

Ni hao (Knee how)	Hello
Ni shuo shenme (knee shun muh)	What did you say?
Nuer (New-are)	Daughter
Peng you (pung yoh)	Friend
Píngguǒ zǐ (Ping-gwoh zzz)	Apple seed
Shenme (Shun muh)	What
Shi de (Sher-duh)	Yes
Ta bing le (Ta bing luh)	He/she is sick
Ting le (Ting luh)	Stop
Tudou (Two dough)	Potatoes
Waiguorens (Why gwoh runs)	Foreigners
Wo gei ta qian (Whoa gay ta chee an)	I gave her/him money
Xiao (Sh-oww)	Title for a young girl or woman
Xiao liwu (Sh-oww lee woo)	Small gift
Xie xie (shay-shay)	Thank you
Yóutiáo (Yo-tee-oww)	Deep fried dough sticks
Zai jian (Zie-jee-ann)	Good-bye
Zaofan (Zow-fon)	Breakfast
Zao, peng you (Zow pung yoh)	Morning, friend
Zǎo shàng hǎo (Zow shong how)	Good morning
Zhi dao (Jer dow)	Know
Zuo xia (Zwoh sha)	Sit down

About the Author

Photo © 2012 Eclipse Photography Studio

Kay Bratt is a child advocate and author, residing on the banks of Lake Hartwell in South Carolina with her husband, daughter, dog, and cat. Kay lived in China for over four years and because of her experiences working with orphans, she strives to be the voice for children who cannot speak for themselves. Over the years, she has volunteered for numerous nonprofit organizations, including Court Appointed Special Advocates (CASA), An Orphan's Wish (AOW), and Pearl River Outreach. If you would like to read more about what started her career as an author, and also meet the children she knew and loved in China, read her poignant memoir titled *Silent Tears; A Journey of Hope in a Chinese Orphanage*. Connect with Kay Bratt or subscribe to her newsletter at kaybratt.com.

Made in the USA
Las Vegas, NV
25 October 2021

33038136R00152